MW01520066

Arabella's Secret ~ Book Two

By Nancy M Bell

Digital ISBNs
EPUB 9781772990980
Mobi/Kindle 9781772995237
Web/PDF 9781772991000

Print ISBN 9781772991017
Amazon Print ISBN 978-1-77299-537-4

Books We Love
A quality publisher of genre fiction.
Airdrie Alberta

Chapter One

Arabella Angarrick leaned on the ship's rail gazing at the spot on the horizon where the tip of Cornwall was lost from sight hours ago. She searched for the strains of the selkie's song under the hiss of the sea against the ship, the rumble of engines, and the wind whining in the superstructure. Common sense told her she had far outdistanced the pod of selkies who gathered to wish her farewell, but she was reluctant to give up the tenuous grip on her homeland.

"Oh, Vear," she whispered. "How am I going to live without you?" Her hands dropped to caress the still flat stomach beneath her coat. "I never had the chance to tell you about the baby. Maybe that's for the best..." Her voice was lost in the wind and tears ran cold down her cheeks. The deck pitched underfoot forcing Arabella to clutch the rail.

The sun buried itself in the bank of clouds and the chill air cut through her woolen coat. Wiping the tears away with the back of her hand, Bella made her way to the first class cabin her future husband booked in her name. She shrugged out of the damp outer garment and hung it on a hook behind the door. The rise and fall of the floor made her stagger a bit when she crossed to the narrow bed. A folded card on the dressing table informed her dinner would be served at 7 pm in the main dining room. Or if she wished, the lady could order room service from the steward.

Bella dropped onto the bed and hid her face in her hands. How in the name of all that was holy had she got herself into this fix? If only Sarie was here to help her make sense of the conflicting feelings swirling through her. Cold dread settled in her gut as the realization she might never see her best friend again became startlingly clear. She twisted the diamond ring on her left hand with nervous fingers. It was humiliating, that's what it was. Bella used the anger to push the fear to the back of her mind for a moment. Packed up and shipped off to Canada in disgrace by her da and the parish priest. Just who did they think they were, ordering her around, giving her no say in the matter?

The anger faded and Bella had to admit she was given a choice. "Some choice." She snorted and glared at the twinkling diamond. "I can marry Daniel Bloody Treliving who is the biggest scut that ever lived, or I can be shipped off to the wilds of Alberta to be the bride of the some rancher who has bought and paid for me." To be fair, D'Arcy Rowan had provided first class passage for her and ensured she would be met in Halifax and transferred, along with her trunks, onto the first of two trains that would take her half way across the country to some dusty prairie town. Mr. Rowan spared no expense, so presumably he must be fairly well off. She'd thought the ship would land in St. John, New Brunswick and she'd have to transfer to Moncton to catch the train. Apparently this ship was headed to Halifax, Nova Scotia and the connection to the train was better.

What was he like, this man she was supposed to share her bed and her life with? The one letter she received from him was civil enough, and he had a good hand...Unless someone else penned the letter for him? Dear Lord, what if he was totally unlettered and horrible? She twisted the ring on her finger again, drawing it on and off over the knuckle. Maybe she could just disappear when the ship made land? There was a few dollars in her hand bag, not really enough to set her up in a strange place, but maybe enough...She was unsure how the strange looking currency used in the colonies translated into British Pound Sterling.

Bella let the notion die. If only she wasn't expecting a child, things would be so much less complicated. It would be hard enough to make a living in strange surroundings if she were unencumbered, but with the child growing in her belly and soon to be noticeable to anyone with a pair of eyes, her chances of landing a job was slim to none. She sighed. There was nothing to it, but to carry on and hope D'Arcy Rowan was a decent human being who would treat her well. The man knew he was getting a two for the price of one deal with her, and the fact hadn't seemed to faze him, so maybe it would be okay after all.

Fresh pain speared her heart. But Vear, oh Vear Du, without him it was like a piece of her soul was missing. He'd never know their love had created a child. Really, there wasn't even any reason for him to suspect such a thing was possible. A consummated love affair between a mortal and selkie wasn't unheard of, but it was certainly not encouraged. Oh, yes, she'd heard the tales from Scotland about the men who hid their selkie wives pelt so they couldn't return to the sea. And women who did the same. But it had never been like that between Vear Du and herself. No pelt hiding, or trying to hold him against his will. No, he'd come to her willingly and pledged to stand by her. Until the damned Council of Kernow intervened.

The council of immortals banished her selkie from the world of man for his transgressions, she snorted in derision, and there seemed to be nothing anyone could do about it. Bella's problem was of no concern to them, the bastards. Of course, they didn't know about the baby. They might have been a bit more concerned with her if they realized she was carrying a half-blood. A shiver coursed through her. Lord only knew what they would have *decreed* if they'd realized the full scope of Vear's *crime*. She lifted her lip in contempt. What crime was there in loving someone?

A tap on the cabin door interrupted her miserable thoughts. Running her fingers through her wind tossed hair, Bella got to her feet and smoothed the skirt of her dress. A glance in the tiny mirror showed her she at least looked somewhat presentable, so she crossed the rolling floor and opened the door.

"Yes?"

"I'm here to escort you to the dining room, Miss Angarrick," the uniformed steward informed her with a stiff half bow. He extended his arm. "The sea is a bit rough this evening, miss. Allow me to assist you."

Bella took the proffered arm, slipping her hand into the crook of his elbow. "Thank you, Stephan." She read the polished name tag on his left lapel.

"This way then, miss."

* * *

The crossing was miserable in Bella's opinion. Although the steward and other passengers assured her the seas were fair, to her it seemed all the ship did was pitch like a horse with a burr under its saddle. The thought made her miss Raven, and Sarie, which in turn sent her to her cabin in tears more than once. She spent the five days it took to cross the Atlantic writing to Sarie. The letters couldn't be mailed until she made landfall in Halifax, but it was comforting to be able to share her experiences. In some small way it made her feel less alone and abandoned.

She often woke in the middle of the night with her heart pounding and the pulse roaring in her ears louder than the wind and waves pummelling the ship. The last night at sea found Bella unable to sleep at all. She huddled in her berth, back against the wall with her knees pulled up to her chin, wrapped in the blankets. The cabin was all greys and blacks in the faint light from the tiny night light by the door. Bella buried her face in the quilt and gave in to the despair which overwhelmed her. How in the name of all she held holy was she to marry some man she had never met? Vear, her heart cried. *Am I supposed to lie with this strange man, let him touch me in those intimate places and act as if I like it?*

Throwing the covers away, she got to her feet clutching a rail for support as the ship rolled. The other hand cradled her stomach and she was glad she had forgone dinner as bile rose in her throat. Letting go of the rail, she paced the tiny cabin, staggering now and again on the unsteady floor. *I can't do this, I just can't. Better I should throw myself overboard tonight than face what the next days will bring. What is there to live for anyway? I've lost Vear, I'll never see Sarie again, or Raven...* The bleakness of her future crashed down on her, she crumpled to the floor landing on her knees, the carpet rough on her forehead. Bella wrapped her arms around her middle and gave in to the wracking silent sobs that shook her.

"Bella, my sweet Bella. Don't weep so. Even though we are apart, I am always with you."

Her sobs broke off abruptly and she glanced wildly around the shadowed cabin. The wind wailed outside the small porthole and the sea thundered against the bulkhead. *"Bella, don't despair."* Her heart leapt painfully in her chest and she used the edge of the bed to lever herself upright. Surely the shadows in the far corner were more than shadows. They seemed to have a solid substance to them. Wiping her bleary eyes Bella wobbled toward the corner where the darkest shadows gathered. Anguish surged when her searching fingers encountered only the polished panelling of the cabin wall. *"In your heart, dear one. I am with you. Dream of me and I will come."* The soft voice faded and she slid down the wall to curl into a ball on the floor.

"Vear? I love you," she whispered. "You may never know this, but our love grows inside me." *The baby, I can't give up. I can't end things by leaping into the sea. I have his child to live for and this D'Arcy Rowan has promised to accept the baby as his own, no matter if it's girl or boy. Sarie would say I owe it to the poor innocent that depends on me for its life. She would say, I have made my bed and now I must lie in it. And so I shall, I guess. At least it's not Daniel Treliving's bed I'm forced to lie in.*

Too exhausted to try and gain her feet, Bella crawled across the cabin and dragged her body up onto the narrow bed. She lit the tiny bedside lamp and began yet another letter to Sarie.

Dear Sarie,

Although this passage only takes five days and tomorrow we'll make landfall in Halifax, I feel like it has been forever since I saw you. God, I miss you so much. This must be the hundredth letter I have written to you. Some of them (most of them, to tell you the truth) I have torn into pieces and tossed into the sea. When I re-read them I realize all I have done is whinge and complain about how unfair this all is and I am embarrassed for you to see how I have wallowed in self-pity most of the voyage. So you remember how fearless we were, you and I? We outwitted Da and the odious Daniel by hiding in the cave in Lamorna Cove. When I think of it now, I can't believe I actually climbed out my bedroom window and slid across the roof tree to escape my fate. You were there with me every step of the way.

Now, I am adrift without you to anchor me. Sarie, I'm scairt. So bad I think I will go mad. It is all I can do at times not to run screaming and tearing my hair out down the blasted corridors of this Godforsaken ship. I've no bravery or daring do in me anymore. Tonight I seriously thought about throwing myself overboard. The seas are stormy (in my estimation at least, the steward assures me the seas are actually quite mild) and I believe it would not take me long to succumb to Poseidon's embrace.

But the strangest thing happened. I know you will think I'm barking mad, but I swear it is true. I heard Vear Du as if he was right here in the room with me. Then I remembered that I carry a part of him growing within me and realized I couldn't selfishly give in to my desires. I know what you are thinking and what you would say if you were here. You see, even though I may never see you again, you are still my lode stone, keeping me from being a total wreck.

Should you be able to get a message to my selkie please let him know where I am and that I didn't leave Cornwall willingly. Perhaps Gwin Scawen has ways? But don't let him get himself in trouble over this and please, please, don't tell him or the selkie about the baby. You see, I am finally thinking of someone before myself. You must be astounded, I'm sure. I just can't imagine what the bloody Council would do to him if they discovered my secret.

Thank you, dear Sarie. Although you won't know this until I can post this letter and it finds its way to you, you have once again helped save my sanity and enabled me to find a way to go on.

Love Always
Bella

She folded the thin sheets, pulled open the night table drawer and tucked them between the pages of the novel along with the other missives to her friend she planned to mail once she was on dry land once more. Closing the drawer with a snick, Bella checked the time on her watch and propped herself up on the pillows. She pulled the quilt up to her chin and stared into the darkness waiting for the dawn she wished would never come.

Chapter Two

Bella scrunched her eyes shut and cursed under her breath when the steward rapped on her door.

"Breakfast is being served, Miss Angarrick," he called. "Will you be going to the dining room, or shall I bring you something to the cabin?"

"Thank you, I believe I will go to the dining room this morning," she answered.

"As you wish, miss. We'll be in port in four hours or so."

"Thank you," she repeated. Swinging her legs out of the bed, she washed and dressed, selecting a suitable outfit for travelling. With a glance at her things strewn about the cabin she tossed her head and closed the door behind her with satisfying snap. Time enough to set things to rights after she ate, it would fill the time before they reached Halifax, and give her something to think about besides the horrible feeling in the pit of her stomach.

The dining room was crowded but Bella found a place at a table by the wall. She ordered tea and toast along with some pastries. The strong sweet tea was hot and warmed the cold pit of her stomach. The pastry was enticing, but she found the raisin scone stuck in her throat. The waiter refilled her tea cup and Bella contented herself with nibbling on the toast. Around her the conversation rose and fell, excitement pitching the voices higher and louder than usual.

When her nervous stomach dictated she should eat no more, she folded her napkin and placed in on the table before allowing the waiter to pull her chair back. She stood on slightly wobbly legs, smiled at the man, and made her way back to her cabin.

The sight of the mess she left earlier that morning was depressing. Her gaze swept over the confusion of personal items, odds and bobs, and clothes flung every which way. Heaving a sigh, Bella dropped her small purse on the bed and began to set things to rights. During her absence someone had brought her trunk up and it stood open in the middle of the small room. In quick order she folded and stashed her clothing neatly into the bottom before replacing the divided tray which fit over them supported by an inner lip. Here she packed some books and papers which she wouldn't need until she reached Alberta.

She pulled a small valise from under the bed and began to fill it with a change of clothes and some toiletries she would need on the train. Having a change of heart, she removed the novel with the letters to Sarie tucked inside from the trunk and shoved it into the side pocket of the travel bag. The letters could be mailed from

Halifax and any other messages she composed in the days that followed could be mailed once she reached her destination. A surge of homesickness almost brought her to her knees when she thought of Sarie and the wind swept cliffs of home.

No, not home any longer. Cornwall was her past, and now she needed to figure out how to survive her future. Hands on hips she surveyed the now uncluttered cabin. One last check of the drawers and tiny cupboard as well as under the bed assured her all her possessions were safely packed in either the trunk or her valise.

Bella glanced at her watch. Only another hour and they'd be in Halifax. She locked the trunk and placed the valise on the bed. Someone would collect the trunk, but leave the bag for her to carry off the ship. Excitement mingled with fear as Bella left the cabin and hurried up to the promenade deck. Other passengers were already at the rail anxiously peering at the hazy horizon, searching for the first sight of land. She joined them, finding a place at the rail by an older couple the woman clinging tightly to the man's arm.

"Can you see it yet, Harold?" The woman's voice quivered.

"Not yet, pet." He patted her arm.

"What if Samuel isn't there to meet us? What will we do?" Grey hair blew across her face, escaped from the scarf tied about her head.

"Now, Alma. Samuel promised to meet us and so he will. Think how wonderful it will be to see the grandchildren."

"Are you just visiting, or have you come to stay?" Bella inquired breaking into the couple's conversation.

"Oh, hallo, miss. We're immigrating to Canada. Our son, Samuel has been here three years now and he's paid our passage so we can come live with him and his new wife," Harold replied.

"Three grandchildren we've never met," Alma added. "But, it's all so big and strange. What if I don't like it? What is *she* doesn't like us?"

"Alma, her name is Araminta, and Samuel assures us they are both looking forward to our arrival. Don't go borrowing trouble, my dear." Harold covered her thin hand with his where it rested on the rail.

"What about you then, miss? Are you here on a visit? Pretty young thing like you." Alma regarded her with eyes that seemed to miss nothing.

"No, I'm on my way to Alberta to marry a rancher. I'm afraid this move is permanent, not a visit at all," Bella answered.

"How sweet, on your way to reunite with your sweetheart, are you?" The old woman smiled.

"Umm, yes. Of course—"

"I see it!"

"Land Ho!"

17

"Dry land at last!"

The excited cries saved Bella from having to answer the awkward question. "It was nice talking with you, but I'm afraid I really must go see to my things." She took her leave of the elderly couple. "Best of luck in your new home."

"And you, my dear." The couple waved in farewell and turned back to the rail.

Bella unlocked the cabin door to find the trunk gone and only her valise sitting forlornly on the bed. It looked as lost and alone as she felt. She found the harried room steward and asked if he could possibly bring her a pot of tea. With ill-concealed impatience he promised to see to it and returned twenty minutes later with a tea tray. He set it on the bed side table.

"We'll be docking in fifteen minutes, miss. Just make your way up to the gangway once the captain gives the all clear. You're First Class so you'll be one of the first. Your trunks and belongings will be dockside. I believe the porters should already have the contact information and paperwork to transfer them to the train station." He tipped his hat and hurried out.

Bella sank onto the bed and poured a cup of tea with a hand that barely shook. The familiar act of sipping the hot liquid helped steady her nerves, and by the time the pot was empty and the all clear was announced for First Class passengers, she was feeling almost like herself.

"Right, Bella. You can do this." She gathered up her coat, small purse and valise, pausing before she opened the door to take a deep breath. She closed her eyes against a wave of vertigo and waited for it to pass. Bella opened the cabin door and bravely stepped into the corridor.

A small group gathered at the head of the gangway waiting for the mooring to be secured. Bella joined them, clutching the valise like a life line. Below her, the docks swarmed with life, people of all sorts pushed and shoved their way along. She spied a knot of people who were obviously waiting to greet the newly arrived passengers. The huge red brick building loomed oppressively over the chaos of the docks. How was she supposed to find her escort? There was a name on the paper jammed into her purse, but what good would that do her in the madness unfolding before her?

"Miss Angarrick?" A junior office appeared at her elbow.

Bella stifled the urge to jump and turned to him. "Yes, that's me."

"Petty Officer Johnson, miss." He touched the brim of his cap. "I'm to accompany you to shore and ensure you are safely delivered to your on-shore escort. It has been arranged for your trunks to be transferred directly to the train station, so you have no need to concern yourself with them. Do you have all your other belongings with you?"

"Oh, yes. This is everything." She indicated the valise at her feet and patted the purse on her arm. "It's very good of you to see that I'm alright once I disembark. I've been ever so worried about getting lost in all this." Bella waved a hand at the seething mass of humanity below.

"Very good, miss. Ah, it appears we are ready. Come, I'll take you down first." Petty Officer Johnson collected the valise from the deck and offered his arm.

"Thank you ever so much." She smiled up at him and tucked her hand into the crook of his arm.

"My pleasure, miss." He threaded their way through the other passengers and waited for her to step onto the gangway a little in front of him. When they were half way across, the rest of the First Class passengers followed, the gangway swayed a bit under the increased traffic. Bella gasped and clutched the officer's arm. "Almost there, miss. No need for alarm," he assured her.

Now she was on solid ground it felt odd not to be moving. The mass of humanity swirled around her, the scent of unwashed bodies, dead fish, and excrement stung her nose. The Petty Officer shouldered a way through the crowd and Bella was grateful to follow in his wake. Presently he opened a door and led her into a large empty hall. It looked more like a huge hanger or warehouse than anything else. Bella glanced around in bewilderment.

"Ah, here we are, Miss Angarrick." Johnson towed her toward a row of chairs outside an office set into the far end of the hall.

She hadn't a chance to settle into one of the hard straight backed chairs before she was escorted into the office and asked to produce her paperwork. The grey haired man perused them carefully, his face expressionless. Bella experienced a moment of panic. What if he didn't find things in order? What was she supposed to do then? Would they put her back on a ship returning to England? Her vision blurred and she fought to control the racing of her heart.

"Everything seems to be in order here, Miss Angarrick. I see here you're headed to Alberta to be married. Welcome to Canada and please accept my best wishes on your upcoming nuptials on behalf of the Queen." The immigration official handed her back the bundle of papers and entered something in a ledger.

"Thank you," she stammered and got to her feet. "May I go now?"

"What? Oh, yes of course, be off with you." He waved a hand at her without glancing up.

Bella left the office on trembling legs and was relieved to see Petty Officer Johnson waiting for her.

"All set then, are we?"

Bella nodded, not trusting her voice. It was all so very final now, no turning back, no use wishing she could re-board the ship and return to her beloved Cornwall. She walked beside her

21

escort in a daze and blinked in surprise when he led her back out into the sunlight. Johnson paused and glanced about before setting off again. Bella trailed along behind him until he stopped to speak to a man with a fedora perched jauntily over his dark curls. She stood a little to the side and waited until Johnson turned and introduced her to the gentleman.

"Miss Angarrick, this is Mister Adamson. He will take you in hand now and see you safely to the train. It's been my pleasure to be of service to you, miss." Johnson touched a finger to the brim of his hat and departed, leaving her valise by the man's feet.

"Hallo, Mister Adamson." She extended her hand.

"Call me Joe, Miss Angarrick. Your train don't leave for a few hours. Would you like me to take you directly to the station, or would you prefer a bite to eat and bit of a tour of Halifax?" Bright blue eyes regarded her quizzically.

"My trunks...?"

"They'll be offloaded shortly and I've already arranged for me mates to deliver them to the train in plenty of time. Nothing to worry your head about. Your man in the west has paid handsomely to be sure you won't be inconvenienced in the least. Now, what would you like to do?"

Bella checked her watch. She was surprised to see it was half-past one. "Perhaps some lunch would be in order?"

"Of course. Right this way. I know a nice place what serves good food for a good price. Just a short ride from here." Joe picked up her valise and led her toward a pony cart. He placed the valise in the bed of the cart and offered Bella his hand to assist her up onto the seat. "Hope you don't mind the mode of transport, it's a mite easier to find a place to park Horace here, than it is to try and park a motor car," he apologized and climbed up onto the seat beside her.

Bella clutched her purse on her lap and glanced around as the cart pulled out of the crowded yard. "Oh no, this is fine. I like horses better than motor cars any day." She smiled at him. The streets were narrow and many of them seemed to go uphill. Once they were clear of the harbour and docks, the houses were clustered close together and painted in a myriad of pastel colours. Her exploration of the city was interrupted when Joe halted outside a corner diner with a huge neon sign emblazoned across the front.

After a hearty lunch of clam chowder and fish and chips, accompanied by non-stop chatter from the proprietor who seemed to be an old friend of Joe's, Bella climbed back onto the pony cart. She was fascinated by the scenes of everyday life she observed as they passed by. The activity near the docks reminded her of Newlyn Harbour, but on a far larger scale. They arrived at the train station and Joe accompanied her to the ticket office carrying her bag. Bella dug in her purse and produced the ticket D'Arcy had sent her. The ticket master took it, and after checking the document over, stamped it and handed the paper back to her.

"Waiting room for ladies is over there." He pointed. "You can wait there until your train arrives. Show your ticket to the conductor and he'll help you find your berth in the sleeping car. First Class passengers eat in the dining car, and there's a ladies' lounge car as well. Once you're aboard the steward will see to your needs."

"Thank you," Bella managed to stammer. The whole process was overwhelming and everything was strange and unsettling. Even the accents of the people were odd and she often found it hard to understand them. It was like English mixed with Cockney slang, and a smattering of Gaelic thrown in for good measure.

"Are you okay, miss? You look a might pale, if you ask me," Joe inquired peering into her face.

"I'm feeling a bit poorly, actually. Do you think I could sit down for a minute?" Bella swayed on her feet.

"Here now, just hold onto me and we'll find you a seat." Joe led her to a chair set by the window. "Just sit here now and I'll get you a glass of water. Just wait here." He hurried off and returned in a few minutes bearing a carafe and a glass. "Here you are, Miss Angarrick. Just take a sip of this. You'll be feeling fit as a fiddle in no time flat."

"Thank you, Joe." She took the glass he had filled with water from the carafe and sipped it gratefully. Her head cleared and her vision steadied. "I feel much better now. Thank you for your kindness."

"Think nothing of it. The train should arrive in about half an hour. I'll make sure you get on board and find your berth and all before I leave you. What you need is a good night's rest. Come tomorrow morning you'll be right as rain. Imagine, this time tomorrow you'll be almost to Montreal. Hardly seems possible, does it?"

"But I'm not going to Montreal," she exclaimed in alarm. "I'm supposed to get off at Edmonton, in Alberta!"

Joe laughed and patted her hand. "No need to be upset. Montreal is just on the way to your destination. You will need to change trains there, but all the arrangements are already in place to see you safely on your way. There's nothing to worry about, not a'tall. "

"How much farther is Edmonton from Montreal?" She stumbled a bit over the unfamiliar names.

"Quite a ways, I'm sure. Takes about three and a half days to get to Alberta from there."

"That long? How big is Canada?" The sheer magnitude of the distance she had to travel suddenly became all too clear.

"Well, it's a big place to be sure. Especially compared to the old country. I've heard once you get to the prairies there's miles and miles of

25

nothing but flat land. Can't imagine it meself. No trees or nothing."

"Oh. I didn't realize it was so far," she said faintly.

"It'll be alright, dearie. Your man out there has made sure the trip will be as pleasant as possible. You'll make out okay. A lot better than some mail order brides, I'm sure."

"I'm not a mail order bride," she started to say and then thought better of it. Let the man think what he wanted. There was no way Bella wanted to explain the real reason for her flight from England.

Chapter Three

In due time the train huffed its way to a halt at the platform. Bella bade her companion farewell after he handed her over to the gentleman in a smart uniform who helped her step aboard. In short order the Pullman porter took her to the sleeping car and showed her where to stow her valise, assuring her it would be quite safe there. Then he demonstrated the method of moving from car to car safely while showing her where the dining car and ladies lounge car were located. He left her sitting at a small table by a window with a pot of tea. She smiled gratefully and leaned her head back for a moment.

Beyond the window life bustled by, oblivious to her inner turmoil. Bella had never seen so many people in one place in her life. The mob seethed in an ever changing sea of motion, every person appeared to be in a hurry and intent on their individual tasks. The crowd pushed and shoved by each other in a single minded purpose. She closed her eyes for a moment, too overwhelmed to take it all in. Fatigue licked at her fragile composure and tears pricked the back of her eyes. She itched to leap up and run away from all the commotion, the inclination so strong she actually started to get up from the chair.

Taking a deep breath, Bella sank back on the cushioned chair. "Where would you run to, idiot woman?" she muttered under her breath.

"Shall I pour the tea for you, madam?" A uniformed cat attendant stood at her elbow.

She looked up in surprise. "What? Oh, no thank you. I can do it." Bella smiled at the man.

"As you wish." He nodded and moved on down the car.

Her hand trembled only slightly when she lifted the large silver teapot and filled the bone china cup set on a matching saucer. Both teapot and cup and saucer bore the logo of the rail company. She added generous dollops of mild and sugar to the liquid and stirred with a tiny silver spoon. It was all so very posh and not at all what she was used to. No heavy crockery tea pot and chipped mugs like in the kitchen at home. It just added to the strangeness and feelings of alienation threatening her grasp on normalcy.

Bella stifled the urge to laugh. *Normalcy?* Would anything ever feel normal again? Somehow, she doubted it. Outside the window, the tempo of the activity seemed to have picked, porters almost running as they rushed to finish last minute tasks and a few tardy passengers hurrying down the platform clutching tickets fluttering in their hands. Bella sipped her tea and concentrated on the scene, willing herself not to think about anything else. *Else I will surely go Bodmin. No one in this new place will even know what I mean if I say that.* A new wave of disassociation swept over her.

Action on the platform dwindled, the sound of slamming doors up and down the train echoed against the wooden walls of the station. Whistles blew loudly and Bella leaned forward as the train began to move. The progress was slow at first, but quickly picked up speed and left the huddle of buildings behind. By the time she had finished most of the pot of tea and all of the fancy biscuits that came with it, the world outside the window consisted of rolling farmland and forests. In the distance she could often catch the blue gleam of the Atlantic Ocean. The tracks followed the wide ribbon of a river. It seemed immense to Bella, far wider than the Tamar, or even the Thames. She supposed this must be like the Thames estuary, broadening out as it reached the sea. Bella expected the waterway would narrow as they went further inland and was surprised when it didn't do so.

After a time, she tired of gazing out the window at the landscape and got to her feet. The sky was darkening toward evening and her body demanded food, even while her nervous state rejected the idea. There were other ladies in the car, all of them with travelling companions. The murmur of conversation and quiet laughter rose from the intimate groups gathered at small tables throughout the lounge. Bella was disinclined to speak to anyone, but perversely also felt oddly left out with no one to giggle with. *If only Sarie were here, what fun we could have.* Bella's throat tightened and she banished the thought from her mind.

"May I be of service, miss?" The car attendant approached her.

"Which way is the dining car?"

She thanked him after he pointed her in the correct direction and made her way to the indicated car. Tables spread with immaculate white linen and set with fine bone china greeted her. Night had fallen and the shades were drawn across the windows down the length of the car. Many of the tables were occupied, but a uniformed attendant led Bella to small table set for two.

"Will anyone be joining you, miss?" The man asked while seating her and placing a heavy linen napkin stiff with starch across her lap.

"No, I'm afraid. I'll be dining alone," she answered. The whole process was slightly daunting. Bella had never been treated with such deference. She felt like she was playing the fraud. It was extremely odd to be treated like the Queen of England when in reality she was pregnant out of wedlock and sent away in disgrace to some foreign place.

"As you wish, miss." He handed her a large open menu, complete with a gold tassel. "Would you like tea or coffee?" With a deft hand he filled a goblet with ice water without spilling a drop.

"Tea, please." She smiled at him.

While she waited for her meal to come, Bella entertained herself with examining her fellow travellers. It was an activity she used to enjoy with Sarie on their infrequent trips to Truro, or on even rarer occasions to London. Giggling behind their hands, they would invent wild and crazy stories about the passengers nearby. By long habit, she found herself turning to speak to Sarie, and was bereft when she remembered she was alone. The waiter appeared with her meal on a silver tray. He set it before with a flourish.

"Are you quite alright, miss?" The man peered down at her with a concerned frown.

"Oh, yes. Thank you. Quite alright," she replied. *Bloody hell, I must learn to hide my emotions better if even complete strangers can see I'm upset. What will Mister Rowan think if I walk around with a face on me like death warmed over?*

Bella finished her meal and found her way to the sleeping car with a sense of relief. At least safe in her sleeper, she could drop her pathetic attempt of putting up a façade of normality and give in to her tears. After using the water closet—what was it they called it on this side of the pond? The bathroom?—she crawled into the berth and lay staring at the ceiling inches from her nose. The repetitive clack of the wheels irritated her and the swaying of the carriage made her slightly nauseous. Eventually, exhaustion overrode her agitation and she fell into a fitful slumber.

She woke early and ate breakfast in the almost deserted dining car. Collecting her valise she settled in the ladies lounge and gazed out the window at the gently rolling Quebec countryside. How odd, she reflected, that most people in this part of the country spoke French. At least that's what she'd been told and had no reason to doubt the information.

Before noon, the train pulled into Montreal and Bella was caught up in the business of leaving one train and boarding another. Once more, there was a man waiting to greet her and smooth the changeover to the train that would take her across the country to Alberta. The gentleman in the tweed cap assured her the trunks were transferred to the baggage car and handed her over the Pullman porter. She stepped up onto the train and went through the process of finding the sleeper car with her berth in it and leaving her valise there in care of the car attendant. She found the ladies lounge and dining car without any fuss this time and settled herself in the lounge by a large window.

She'd no sooner ordered a pot of tea before the doors slammed, whistles blew and the engine steamed out of the station. Bella leaned back, tea cup in hand, and watched the suburbs of Montreal flash by. It was soon replaced by green hilled farmland spotted with black and white cows grazing in velvety pastures. After a time, she wearied of looking at the scenery and removed the novel from her hand bag. One of the letters to Sarie fluttered to the table. She retrieved it and shoved the paper into her purse. She didn't feel like writing yet another letter and was annoyed at herself for not remembering to find a post office either in Halifax or Montreal.

Bella consulted the schedule in her bag. The train was supposed to have a stop in Ottawa and Toronto, and then Winnipeg. She would have to find the opportunity to mail the letters at one of those places. The novel was a mystery whodunnit, not something she usually read, but it took her mind off her own troubles and passed the time. Tiring of the complicated plot and at a total loss to even guess who the murderer was, Bella wandered to the dining car and ate lunch. Afterward she returned to the lounge car and gazed at the Saint Lawrence River wide and blue sparkling in the sun. Before long they crossed the broad Rideau River into Ontario. The capital city of Canada seemed small and inconsequential so Bella who was used to the ostentatious parliament buildings of London and the imposing presence of Big Ben in his clock tower. Compared to the ancient timelessness of British cities and towns everything here seemed to be raw and new, with no patina of centuries of wear and tear to give it character. It looked as alien as Bella felt.

The tracks ran beside the waterway for miles, the train made a brief stop in Kingston where she could see a fort of some sort perched on a rise by the river. She stopped the car attendant to ask what it was.

"That's Fort Henry, miss. It's a historical site now. If you're planning to stay in the area it's well worth the time to go and visit it."

"Thanks, but I'm bound for Edmonton. I'm sure I'll never get back this way," she replied.

He nodded and moved on down the car to tend to the other occupants. Bella craned her neck to see the battlements better. Did they have interesting things like this where she was going? It would be exciting to explore. The train rolled on through the gently Ontario countryside, Bella tired of the view and returned to her novel. She looked when the outskirts of Toronto came into sight and the train slowed slightly. When it came to a stop in bustling Union Station in the heart of the city, Bella disembarked after being assured by the Pullman porter that she had plenty of time and the train would not leave without her.

The noise and crowds reminded her of Paddington or Euston, but the resemblance stopped there. Voices rose and fell in cacophony of different languages, even the smell of the city was foreign to her. The huge vaulted ceiling and arches of the main lobby was impressive. She bought a newspaper from a young boy, and after finding a post office and purchasing the required postage stamps, she mailed the handful of letters to Sarie and hurried back to the platform where her train waited, belching smoke from its stack.

The porter helped her up the step into the train and gave her a friendly smile as he released her hand. Bella thanked him and found her way to the lounge as the train pulled out of the cavernous vault of the station. In a short time the scenery passing by changed from pastoral to more rugged country. In a few hours trees and rocks hemmed the tracks on both sides. It seemed the coniferous forests and stark granite cliffs and boulders would never end. Occasionally lakes and ponds filled with water lilies broke the monotony of the sombre spiked spruce and pine that dominated the forests. For a time, the tracks ran beside a huge body of water. The car attendant informed Bella it was Lake Huron, he advised her if she thought it was huge to wait until she saw Lake Superior. The natives called it *Gitche Gumee*, the big waters. Since she seemed interested he went on to tell her it was the largest lake by surface area in the world and the third largest if measured by volume. Bella listened politely, but with only half an ear. Her thoughts were miles away on Cornwall's coast with the Atlantic throwing itself at the cliffs. She smiled and thanked the man before he moved on.

The open novel lay on her lap, but the inclination to discover what dilemma the heroine had gotten messed up with deserted her. Bella's head bobbed sharply startling her. *Bother and damn, I must have dozed off.* She blinked and turned toward the window. More trees crowded the edges of the railway, the sky above a vivid deep blue that reminded her of the deep waters Mounts Bay. Her broken sleep of the previous night was catching up with her. She rubbed her stinging eyes with her hand and sighed. Giving in to the lethargy that sapped her strength, Bella shifted in her seat, leaned against the window and closed her eyes.

"Bella?"

She stirred in her sleep. *I must be dreaming. Vear? Is that really you?*

"I told you I would never leave you. I am always in your heart as you are in mine."

But how can that be? The rational part of her brain argued with her sleeping mind. *I'm thousands of miles away, and the Council has forbidden any contact.*

"Even the Council of Kernow cannot control my dreams—our dreams. In the luminous in-between place that exists between waking and deep sleep, on the threshold of dreaming, we can meet and speak the words of our heart."

Are you sure? I'm afraid. Afraid of what they could do to you, or to me, for that matter. Does their power reach even to Canada?

"There is no reason to fear, dear one. No one can touch us here and we have broken none of rules they have decreed we must abide by."

But can their power touch me here, across the sea in Canada? Bella persisted, fear cold in her belly. She resolutely blocked all thought of her unborn child from her mind. Vear must never know or he'd move heaven and earth to come to her and no good could ever come of that. Lord only knew where the Council would banish him to if that came to pass.

"No," the thought came slowly and cautiously. *"I do not think their power or jurisdiction reaches that far. In any case there are other powers at work in the new world. Ancient, powerful ones who lay claim to those lands. Alien to me in touch and feel, but not unkind if shown the respect they demand. Do not fret, dear heart. You are protected."*

A shuddering breath escaped Bella's lips and she felt on the verge of tears. *I miss you so much. I don't know how I can go on without you. How can they make something so right into something so horrible? I never wanted to leave Cornwall, and yet here I am, halfway to some Godforsaken place I know nothing about.*

"Bella, my love. It was not the Council who exiled you from your homeland. You must look to your very human mortals for that blame. It was a choice you made, as well." The nebulous dream voice reminded her.

Some choice! Her dreaming voice laughed bitterly. *Stay and be married to Daniel Treliving, becoming his property, his chattel, that he can abuse and misuse as he sees fit.* She shuddered. *I have already had a taste of what he is capable of. And,* she hesitated, taking care with her words least she give away her carefully guarded secret, *there are others to consider.*

"What others? Sarie and her mother? Treliving cannot harm them. Surely, you realize

Sarie has guardians and friends, as does her mother."

I have my reasons, Vear. Please don't press me.

"There are things you aren't telling me, Bella. What secret are you keeping? Has something happened to you, has someone threatened you?"

Vear, just remember I will always love you. Please, hold that close to your heart and believe in my love for you. Nothing else really matters between you and I.

"You are afraid of something, Bella. I will know what secret you hide from me..."

The train jerked and Bella woke with a start, her heart racing. "No, no, no. He can never know. I must be far more careful."

"Are you alright, my dear?" A motherly woman touched Bella's shoulder. "You seemed to be having a bad dream."

"Yes, I'm fine, thank you. T'was just a dream, that's all." She smiled tremulously. "I appreciate your concern."

"Would you like to share a pot of tea with me? From your accent I would say you hail from Cornwall. Am I correct?" The woman inquired.

"That would be lovely. I'm surprised you recognize my accent, how did you know?" Even though the woman was a stranger, she seemed genuinely concerned, and more importantly, Bella wanted to avoid falling asleep again at all costs.

"My husband is from north Cornwall, near Tintagel. He's been in Canada for over a decade, but still maintains the lilt and cadence of the speech. Here, dear, come join me at my table and I'll order a nice pot of tea and some biscuits. Roland says a good cup of tea can make any problem go away." She smiled and offered Bella her hand.

"That would be very kind of you," she replied. "I'm Arabella, but my friends call me Bella." She took the woman's hand and got to her feet stiffly. "Oh, my. I've been sitting in spot far too long."

"Come along then, Bella. I'm Caroline, Caroline Logan." She led the way to secluded corner table at the front of the car, the shade drawn half down over the window. She settled herself, beckoned the car attendant and requested the promised tea and biscuits. "We can open the shade if you like. I just find all the trees and wilderness quite depressing, don't you know. I'm far more used to the open prairie now."

Bella seated herself across from her new friend. "No, it's quite fine the way it is. It doesn't seem like the trees and rocks and lakes will ever end. It's all so, I don't know, raw and new, and it frightens me in a way," she confessed.

Caroline patted her hand and smiled. "Well then, we shall find something more pleasant to talk about."

The attendant arrived with the promised tea and refreshments. Bella spent a few happy hours chatting with her new friend and began to feel more like her old self.

"Where are you headed for," Caroline inquired as she poured more tea into the younger woman's cup.

"Alberta, a town or city called Edmonton."

"Is that where you're planning to stay?"

"Oh no. From there, Mister Rowan is supposed to meet me with a motor car and then take me to a ranch outside some place called Pincher Creek. I understand it's a long journey from the train station, but the train doesn't stop any place closer," Bella explained.

"And, is this Mister Rowan an acquaintance of yours? You're very young to be travelling such a distance on your own." A small disapproving frown creased Caroline's forehead.

Bella blushed in spite of herself. "Well, actually...he's my fiancé." She left the sentence hanging and hoped the woman would let the subject drop.

"I see." Caroline studied her face, plainly not about to let Bella change the topic. "Just how well do you know this man?"

"I don't, really. He's an acquaintance of the priest of my parish and Father Boyle swears he is a kind and honourable gentleman. Da says it's the best I could hope for," her voice wavered slightly under the woman's intense scrutiny.

"Any you, Arabella, what do you hope for? I can't imagine you have decided to trek half way across the world of your own accord."

"I have promised to be the best wife I possibly can, and to try hard to learn the things I need to know to help my future husband on his ranch," Bella said stoutly.

"You can cook then, dear? And sew and bake?" Caroline raised an eyebrow.

"I've kept house for my Da since I was a little, and I'm sure I will learn the new ways fast. I have ever so many cookery books to help me."

"If you say so, dear." Caroline didn't sound convinced. "Here let me pour you another cuppa." She upended the tea pot and emptied the last of the contents into Bella's cup.

"Thank you, Caroline."

Chapter Four

The train left Winnipeg behind and continued westward. On either side of the rail line the land spread away to the horizon in a monotonous vista of undulating acres of green. Bella's head ached from trying to make sense of the vast distances. How could there possibly be so much vacant land? She imagined the whole of England, or Cornwall at least, could fit into the immense country stretching as far as she could see.

She felt suddenly small and insignificant and totally out of her depth. She wished Caroline were here to talk to, but the woman had left the train at Winnipeg. The faint, and barely acknowledged, possibility that she could run away and somehow make her way back home if D'Arcy Rowan turned out to be horrible, died a thousand deaths. There was no way she could ever manage to travel so far.

Besides, common sense raised its head and forced her to admit that Da would just ship her away somewhere else. Or else force her to the altar with Daniel. As the prairie slipped past the window, Bella took pen and paper from her valise and poured her heart out to Sarie. A single tear slid down her face as she folded the thin sheets of onion paper and addressed the letter. She should have time at the stop in Saskatoon, Saskatchewan to find a post office, buy a stamp and send the letter on its way.

Saskatoon came and went, she gave her letters along with money for postage to a conductor who promised to mail them for her. Bella dozed in her seat in the lounge car. She hadn't slept well last night again. Each clack of the wheels on the track grated on her nerves and whispered incessantly—mistake, mistake, mistake, you made a mistake. Growling under her breath, Bella surged to her feet and prowled from the ladies lounge to the dining car and back again. Sitting still left her too much time to think, and thinking was the last thing she wanted to do.

"Welcome to Alberta," the car attendant greeted her when Bella tired of her pacing and returned to the lounge.

"What?" she asked startled. "What did you say?"

He looked at her strangely. "Welcome to Alberta, miss." The man continued on his way shaking his head.

Bella collapsed into the nearest empty chair, her trembling legs threatening to let her down. "Alberta. I can't do this, I can't do this. I can't." She buried her burning face in her hands and wished the floor would open up and swallow her. Time was running out, and soon she would step off the train and meet the man who she would share her life, and her bed, with.

The last thought brought bile up her throat and painful spasms in her belly. Da's words echoed in her head. *You will be expected to fulfil your marital duties as his wife.* She feared for an awful moment she might be ill all over her shoes. Heat flooded her body at the thought of the intimacies she shared with Vear Du. With him it was wonderful and magic, but the thought of sharing those acts with a man she didn't even know, let alone love, sickened her.

It would be worse than what Jan Tregeagle did to her, because she would have to be a willing participant, not a spell bound victim. From the information she was given, D'Arcy Rowan was forty-two years old. Twice her age for God's sake. He was an old man, almost as old as Da. He'd be entitled to do with her what he wished, put his hands on her and expect her to welcome him into her body. *It's so unfair! This is all a bad dream and I'm going to wake up safe in my bed and hear Da downstairs banging around in the kitchen. I just need to wake up, that's all.* She pinched her forearm hard enough to leave a mark. It hurt like the dickens and she didn't wake up at all. "Bloody Hell, Bella. Don't be such a fool. You can't wake up because you're already awake." She rubbed the red mark on her arm.

Only a few more hours of freedom and she might as well make the most of it, she supposed. The longing to be with Vear shaded everything with desperation and a weird sense of disassociation from the reality of her situation.

With a weary sigh, she rested her head on the back of the upholstered club chair and closed her eyes. She was so tired, but her mind refused to be quiet. The swaying of the car and the infernal chattering of the wheels set her teeth on edge. She clenched her jaw to keep from screaming.

"Bella, my bright star. How fare you?" The deep voice vibrated in her bones. She started, but refused to open her eyes.

Vear, is that you? Oh my God, what am I going to do? I'm scared half to death and I just can't let anyone touch me like…you know. That was something special just between us, and…I need you so…

"Bella, Bella. Calm yourself, my bright love. We have so little time, can we not spend it talking of our love?"

But what am I supposed to do? I can't let him…I can't be his wife in that way. I thought I could, but can't."

"We knew what we risked when we let ourselves love each other. It was a gamble, and we lost. Now, we will do what we must to survive. You and I both. There is so little time." The inner voice became rough and worried. *"I love you, Bella. I always will. In time we'll be together again. I don't know how or when, only that I will make it happen."* His presence faded from her mind.

Bella groped through the threads of her dreams and scattered thoughts, seeking to follow him, to hold onto to some small part of the selkie's dream. Shades and shadows confused her and her feet missed the path, leaving her wandering in thick curtains of mist and rain. She began to run, slipping and sliding on wet grass and mud. Through the shifting mists she was certain she saw the darker figure of a tall man just ahead. Surely if she ran just a bit faster she would catch up to him and he'd take her in his arms. "Vear, wait up!" she called.

In her haste she tripped over a protruding chunk of Cornish granite buried in the pathway. She sprawled face first onto the path. Boots squelched in the puddles as the figure she'd been chasing made his way back to her. She struggled to raise herself up on her elbows, still gasping from having the wind knocked out of her. A large hand entered her line of sight, she grasped it and looked up, a smile of welcome on her lips—and screamed in terror. Daniel Treliving glared down at her from under the peak of his battered cap, his fingers biting into her wrist.

"Miss? Miss? Are you alright?"

Bella came fully awake and flinched away from the gentle hand on her shoulder. She looked wildly around, disoriented for a moment, before her thoughts settled and she recognized her surroundings.

"Miss?" The car attendant peered down at her.

"Yes, I'm fine. I must have dozed off. I must have been dreaming," she managed to answer him.

"Seemed like a bad dream, if you'll pardon me saying so, miss."

"A night mare more like." She forced a weak smile to her face. "I'm fine now, thank you for your concern."

"If you say so, miss. We'll be arriving in Edmonton in an hour or so, would you like something to eat. It might make you feel better." He smiled at her with kind eyes.

Her stomach clenched and she forced herself to relax. "Yes, a cuppa would be splendid, and some biscuits perhaps?"

"Right away, miss." The car attendant scurried off to carry out her biding. He returned a short time later with a tray laden with tea, biscuits and a ham sandwich."

Bella thanked him gratefully and gazed out the window as the last light of day leaked from the sky to the west. The blazing red-orange ball of the sun had slipped behind the jagged silhouette of the mountains earlier. The sky was a deep blue, so intense it took her breath away. The sandwich stuck in her throat, but she made herself choke it down. The tea helped, but did nothing to warm the cold fear in the pit of her belly.

Mistake, mistake, mistake. You made a mistake, the train chanted as the rails carried her closer and closer to her fate. *Please God, let it be alright. Let him be kind to me.* Bella prayed earnestly as she hadn't since she was a child and wanted a pony of her own.

The dark prairie soon gave way to a smattering of lights strewn haphazardly across the land as the train approached the outskirts of Edmonton. As it penetrated deeper into the city proper factories and rows of houses illuminated the night. Panic closed Bella's throat, it wouldn't be long now before she met her fiancé. She peered at her reflection in the window glass, not perfect, she decided, but it would do well enough. The passing structures were strangely alien and exacerbated the panic building within her.

Everything seemed built of wood, although there were a few brick structures. Where were all the stone buildings with the patina of years of weather softening their starkness, and the narrow curving streets that felt so safe and comforting as they curled through the town? From what she could glimpse from the window, the through fares here were wide and straight, the buildings sitting well back from the edges as if they feared to sit too close to the traffic streaming by. Bella got to her feet and smoothed the skirt of her rose linen skirt. Unable to stave off the inevitable, she made her way to the sleeper car and retrieved her valise and coat. D'Arcy had written to Father Boyle and advised that Bella should be aware the Alberta weather could be capricious and warm clothing was a necessity. She shrugged into the blue woolen garment which reached past her knees. It was rather awkward to walk in, and she hoped it was suitable. The colour did look nice with her eyes she noticed when she checked her appearance in the small mirror.

Bella swayed a little and caught the edge of the berth for support. The train slowed rather abruptly and then jerked forward again. "Bother and damn," she muttered. She did a last minute search to ensure nothing was left behind. Stepping into the corridor, she felt suddenly bereft. The small berth took on the aspect of safe haven, and now she was leaving that safety and stepping out into the unknown. She swallowed hard and resolutely went to find a place where she could see the station as they approached.

Edmonton looked quite pretty, spread out with her lights glittering like jewels reflecting in the waters of the wide river the train passed over via a bridge suspended high over the water. An imposing cliff on the far side was topped with a cluster of buildings. The more undesirable aspects that are present in any city were softened and obscured by the darkness. At the moment it looked more like something out of a fairy tale. Once across the river, they travelled past various buildings Bella was hard pressed to know what function they served.

Sooner than she would have liked, the train entered the harsh glare of the station lights and jerked to a stop. The steam engine released a loud hiss Bella could hear even half way down the line of cars. A general hustle and bustle of passengers preparing to de-train ensued. A Pullman porter assured Bella her trunks would be offloaded and kept secure until she could claim them. She thanked him and turned to peer out the window at the people clustered in the circles of light cast by the station house lights. *Why, I don't even know what the man looks like.* The realization gave her pause. *However will I know which person is Mister Rowan?*

"You can get off now, miss," the porter said. "The doors are open and the steps in place. It's been a pleasure having you onboard."

"Thank you," she replied and gave him a tremulous smile.

"It will all come right, miss. Don't you worry. I've seen hundreds of women ride this train west to be the brides of men they've never met. You'll get used to it." He patted her hand and hurried off.

Taking a deep breath to quell the panic, Bella moved into the stream of passengers heading to the door at the far end of the car. She hesitated a moment on the threshold before stepping down onto the wooden stool and then onto the platform proper. Clutching her valise and purse, she ventured toward the station house, glancing around hoping to see someone looking for her. A cold wind whipped down the platform picking up bits of paper and refuse, hurling them skyward and spinning them about before either dropping them back to the platform or carrying out of sight. Bella shivered. *Bloody hell, it's freezing.* No one in particular seemed to be looking for her, so she joined the crush of people inside the station house. She spied a man in a Canadian Pacific uniform, the brass buttons winking in the overhead light.

"Excuse me, sir. I'm supposed to be meeting someone, but I can't seem to find them. I'm hoping you can assist me," Bella said when the man had a moment free.

"Could I have your name, miss, and the name of the person who is supposed to meet you?" He consulted a spiral bound pad he pulled from a pocket.

"Oh, of course. How silly of me. I'm Arabella Angarrick and I was expecting to be met by a man by the name of D'Arcy Rowan."

The railway man frowned and flipped pages in his notebook. "Why don't you take a seat over by the wall, there?" He pointed to a long wooden bench. "I'll go see what I can find out for you. There's been a couple of telegrams today for passengers on this train, but I don't see anything for you."

"My trunks—" Bella waved toward the platform.

"They'll be fine. Someone will watch them until you collect them. I'll be right back." He hurried off toward a door on the far side of the room.

Bella wandered over to the long bench and sank down gratefully. Even though the baby wasn't showing yet, she found herself becoming exhausted much more easily. It was irritating and very inconvenient, to say the least. She set the valise by her feet and attempted to assuage the impatience thrumming through her by

51

observing her fellow passengers. A sharp pang of loss stabbed her, Sarie should be here take part in the game. It wasn't near as much fun without her.

"Miss Angarrick?"

"Yes?" Bella looked up sharply.

"Yer Arabella Angarrick?" The grey haired man looked her up and down as if he were assessing a horse for suitability. "Not at all what I was expectin'."

"Pardon?" She blinked. "What do—"

"Trunks still out there?" He nodded toward the platform and stalked away when she nodded. He looked back before he opened the door and frowned. "C'mon, missy. Shake a leg."

Fighting back the urge to scream or cry, or maybe both, Bella got to her feet and followed him. She exited back onto the platform and found he had already claimed her trunks and was loading them onto a dolly of some sort."

"This all of 'em?" He started pulling the low wooden cart down the platform toward the exit. The metal wheels clunking over the joins in the floor boards.

Bella trailed along behind, still carrying her valise. *What have I agreed to? I should march right back to the ticket booth and buy a ticket to Halifax and then get on a ship and go home. This is barmy. The bloke isn't forty, he's got to sixty at least.*

"Get a move on, woman." Her escort stopped at the far end of the station. "I ain't got all night, ye know." When she caught up to him, he continued into a car park and stopped by a large dark coloured vehicle. The thing was huge, far bigger and longer than any auto Bella had ever seen. The man, whose name she still didn't know for sure, opened the rear of the car where she expected the boot to be. Instead it opened more like a gate and inside she caught a glimpse of a flat bed. He hailed a one of the railway men working in the area and with his help, Bella's trunks were stowed in the back of the motor car. She stood quietly by and waited. Her companion slammed the door shut and went around to the driver's side and got in.

Bella hesitated. Was she supposed to just get in the car or was there some other plan? She was all at sea, should she just get in?

The passenger door swung open and the grey haired man's angry face peered out at her. "You comin' or what, woman? I'm a'leavin' so if yer comin' get yer arse in the car." The face disappeared and the engine burst into life.

Anger replaced uncertainty, Bella stormed over and flung her valise and purse onto the wide seat and glared at him. She opened her mouth to give him a piece of her mind, but he let the clutch out and the car started to roll. In an instant she decided that being left alone in the dark in a strange city was less attractive than going with the bleeder in the vehicle. She scrambled into the seat and slammed the door. Once she seated she turned to glare at him.

"Look, I really don't…"

The rest of the words fled her mind when the cowboy at the wheel floored the gas pedal and the metal monster leaped forward, throwing Bella back against the seat. She gripped the dashboard with one hand and the side of her seat with the other. The diabolical little man looked her way and cackled.

"Hang on, missy."

Bella didn't know which was worse, closing her eyes or keeping them open. Streetlights became a stream of brilliance as they careened through the streets. She was thrown about as the maniac driver dodged cars and lamp posts. *This is the man I'm doomed to spend the rest of my life with? On the bright side, given his driving habits, my life might not be that long.* The thought of the unborn child she carried gave her courage.

"Would you slow down, for pity's sake," she yelled at him.

"Ain't goin' that fast, missy. This here machine gots a V8 engine, she can hit 70 miles an hour." He careened around a corner, leaning forward over the wheel and cackling the whole time. "YeeeHawwww!"

Bella let got for an instance and clapped her hands over her ears. A moment later, she was forced to hang on again. The car hurtled down a road clinging to a steep cliff overlooking the river. She closed her eyes and prayed for deliverance.

"That there's the South Saskatchewan." He waved one hand at the water looming on her left.

"Would you keep your hands on the wheel, please?" Her voice rose to a screech.

"What're ye getting' all het up about?" He turned to look at her.

"Eyes on the road!" she ordered.

"Wimmen." He shook his head. "Cain't figure 'em out, no matter how ye try."

Reaching the flats by the river, the car accelerated again. Bella had never gone so fast and if she hadn't been terrified it would have been exhilarating. In her present exhausted state it only served to increase her anxiety. If Da were here she'd kill him with her bare hands, and Father Boyle along with him. *Kind and respectable, my arse. D'Arcy Rowan is a card carrying crazy man. He's barking mad, belongs in Bodmin!* The lights of cars and lorries streaked by. He made a sharp right into a narrow road way and came to a jarring halt in front of a hotel.

"Home sweet home. This is where yer bunkin' for the night. Tomorrow we'll head for the south country," he informed her. "Lessen ye need somethin' from them trunks of yers, I'll jest leave 'em where they sit fer the night."

"No, I don't need them. I've got the necessities in my valise." She would have said more but he was already out of the car and standing by the hotel door tapping his booted foot impatiently. Her temper flared, but she was

55

too tired to give vent to her anger. With no grace whatsoever Bella scrambled from the death trap of a car, gathered her belongings and joined him. Without a word he went inside without looking to see if she followed. Gritting her teeth and suppressing a sigh, Bella pushed through the door and joined him at the front desk.

If the disagreeable urchin thought he was going to share her bed tonight, he was sadly mistaken. He was rude, and short, and unkept, and…and…she wasn't his wife yet! She ended the thought triumphantly. A room key was thrust unceremoniously into her hand as he passed. Clutching it, she trailed behind him up the stairs.

"This'un yers," he said, stopping by a door near the head of the stairs. "Just holler iffen ye need something, I'm right next door." He didn't wait for answer, just inserted his key in the lock, slipped inside and shut the door with a snick.

Bella stood stock still, quite astounded by the man's abrupt mannerisms and his total lack of regard for her. *He expects me to agree to marry him? But I have to, I guess. I've no place else to go, and to Da's way of thinking, the man's bought and paid for me. He'd yell and screech and say I'm lucky any man will take me in my condition. Like I'm damaged goods or something. This guy makes Daniel start to look good. Although, on second thought, scupper that. I don't thing D'Arcy is mean, just rude and ignorant. I can learn to deal with that.*

"Ye gonna use that room or stand in the hall all night?" His head poked out the door next to hers.

"What? Oh. No, I'm just going in. Had trouble with the key," she lied.

The room was clean and she was pleased to see it had its own water closet. No traipsing down the hall in the middle of the night. Seemed like she needed to pee all the time lately. After a quick wash, she changed and slid into the bed. The curtains shut out the lights of the city and she could almost pretend it was London or Truro behind the curtains and not strange and alien Edmonton. She thought of Vear as she slipped into sleep, but no dreams came to her.

Chapter Five

Loud pounding on the door woke her. Bella struggled out of the tangled nest of covers and blinked sleep from her eyes. "Alright, alright. I'm coming, Da," she called.

"Ain't yer pa, woman. Git yer ass in gear, we got us a long way to go today."

Reality came crashing down on her. She wasn't in her own bed in Penzance, she was in Edmonton and the man outside was some crazy rancher bloke she'd stupidly, or so it seemed now, agreed to marry sight unseen. Morning was not her strong suit, and she spoke without thinking.

"Take your hurry in your hand, man. I'll be down in a few minutes." She flopped back on the bed and pulled the covers over her head. He could just bloody well wait for her she decided mutinously. The door handle rattled and she was glad she remembered to lock it last night.

Twenty minutes later she descended the stairs to find the lobby empty. *Did the bloody bastard leave without me?* Leaving the valise by a chair she approached the front desk to return the room key.

"Miss Angarrick, thank you. Your travelling companion asked me to tell you to wait for him here. He's just gone to refuel the car. You're quite welcome to make yourself to home until he returns."

She thanked the man and settled herself to wait. Ten minutes later the car pulled up outside the lobby doors. Bella gathered her belongings and marched out to meet him. She nodded stiffly as she passed the driver side, flung the valise into the back seat, and with as much dignity as could be mustered, slid into the passenger seat. Without a word of welcome, or anything else for that matter, the wiry little man put the car in gear and roared out of the hotel lot. His driving hadn't been improved by a nights' sleep it seemed. The big boat of a vehicle soared down the highway once they left the precincts of Edmonton behind. Like a bird of prey it swooped down on the slower vehicles before it, swept around them and left them in its dust.

The awkward silence stretched Bella's nerves to the breaking point. What was wrong with the bloke? If this was what her life was going to be like she might as well throw herself out the door and put an end to it right now. At least she would exercise some control over her own destiny in that case. Her fingers closed on the handle at her side before common sense took over. Sighing, she returned her hand to her lap. Turning her head toward the window so she didn't have to look at the fiendish driver, Bella studied the land passing by. Rolling hills and scattered trees lined the road. Though she searched the western horizon there was no evidence of the range of mountains that was supposed to be there. Maybe that was a lie too, she mused, stealing a quick glance at her companion. Nice and respectable? She snorted and quickly turned it into a fake cough when the object of her scorn spared her a speaking glance.

A highway sign declared they were approaching some sort of civilization. It sounded like some kind of a zoo, Red Deer. What kind of name was that for a city? The frenzied flight of the car slowed when they passed the outskirts. Bella straightened up and peered out the window. The highway seemed to be bounded on either side by restaurants and petrol stations. Her stomach growled in protest of the lack of breakfast.

"You hungry?" The wizened man grinned as if he could read her mind.

"I could eat," she replied, refusing to look at him.

"I'm gonna stop for a cup a joe. If you're quick you should be able to rustle up somethin' to eat." He took a turn off onto a side road and pulled into a gas station come restaurant.

Bella had the door open before the car rolled to a stop. Her bladder was ready to burst but she'd be damned before she'd admit anything like that to the hateful little man. She hurried into the store, asked for the water closet, remembering too late it was called a bathroom here, and after a brief exchange she scurried to relieve herself. Taking a few precious moments to freshen up, she emerged from the bathroom hallway at the rear of the store to see D'Arcy leaning against the fender of the car sucking on a large cup of coffee. Quickly scanning the items on offer she chose an egg salad sandwich which claimed it was prepared by Hattie's Homemade Goodness. A bottle of club orange completed her choice. It took a moment for her to figure out the right amount of money to give the clerk. The coins and bills were so different from the familiar currency of home.

"Took ya long enough," the little man drawled when she approached the car. He pushed away from the fender and got in, placing his coffee in a fragile looking holder of sorts.

Bella didn't dignify his comment with a response and managed to get back in without squishing the sandwich too badly. The driver took one long swig of his joe, as he called it. and the vehicle took flight down the highway again. She concentrated on eating and attempting to drink without breaking her teeth on the neck of the pop bottle. Every time she brought it up to drink the fecking car hit a bump or swerved, Bella swore the little bastard was doing it on purpose. The day stretched before like eternity, her back ached and one leg kept cramping and jumping. How much further was this place she was going to live? Exhaustion finally caught up with her, though she fought it her head kept bobbing forward as she slipped in and out of a half-doze. In the end she gave up, rested her head on the window and went to sleep.

"Bella? What is wrong, dear heart?"

Vear? Come and get me, take me home! I don't want to do this. I hate this crazy man...

"Bella, calm down. We both have a path we're destined to walk, there is nothing we can do to change it. We made our choice when we loved each other, now it is far too late to be lamenting that choice."

But Vear...

Her head bounced off the window and muffled a curse. Bella shot a poisonous glance at her companion who responded with a devilish grin.

"Wake ye up, did I?"

"I was just napping," she protested defiantly.

"Then ye've been nappin' fer over an hour." He cackled and the car shot forward at an increased rate of speed.

A highway sign flashed by declaring that Crossfield was 2 miles ahead and Airdrie was 10 miles. Such odd names and none of them with the familiar feeling of home. But this was home now, she reminded herself, and she'd best get used to it.

"We'll be stopping in Calgary for fuel and I'm gonna hunt me down some chow while I'm at it," he informed her without taking his eyes from the road or slowing the headlong pace of the vehicle.

"Fine," she replied tersely.

When they whipped by the Crossfield turnoff Bella strained her eyes but could see no evidence that a village even existed. Since leaving Red Deer the land had become increasingly flatter and the number of trees dwindled. The only thick stands seemed to be clustered around houses. Her curiosity got the better of her pique. Besides, if she was going to spend the rest of her life with this man, she was going to have to figure out how to communicate with him.

"Are all those trees around the houses natural?"

The driver shot her a sidelong glance, his face contorting like he was in pain or something.

"Are you alright?" *Please God, don't let him be having a heart attack while he's driving.*

For a long moment he was silent and his chest heaved. Panic rose in her breast, he *was* having a heart attack. She leaned across the seat, he slapped her hand away when she reached for his wrist to check his pulse.

"Get on with ye." Laughter bubbled up and he laughed so hard tears ran down his cheeks. "Let a man drive, woman."

"What's so bloody funny?" Bella flounced back to her side of the car and crossed her arms over her chest. "I thought you were having a heart attack," she muttered.

He gave one last guffaw, and hawked to clear his throat before he replied. "Them trees are a wind break, a shelter belt. Just 'bout any tree bigger'n a bush ain't natural out here on the prairies."

"Oh," she said faintly. "What's a shelter belt and why do they need one?" If she was going to live her, she needed to know what was what.

He took his eyes off the road long enough to study her face. Apparently satisfied with what he found there, he nodded. "The wind blows somethin' fierce out here, an' the snow drifts. Take the wire right off the posts it will. Wind'll like to take the skin offen yer face sometimes. So we plant trees and bushes to break the wind and help stop with the driftin'."

"How do you know what to plant? If the weather is so harsh, how does anything survive?"

"Wal, it do get plenty dry in the summer, so ye need to use somethin' that's drought resistant, and can stand the battering by the wind. Not to mention the cold. Kin get down to minus fifty."

"So what do you plant?" Bella found she was actually interested in what he was saying.

"Ye start with bushes on the outer edge, to break the full force of the wind and to catch the snow. So, caragana, or barberry, Saskatoon bushes will work too, then you go a bit bigger but still bushy, like lilacs or diamond willow, then spruce trees, maybe two lines of those kinda offset from each other and then cottonwood or poplars."

"Sounds like a lot of work," Bella remarked.

"In the beginin', sure. But once ye spend a winter here, ye'll unnerstan' better." He actually smiled at her.

Be still my beating heart. She grinned in spite of herself.

They passed through Airdrie, she marvelled that the town seemed to be split in two by the highway. It seemed an odd way to construct a town, but it must work, she mused. A short distance later they came to the Calgary city limits.

"Cow Town at last," D'Arcy declared.

"Cow Town? Isn't this Calgary?"

"Yep. Home of the Calgary Stampede. That's why they call it Cow Town. Not that long ago ranchers had to drive their herd into Calgary to the rail head. Ye ever heered of the Stampede over the pond?"

Bella shook her head.

"Wal, ye'll get yer chance to see it firsthand come July. D'Arcy always makes the trip with some of the stock. Last year he won Grand Champion with his big old Hereford bull."

The man kept prattling on, but Bella was hung up on the one remark.

"What do you mean 'D'Arcy always makes the trip'? Aren't you D'Arcy Rowan?" Bella interrupted him.

He gave an incredulous look and dissolved in laughter again. When he regained his composure and was reduced to quiet cackles, he finally replied.

"Ye thought I was D'Arcy?" He engaged in another fit of giggles. "Not hardly, missy. I'm his foreman. Name's Red. Man o' man, D will get a good chuckle outa that. Why would ye think that? Didn't ye get the tellygram thing sayin' he was sendin' me to fetch ye?"

"Of course I didn't, or I wouldn't have made such a fool of myself. It must have arrived after I left." She paused and then plunged on. "What was so important he couldn't come himself, he promised Da and Father Boyle he'd collect me personally when I got to Edmonton. Has he changed his mind about me? Or am I just not worth the effort?" she said bitterly.

"Ye watch yer mouth when yer jawin' about D, missy." Red's eyes glittered dangerously. "Ain't a finer man this side of the Rockies. Maybe in all of Albertie."

"Then why didn't he come and get me like he promised?" Bella interrupted him.

"Man's laid up. Got run over by a pen of heifers a week an' a half ago. He's pretty broken up, gonna take a while to get back on his feet. Up til then, he was plannin' on goin' hisself. He's a good man, D. Ye could do a lot worse'n him, missy." Red glared straight ahead.

"I had no idea. As I said, the telegram must have arrived after I left," she murmured.

"Just sayin', ye'd do well to now go shootin' yer mouth off afore ye got all the facts."

Red took an exit off the highway and drove for a few minutes before he found a petrol station and pulled in. Bella took the opportunity to use the bathroom and splash some water on her face. When she emerged, Red was at the counter paying for the petrol. A couple of packets of crisps lay on the counter by his elbow.

"Ye want any thin'? I got a couple a bags of chips, just go pick what ye want and add it to the pile."

She was stymied for a moment. *Chips?* Chips were deep fried and made to eaten with battered fish. *He must mean crisps, that's it. Lord Almighty, how am I ever going to fit in here? I should have stayed at home and brazened it out.* Bella chose some crisps that claimed to be ketchup flavoured. It sounded intriguing. She added a couple of chocolate bars as well and waited while he paid for everything. Red gathered up the purchases and pushed through the door, Bella followed behind. Once she closed the door, Red pulled away and headed back to the highway. The clouds and haze had dissipated when she glanced toward the west where the sun was retreating. Her breath caught in her throat at the sight of the saw-toothed peaks iced with snow stretching across the horizon. The mountains seemed so close, but in the vastness of this new country distances were deceiving.

"How long would it take to reach the mountains?" She broke the silence of the car.

Red glanced toward the west before he replied. "From here, about a couple of hours, just to get to Banff. To get into the mountains proper, probably three or four hours."

"They look beautiful. Is the ranch near the mountains?"

"Not hardly. It's mostly rangeland down south. We're not far from the Porcupine Hills and the Rockies are a little further on. Pretty country, in my opinion anyway."

"I'd love to see them close up," she murmured.

"Once D is feelin' up to scratch, I reckon he'd be right happy to take you."

"That would be lovely, but I wouldn't want to inconvenience him."

"I reckon D is just mighty pleased ye've agreed to come all this way and get hitched to him. Man's all fired lonely rattlin' around in that big old house a' his. Reckon he'll give ye just about anythin' ye ask fer." Red favoured her with a sharp glance. "Yer not plannin' on takin' advantage of his good nature, are ye?"

"Certainly not! How dare you suggest such a thing? I'm just not that kind of person, I'll have you know." Bella glared at the little man and stuck her nose in the air.

"Don't be getting' on yer high horse, missy. I don't know nuthin' about you and I'm right fond of D. I got no intention of seein' his good nature turned agin him."

"You have a point, I suppose. The other side of the coin is, I don't know anything much about him either."

"I kin tell ye, he's right glad yer comin'. And he's right excited about the extry edition yer bringin' along with ye. Lookin' forward to havin' a young'un running around the place."

Bella's heart dropped and she feared she might faint. "How do you know about...you know?"

Red glanced at her before returning his attention to the road. "Ain't much that D don't share wi' me. I know ye got yerself into a sticky situation wi' some scoundrel. Ain't nobody gonna hold it agin ye here. D is plannin' to let folks hereabouts think the young'un is his, so ye be sure to go along wi' it. Ye here?"

"That's very kind of him," she said softly. "Probably more than I deserve."

"Ye seem like a nice gal, and the nipper's gotta grow up here, he don't need to be the butt of gossip. Growin' up's hard enough wi'out that."

"It might be a girl," Bella ventured. "Will he be upset if it's a girl?" She crossed her hands protectively over her belly.

"Won't make no never mind to D. For some reason he cain't sire no kids. Thet ain't common knowledge though, so mind yer tongue on that score. He's right pleased he's getting' two fer the price a' one." Red winked at her.

"You make me sound like he bought a brood mare," she feigned insult, but dissolved into giggles instead.

"I'm thinkin' ye'll fit in just fine, missy. Long as ye can keep yer sense of humour when things go bad."

"I'll try to remember that."

They were clear of the southern edge of the city now and the land rolled away on either side. To the west the Rockies were bathed in the golden glow of early evening. The March equinox had come and gone, the long prairie days were lengthening. Gold fingers of light illuminated the hill tops and the blush of new leaves on the trees. Red said they were cottonwood and poplars. For the life of her, Bella couldn't tell the difference between the two.

"Jus' wait til May when the cottonwoods look like they're hung wi'snow and the cotton's blowing everywhere. Getting' on yer clothes and makin' ye sneeze. It's right pretty though.

Chapter Six

Bella yawned. The last leg of her journey seemed to take forever, the ribbon of highway stretched ahead as far as she could see. She was hungry again and needed to pee. A glance to her left revealed her companion seemed to be perfectly happy to just keep bowling along without stopping. It was hard to get used to feeling off kilter, she flinched each time a vehicle passed. Everything was on the wrong side of the road, what possessed these people to drive on the wrong side of the road? Whose brill idea was that?

The pressure in her bladder reminded her sharply that they really needed to stop. The side of the road was looking good at the moment, but there were no bushes to hide behind. She cleared her throat and turned toward Red.

"Can we stop at the next petrol station? I really need to use the water closet," she ventured.

"Huh?" He shook his head before he glanced across at her. "What? Sorry I was wool gathering. Sure, I'll pull in the next place I see." He hesitated for a moment. "Don't be takin' this the wrong way, but iffen yer gonna stick around ye might as well learn the lingo. It ain't a petrol station, it's a gas station, an' it ain't a water closet, it's a bathroom. Be a might easier to fit in if folks ain't tryin' to figure out what in the blue blazes yer talkin' about."

"Thanks, I think." She turned back to the window.

Finally another small dusty prairie town appeared on the horizon. Claresholm would be a decent sized village by Cornwall standards, but apparently, it was a town. Bella sighed in frustration. Right now the only thing that she cared about was that Claresholm had a petrol—no, make that gas—station. Red swung the big car off the highway and let her out by the garage door.

"Just nip in and ask for the key. Washrooms are around the side of building. Might as well top up the tank while we're stopped. I got enough fuel to get home, but…" He shrugged.

Bella got out, slammed the door because the latch didn't always catch, and hesitantly entered what she thought must be the garage office. A boy in a battered wide brimmed hat greeted her.

"How can I help ye, m'am?"

"I need…I mean…could I use the washroom, please?" It felt like her face could spontaneously burst into flames. Anxious fingers fiddled with the clasp on her hand bag.

"Sure, m'am." He turned and plucked a key with a thick stick attached to it. Bella stuck her hand out and he passed the odd looking item to her. "Out the door, turn to yer left. Ladies' is the second door. Jest bring the key back when yer done."

Bella fled out the door, forgetting to even thank him. The tiny room had a toilet and a sink crammed side by side, the cement floor was dirty and the smell of old urine was almost too much to bear. She hesitated before setting foot inside, but the urgency of her bladder insisted she press on. Gingerly, she went in and closed the door. A small hook on the back of the door served to hold her hand bag. Holding her skirt up to avoid touching the floor she hovered over the bowl. There was not a chance in hell she was going to actually sit on the yellowed, and far from clean, plastic seat. Her business finished, she straightened her clothes and looked in vain for the chain to flush the mess away. There wasn't any place in the tiny confines to hide something like that, so Bella decided it must be another thing she was going to have to figure out. She spied a tiny lever on the far side of the back of the toilet and pushed it down with tentative fingers. To her relief, water flooded the bowl, and then refilled with fresh water. She was feeling quite proud of herself while washing her hands.

"Are ye dead in there, woman?" Red pounded on the door, shouting at the top of his lungs. "Shake a leg, time's a wastin'. Ye got two minutes an' then I'm leavin', with or without ye." His boot crunched on the coarse gravel and faded away.

Bella finished her ablutions and hurried toward the car. She almost forgot to return the key and had to backtrack in order to leave it on the counter in the office. The attendant being busy washing another customer's wind screen.

"Right, I'm here. You can shove off now." She flounced into the passenger seat.

Red said nothing but gave her a sour look. "Wimmen," he muttered under his breath.

"Blokes," Bella muttered a tad bit louder and glared at him.

He sniffed, smoothed his rusty-red handlebar moustache with one hand and put the car in gear. Although Bella was determined to stay awake, the silence in the car and the effects of the long journey caught up with her. It was dark when she woke up and the stars gleamed overhead. The sky seemed infinite, stretched above the shadowed land, the faint light of the stars just hinting at hills and shallow valleys. On her right though, the mountains reared high and majestic against the deep blue of the sky. Above them, the sky was black velvet, the stars glimmering with diamond sharpness. It reminded her sharply of the sky over Mounts Bay with the Milky Way strung above Saint Michael's Mount like a string of diamonds and pearls.

"Almost home," Red broke the silence.

"Thank goodness, I'm that tired." Bella stretched and yawned. "How much longer do you think it will take?"

"Better part of an hour by my reckoning," Red replied. He took one hand off the wheel to scrub his face. Lines were etched deeply around his eyes and mouth, visible in the faint illumination provided by the dashboard light.

He must be tired too, Bella realized. Driving all that way to fetch her probably wasn't something he enjoyed. She vowed to try and be nicer to the prickly old man. Good intentions and all that, she grinned.

The big car rolled along like a ship driven before a gale. Did everyone drive like maniacs? Bella gripped the door handle and closed her eyes. The road curved a hundred yards ahead and seemed to just disappear. She'd really rather not watch if they were going to plunge to their deaths. Compared to the narrow Cornish roads with their massive hedgerows on either side, the ones she was currently on were just as narrow, but with no comforting overhang of brambles and ivy. They also had the disconcerting habit of disappearing around bends or over crests giving the impression that anyone foolish enough to continue would find themselves airborne. Deep steep sided vales snaked across the landscape, winding up toward the mountains and down across the prairie to what Red called the Crowsnest River and the Old Man River. She opened her eyes, relieved to find they were still on the road and unharmed.

To distract her mind from Red's headlong approach to driving, she thought about the all the new terms she needed to remember. Vale wasn't really an accurate way to describe the arid slashes in the earth, vales should have clear water running in them and green trees and ferns crowding them. Glen didn't work either, or dell…maybe gorge? Like the Cheddar Gorge? Sighing, she eyed Red wondering if he was in a talkative mood. Deciding to try her luck, Bella cleared her throat.

"Red, can I ask you a question?"

"Depends on what it is," he replied without taking his attention off the road.

"Right then. What do you call those huge cuts in the earth we keep driving through or around? Valleys or dales or…?"

"Ye might get away with valley, but most folks refer to them as coulees."

"Coulees?" Bella tried out the word. "How do you spell it? C-o-o-l-i-e?"

"Nope. If my memory serves me correctly it's c-o-u-l-e-e."

"That's an odd word. Does it come from a native word?"

"French, I think. The Metis are half Indian-half white man, and most of 'em were Frenchmen. Don't know why, so don't be askin' me. Coulee with an accent thingmabob over the last e, is their term for flow or moving water."

"But there's no water in most of them."

"Must have been at one time, 'cause that's how they was formed. Least ways that's what D says and he's right smart, so he is. And if we get lots of rain along with the mountain snow-pack melting in June there can be a sight more water than is comfortable."

Bella subsided into silence, her tired mind attempting to assimilate this new information.

The back end of the car slewed a bit when Red turned off the pavement unto a dirt track. A little further on, they came to two huge posts with a third across the top like a lintel. Red braked in a flurry of dust, and then drove between the posts. Bella stifled a yelp of surprise at the sudden noise of rubber tires bumping across something in the roadway. Once through, Red accelerated again.

"What the bloody hell was that?" Bella twisted around looking out the back window.

"Texas gate." Red was succinct.

Bella waited for more, but it wasn't forthcoming. "What's a Texas gate?"

Red chuckled. "Ye sure are one for questions, ain't ye? It's a grate set into the ground to keep the cattle from crossing. Cows ain't smart, but they ain't dumb neither. They won't walk on something that ain't solid like. The gaps are wide enough that a critter could break a leg, but close enough ye can drive a vehicle over 'em. Ye ain't got them things over there in England?"

"They have something like that over at Bosistow Farm, I think. I guess I never paid much attention to things like that."

Red grunted but offered no further comment. Bella searched the darkness for lights or any sign of life. As far as she could tell they were out in the back of beyond headed to nowhere. Her companion didn't seem to have any inclination for conversation, and Bella thought it best to let the hare sit at the moment.

77

The rough edge of his tongue stung more than she was willing to admit. *I do hope D'Arcy is a kind man and not a nutter or a bounder. Gads, what if I've traded in Daniel for something far worse?* It was a sobering thought, and one she hadn't contemplated until just this second. Father Boyle vouched for him, but what if he was just anxious to remove an embarrassment from his parish? Maybe the Bishop would view the situation as a failure on the Father's part to safely guard his flock. She straightened up in her seat and stuck her chin out. Well, she'd just have to make the best of it, that's all.

The car flung itself over the crest of hill and raced pell mell down the other side. Bella's stomach dropped and flipped. In the wide flat area below the lights of a house shone brightly. The shadowy outline of other buildings was barely visible behind what looked like a bunch of round paddocks. Nearer the house, horses grazed on the verge of the road, barely looking up as the car hurtled by them.

"Aren't you afraid you'll hit one of them?" Bella couldn't stop herself from asking.

Red snorted. "Iffen they ain't got the sense not to walk in front of a movin' vehicle they get what they deserve."

She opened her mouth to protest, but gave up the argument before it started. What was the use? Her new life was definitely going to be far different that the one she left behind. More visceral and raw. Bella hoped she could cope with it. And if she couldn't…?

They came to an abrupt halt amid clouds of dust and crunching gravel. Bella abandoned her thoughts and looked around with interest. A huge house loomed in front of her, a set of broad steps led up to a wide porch. A first glance it appeared to only have one floor, but when she got out of the car she could see two gables jutting out of the sloping roof. Compared to the narrow row houses she was used to, it appeared massive and intimidating.

"C'mon, woman. Quit gawking an' grab yer stuff. D'll be wantin' to see ye, and I'll wager he ain't eaten yet either." Red brushed by her, the smaller of her trunks perched on his shoulder as if weighed nothing at all.

Blushing, Bella wrenched open the back door and collected her valise and hand bag. Clutching them to her chest like shield she followed the diabolical little cowboy up the steps and onto the porch. Red was already inside and striding across an open room with a huge stone fireplace on the far wall. Tentatively, she opened the door and stepped into what she supposed must be the living room. "Lordy, Lordy, you could put five of Da's house into just this room." She gazed upward where the peaked roof rose high above her. The massive fireplace was wide and then the stonework tapered as it rose up until it disappeared out the roof. A fire burned fitfully giving off little heat. It was more coals and ashes than an actual blaze.

"Sweet Jaysus, woman. Are ye planin' ta stand there gawking all night? I set yer trunk in the first room on the right at the top of the stairs. In the mornin' I'll get one of the hands to help me tote the others up. Ye might want ta wipe off the travel dust, or whatever it is you wimmen do, afore I take ye ta meet D." Red strode past her, boot heels clicking on the polished floor boards. He stirred up the embers in the hearth and piled on some logs from the basket by the andirons. When he straightened up from his task and she was still standing staring at him, he scowled. "Go on, git! I ain't got all night, and I still gotta rustle up some grub for D, and introduce ye to him. Tomorrow's another day and the sun ain't gonna wait to come up just cause I want it to."

Bella found the stairs that led up to a wide hall open to the room below. She located the door Red indicated and pushed it open. It wasn't large, but it was bigger than her room at home. One of the gables she'd noticed from the drive occupied the middle of the wall opposite the door. The blue checked curtains were closed at the moment. The single light on the ceiling was on, and there was a lamp on the table beside the bed. Her trunk sat in the middle of the floor and she edged around it to investigate the low dresser that stood against the wall behind it. An armoire took up most of one short wall, Bella pulled the sticky door open and was pleased to find it boasted shelves as well as a bar to hang her clothes. The drawer at the bottom was deep and wide. The light coloured wood was smooth under her fingers, she wondered what kind of wood had that soft mellow golden hue.

The sound of Red thumping around downstairs shook her out of her examination of the room. Hastily she poured the cold water in the pitcher into a wide bowl and washed her face and hands. Pulling the small key out of her hand bag she opened the small trunk and pulled out what she hoped was clothing suitable to meet her husband-to-be in. The pale peach sweater and darker skirt out of the same material suited her colouring and Bella thought she looked very mature when she checked her appearance in the mirror. A quick comb through her hair and she declared herself ready.

Closing the door behind her, she descended the stairs and joined Red in the living room where the fire was now giving off a welcome warmth. She crossed the room and held her chilly hands out to warm them.

"I got D's vittles ready iffen ye'd like to take 'em in ta him," Red said. "I'll show ye where the kitchen is, an' the other things yer gonna need ta know."

Bella followed him out of the room and down a small hallway. The kitchen took up most of the rear of the building, or so it seemed. There was a propane range and a huge wood stove that reminded her of the Aga in Mrs. Waters' house. Red bustled around pointing out where things were stored, showing her the pantry and then the wood pile outside the back door under a wide overhang.

"The cold cellar is over there," he waved vaguely toward someplace Bella couldn't see, "time enough tomorrow ta show ya that."

Back inside he took a tray down from a cupboard and pulled a plate out of the warming oven of the wood stove. He placed it on the tray, added silverware, a small pot of coffee, and a mug, along with a jug of cream and a bowl of sugar. As an afterthought he shoved a red chequered napkin under the edge of the plate. Bella watched closely and tried to commit to memory where everything was found.

"Iffen ye'll carry the tray, I'll go in first and let D know yer here. He might need ta use the chamber pot since Maisy left at four and he ain't had a chance since then. Best ye wait outside the door til I calls ye." Red didn't wait for her answer but marched out of the kitchen by a different door.

Gritting her teeth, Bella picked up the tray and followed. The door led into another passageway that must run behind the living room, she supposed. Red stopped and rapped on a door she hadn't even noticed in the dim light.

"D? Ya awake? It's me," Red called.

Bella made out the muffled sound of a voice but couldn't decipher what was said. Red opened the door and went in, closing it behind him. He obviously expected her to do as she was told. She grinned, more the fool him, she thought. But for the moment, she happy enough to follow his instructions. Meeting D'Arcy Rowan was something she was very glad to postpone as long as possible. The tray was getting heavy and her wrists were starting to ache. A chair made out of some kind of branches cobbled together, with a cushioned seat was by the door. Bella balanced the tray on the seat, and leaned on the wall. The scraping of a chair or some type of furniture came through the closed door. The murmur of voices was too faint for her to eavesdrop on the conversation. *I wonder what that old reprobate is telling him about me? Nothing good I'm sure. Well, I could him an earful about the old goat he sent to meet me, and none of it would be pleasant.*

Her heart rate quickened as frustration and anger reared its head. Bother and damn, he was the one that was all fired ready to pretty much buy himself a bride. Why in the name of God would he send someone to meet her who was certain to be rude and annoying? Maybe she'd have to ask him that exact question. *If I'm ever granted entry into the inner sanctum.* Her foot tapped impatiently, waiting had never been her strong point. More scraping, louder this time, caught her attention, along with muffled curses. Bella grinned. Maybe his precious *D* was giving Red a hard time. She could only hope.

When she had just about lost every vestige of her patience, the door finally opened and Red came out. He closed the door and studied her for a moment.

"Ya can go in now. See ya don't upset the man, he's had enough ta bear, as it is. I'll be in the kitchen if ya need me." Without another word he vanished down the shadowy hall.

Should I knock or just go straight on in? She'd forgotten to ask, and she'd be damned if she'd give the little cowboy the satisfaction of going to ask him. Steeling herself, she rapped once and walked in. The square room was smaller than the one upstairs. A bed, a chest of drawers, a narrow chair, and a small table left hardly any room to manoeuvre. She set the tray of food down on the table and turned to the bed.

"Hallo, I'm Arabella," she greeted the man lying on the bed. At least he was fully clothed. Surely he didn't expect her to anticipate the wedding the first night she arrived. She hid her trembling hands in the folds of her skirt.

"Hello, Arabella. As you know, I'm D'Arcy Rowan. Welcome to my home." He stretched out a large callused hand toward her.

Bella moved closer to the bed and placed her smaller hand in his. The huge paw engulfed hers in a firm but surprisingly gently grip. "Pleased to meet you," she said awkwardly. What did one say to the man who had basically purchased you sight unseen to be his wife. Bella was at a loss to find the proper words.

"Pull that chair over and sit down, Arabella. I think there are things we need to get straight between us."

He seemed very formal, almost distant. She did as he asked and settled on the chair by the bedside. Bella folded her hands in her lap and waited for him to say whatever it was he wanted her to know. She was hardly in a position to make any demands, and she wasn't familiar enough with the situation to even know what questions to ask.

D'Arcy sighed heavily and frowned at her. "You're much younger I was led to believe. How old are you?"

The blunt tone of his voice raised her hackles. "I'm twenty-one on my last birthday," she replied stiffly.

"Can you prove that? I'd like to see a birth certificate."

"Whatever for? I'm not lying, you know."

"You look more like sixteen. I've no notion to marry a child, I'm not a cradle robber. Your Father Boyle assured me you were a mature and responsible young woman well suited to life on the ranch here. I'm beginning to think he varnished the truth some." The man chewed at his bottom lip and waved a hand impatiently. "The birth certificate. Let's see it, then if you are what you claim to be."

"Look, let me get the supper tray for you and you can eat while I go get the papers. They're upstairs in my hand bag. I didn't realize I was going get the third degree and have to prove my soundness like some animal you bought at a horse fair." Bella set the tray none too gently across his lap and flounced toward the door.

"Arabella."

His voice stopped her dramatic entrance. "What?" she said through clenched teeth.

"Take the chamber pot with you and empty it would you? That's a good girl."

She whirled around ready to dump the contents of the pot over his head. One glimpse of the look in his eye and she changed her mind. She allowed herself a secret smile. There would be plenty of time to get even. Without uttering a word, she picked up the heavy porcelain pot emblazoned with long horned cattle and marched out the door. She would have liked to slam it, but it was hard enough just to get it shut.

"Where do I dump this?" she demanded as she entered the kitchen.

"In the outhouse out back." Red nodded toward yet another door she hadn't noticed in the kitchen. "Jes' follow the path, ye cain't miss it." She could have sworn the bastard was laughing at her.

"Seriously?" She raised her eyebrows and snarled.

"Ye gonna stand there and hold that thing all night, or are ye gonna empty it? Startin' to stink in here."

Admitting defeat for the moment, Bella managed to open the latch and went out onto a small stoop. The light from the windows showed her a dirt path leading into the dark. Setting her teeth, she stepped off the stoop and followed the path. A hundred feet from the house a tall narrow wooden hut materialized out of the darkness. From the smell she knew she'd reached her destination. Hooking the door open with the toe of her shoe, she held her breath and stepped into the inky black interior. She took the lid off the pot and almost gagged. *Holy mother of God, he's going to regret making me do this.* Muttering curses, she poured the contents down the hole and replaced the lid. She stepped out of the close confines and let her breath out. At least the thing was lighter without the load of excrement. Bella hurried toward the dubious sanctuary of the house.

An eerie howling screech that seemed to come from right behind her set her heart to racing. Her tongue stuck to the roof of her mouth and she couldn't have screamed to save her life. The howl came again, this time answered by another beast on the other side of the path. *Holy Mary mother of God, I'm surrounded, whatever it is that's making that noise is coming for me.* Even as she stood there shaking, more voices joined the eerie chorus. Bella forced herself to move and ran on shaking legs toward the house. Her shoe caught on a root and she fell headlong into the dirt. The benighted chamber pot flew out of her hands and smashed itself into smithereens on the path ahead of her.

Bella fought to drag air into her lungs, she'd knocked the breath out of herself once before when she took a header off Raven. She fought down the panic and made herself breathe in small shallow gulps. The God-awful howling seemed to be getting closer, terror brought her scrambling to her knees. Finally managing to get to her feet, she stood swaying for a moment. One of the beasts howled so close she was sure it was right beside her, just waiting to pounce. She made it to the stoop, avoiding the remains of the pot, and had one foot on the edge when the door flew open and Red burst out with a long nosed gun pointed at her face. Bella screamed, threw her arms over her head and dropped to her knees where she huddled, sobs shaking her body. *Just kill me now and put me out of my misery. Feck, maybe marrying Daniel wouldn't have been so bad after all.*

"Arabella, are ye okay?" Red knelt beside her, the gun on the ground at his side. He put a hand on her arm. "Are ye hurt, woman? I cain't help ye if ye won't talk to me."

She recoiled from his touch and shook her head from side to side. She didn't resist when the man lifted her to her feet. She refused to look at him and stood silently in his grasp.

"Arabella? Are ye…Oh, for the love of Pete!"

Before she could even squeak in protest, the wiry cowboy scooped her up and carried her into the kitchen, banging her knee on the door jamb as he did. He set her down in a cushioned chair by the stove and went outside to retrieve the gun. Bella huddled in the chair with her arms wrapped around her waist. She started when Red came back through the door, the gun resting in the crook of his arm.

"If you're planning on killing me, just do it," she said between sobs.

Red set the gun by the door and came over to her. "I ain't aimin' to kill ye, woman. Where did ye git that crack-brained idee from?" He knelt down in front of her. "Are ye hurt?"

"What do you mean, where did I get that idea from? You came flying out the door with a gun pointed at my head, what was I supposed to think? I know you don't like me and you don't think I can fit in here, but I haven't got anyplace else to go, right at the moment. So you're stuck with me." Anger helped her find her voice.

"I weren't aimin' to shoot ye. Them 'yotes sounded pretty close to the house so I went out to make sure ye were safe. Didn't 'spect to find ye right outside the door lookin' like something the cat drug in." He looked around and then turned back to her. "What did ye do with the piss pot? Ye didn't throw it at the 'yotes did ye? D sets quite a store by that there pot, it were his pappy's."

Bella raised her head and gave big sniff, wiping her nose with the back of her hand. "Well, it's scattered to kingdom come. I dropped it when I tripped over something and fell on my face. Look at my clothes..." She waved at the muck caked on her skirt and blouse.

"You broke the pot?" Red stood up. He disappeared out the door.

"Yes, I broke the flaming pot. Nice of you to be so concerned about my welfare," she said bitterly to the empty room.

"What in the Sam hill is goin' on out there?" D'Arcy roared from his room. "Arabella, what the hell is takin' so long?"

"Bother and damn!" Bella got to her feet and stomped down the hall. She flung the door to his room open and marched over to the bed. "I took your damned pot out to dump it, a pack of demon dogs tried to kill me, I fell, I broke the bloody thing and then your man tried to kill me. I'm done here, I'm finished. First thing in the morning, I'm leaving." She whirled around and stormed out of the room.

"Arabella Angarrick, you get you sorry ass back in here this minute," he bellowed.

Bella kept going, she swept through the kitchen just as Red appeared with the remains of the pot gathered in his shirt tail. Without slowing down, she stomped into the fireplace room and up to her room. The door didn't appear to have a lock, so she jammed the back of a chair under the handle and then for good measure shoved the chest of drawers in front of it. The muddy clothes she stripped off landed in a heap on the floor. The pretty peach outfit was beyond repair, but that was the least of her worries at the moment. She shivered at the touch of the cold water on her skin, but persevered until she was clean again. Unlocking the small trunk, she pulled out a long flannel nightie and drew it on over her head. The room was chilly and the wind whined outside her window. The curtains billowed as a draft found its way through the frame, she crossed to pull them closed but paused to look out into the dark night. Above the wail of the wind whipping around the building, the hair raising howl she'd heard earlier came again. Shuddering, she pulled the curtain tightly shut and stood in the centre of the room, uncertain what to do next.

It was cold in the room. Bella wanted a cup of tea in the worst way, but she certainly had no intention of going downstairs to make one. The thought of running into the Red, or worse yet, being summoned into the man of house's presence was something she wanted to avoid. *I need time to think, figure out how I'm going to get myself out of this mess. I should have known better than to trust Father Boyle. He's all fire and brimstone and I bet he knows about who the* father *of my baby is.* Arms wrapped around her middle she paced the room. There was no easy solution. She was stuck out here in the middle of nowhere, with no way to get back to anything that even resembled civilization. *I could steal the car...but I need a map. I don't know how to get back to the highway or which way to go once I get there. One thing's for sure, I'm not staying her one minute longer than I have to. There has to be a way, there just has to.*

Bella stopped pacing, tendrils of frigid air snaked around her bare ankles. She pulled back the thick quilt and blankets on the bed and crawled in. The sheets were freezing, but she wrapped the bedding around her anyway. It wasn't any colder than back home, but here she had no warming pan to chase away the chills. With the covers pulled up to her chin, she leaned against the head board and pulled her knees up, wrapping her arms around them under the blankets. The light switch was conveniently located within reach of the person in the bed, Bella flicked it off and stared into the shadows illuminated by the faint light of the stars.

Chapter Seven

Bella was in no better mood when she woke the next morning. Dressing quickly she went down to the kitchen, pleased to find the place empty. The big cook stove was warm, she stirred the coals and put the kettle on the hob. She selected a log from the bucket by the stove and placed in on top of the hot coals. Satisfied it had caught, she hunted through the cupboards looking for bread. Finding a half loaf, she took a knife from the drawer and sliced two thick pieces. A toasting fork lay by the stove, before long she had two nicely browned slices slathered with butter and a thick dark blue jam. She thought it might be blueberry, but it tasted different. Maybe Red would tell her what it as. If he was still speaking to her. The kettle spit hot water onto the stove, she wrapped a dish cloth around the handle and lifted it off the stove. Once the pot was full, she put the kettle on the back of the stove.

She was just finishing her toast and had poured the last of the tea into the thick mug she found in one of the cupboards, when Red stamped into the room.

"Morning," she greeted him without looking up.

"Mornin'. Didn't 'spect to see ye this early." Red poured a cup of coffee and took a seat at the table across from her. "Have ye bin in ta see D yet?"

Bella shook her head, eyes on the dregs of tea in her mug. "What were those things last night?" She looked up and met his gaze.

"Them was 'yotes, coyotes. Don't usually come down this close to the house."

"What are coyotes? Some kind of dog?"

"Wal, I guess you could say that. They ain't dogs, but they are related. Pesky buggers, they is."

"Why were they attacking me?" She swirled the last of the tea around her mug. "Do they eat humans?"

Red snorted and Bella suspected he smothered a laugh. "Weren't attacking ye. Ye'd know it they was. Most likely they was jes' snooping around hopin' to find some chickens or garbage to steal. 'Yotes won't bother ye lessen ye was already hurt out on the range somewheres. Cowards most of 'em."

Remembering the events of the last evening, she glared at him. "Why were you charging at me with a gun last night? I don't want to be here anymore than you want me here, but there's no call to murder me." She stood up and carried the mug to the sink.

"Aw, c'mon, girl. Weren't planin' on murdering ye, I was gonna put some buckshot into those 'yotes if I could git 'em in me sights.

Ye scairt the pants off me, lurkin' outside the door like that."

"I wasn't lurking," Bella protested whirling around. "I was trying to get to safety. You scared me half to death."

"Wal, I'm right sorry, fer that then." He paused. "I let D know 'bout the piss pot ye broke."

"Oh really? And what did he have to say about that?" She leaned against the counter.

"He was a might upset, fer sure. But after I told him about the 'yotes being down close to the house and all, he just kinda shrugged it off. Surprised the pants offen me, I can tell ye."

"I suppose I should go and apologize for it, even if it wasn't my fault, seeing as how it was something he valued."

"Ye can take his breakfast in to him, if ye would," Red offered.

"Sure, why not." Bella shrugged.

Red pulled a tray out of the warming oven and handed it to her, the handles wrapped in dish clothes to save her hands. "He'll be waitin', so ye'd best go git."

Bella nodded and took the tray down the hall. She hesitated outside the door, took a deep breath, and knocked at the door with the toe of her shoe. "Breakfast," she called.

"Come!" The deep voice carried easily through the door.

"She pushed the door open and backed into the room. The small table was beside the bed so she set the tray down and removed the covers on

95

the dishes. "Is there anything else you need?" She backed away a few paces. Being careful not to meet his gaze, she continued. "I suppose I owe you an apology for breaking your chamber pot. I didn't do it on purpose, those demon things were howling, sounded like they were right on top of me. I tried to run back to the house, but I tripped on something and well..." She looked up and raised her hands, palms up. "I am sorry, I hope you aren't too angry with me." She waited for a moment. "Right then. I'll leave you to your breakfast."

Bella hadn't gone two steps before he stopped her. "Arabella, we need to talk, you and I. Maybe after I've finished breakfast we can share a cup of coffee and jaw for a bit. There are things we need to set straight between us. Does that suit you?"

"Of course. Whatever you wish, Mister Rowan." She called him by name for the first time and scurried out the door before he could find an excuse to keep her any longer.

"Wal, I see ye survived." Red observed when she returned to the kitchen. To her surprise, he grinned at her and tossed her a dish towel. "Here, missy. Ye can dry while I warsh these here dishes."

Wordlessly, she caught the cloth and moved to the draining board. Working in companionable silence, the dishes were done in record time. Red took the wet towel from her hand and hung it over a bar on the side of the cook stove. He poured two cups of coffee and set them on the table.

"Time for a break." He gestured for her to sit opposite him. "Are ye still fixin' to skedaddle outa here this mornin'?"

"Arabella!" D'Arcy's deep baritone rumbled down the hall.

"Bother and damn," she said under her breath. "The master calls and I must answer," she joked. Straightening her back and sticking out her chin, she sailed out of the kitchen and down the hall. Half way down the hall she realized she'd forgotten the coffee pot, spinning around she retraced her steps. Red looked up when she returned to the kitchen.

"That was quick," he remarked.

"Forgot the damn coffee pot." Bella took a clean towel to protect her hand and picked up the somewhat battered pot from the stove top. She snagged a thick mug from the hook on the underside of the cupboards as she passed, it clanked against the others hanging there and she winced. Just what she needed to do—break more crockery. She grinned at Red and headed back toward the hall door. "Off to beard the lion in his den." She grinned.

The room was half in shadow, D'Arcy was sitting up, leaning on pillows piled against the headboard, his face dark as a thundercloud. The breakfast tray lay overturned on the floor, he had one leg over the edge of the bed and free of the covers. He paused in the act of throwing the quilts to the foot of the bed.

"My stars! What do you think you're doing?" Bella set the coffee pot and mug down and hurried to the bed. "Red says you're supposed to stay in bed and rest. What happened?"

The big man subsided against the pillows, features pinched with pain. "Dang stupid thing slid right off the bed. Now look at the mess. Good God Almighty, I sick and tired of being useless." His fist pounded the mattress beside his thigh.

Bella flipped the blankets back over him and knelt to pick up the tray. His bare leg still hung over the edge of the bed, just in her line of sight. "Do you need assistance getting comfortable?"

He growled a response under his breath and she was pretty sure it was a good thing she couldn't make out the words. After a few attempts to swing his leg unto the bed, D'Arcy fell back against the pillows with a groan. Wordlessly, Bella got to her feet and carefully lifted the limb, the dark curly hairs rough on her palms. She slid his leg under the covers. She bent to retrieve the tray and placed it back on the small table. Hands on her hips, she surveyed the mess on the floor. A quick glance around the room failed to reveal anything to clean up the remains of his breakfast. She retrieved the mug from where it lay just under the edge of the bed and filled it with fresh coffee.

"Here, you look like you could use this." Bella handed him the mug. "I'll be right back, I need to fetch something to wipe all this up with." She waved a hand over the mashed pancakes and eggs.

Her husband-to-be only grunted and cradled the hot mug in his large hands. She waited a moment, but when he made no effort to speak she left the room. *What in heaven's name is wrong with the man? I wonder how bad he's hurt?* The questions bubbled in her head as she entered the kitchen. Red looked up in surprise when she came in the room.

"What is it? Somethin' wrong?" Red half rose from his seat before Bella shook her head.

"Not really. I need to find some old rags or something to clean up a mess—"

"Let me, it ain't proper for a young'un to deal with that kinda thing." Red pushed back his chair and dumped the remainder of his coffee down the drain.

"I've cleaned up far worse when Da was on the rampage," she assured him.

"Your pa?" The man looked outraged and Bella for the life of her couldn't fathom why he as do upset. "That's jes' wrong. Ain't right fer a daughter to be wipin' her pa's arse—"

"Oh my stars, Red! It's not that kind of mess." She dissolved in helpless laughter. "Let me assure you if it was that mess, I'd be letting you handle it. The tray fell off the bed and the floor is all pancakes and eggs, I just need a bucket and some rags."

Red rummaged in a cupboard and produced the items she requested. Still giggling, she went back to sick man's room. The door was still ajar but she rapped once before going in. D'Arcy was still in bed looking madder than a nest of hornets.

"Right, I'm back then," she greeted him. When he remained silent, she gave a mental shrug and went about setting things to rights. When the floor was as clean as she could manage, Bella set the bucket out in the hall by the door, poured herself some coffee and perched on the only chair in the room. He was the one who summoned her so she was damned if she was going speak first.

D'Arcy stared at her so long she began to be very uncomfortable. The scowl twisted his features into an evil mask, the lowered eyebrows shaded his eyes which only made the impression stronger. Bella shifted in her chair and straightened her skirt. The rustle of the bed clothes sounded loud in the silence as the big man shifted his bulk in the bed. He exhaled sharply, bringing her attention back to his face.

"Have you brought the papers I asked for last evening?" he growled, finally breaking the silence.

Bella was taken aback and racked her brain wildly. *What papers?* Last night seemed so distant now. Her confusion must have shown on her face.

"The birth certificate I asked for. I refuse to marry a child. I'm warning you, if those papers don't say you're of age, you're going back where you came from. My lawyer will look at

100

them too, just in case they're a forgery," he growled.

"I don't have them on me, no. But of course I can show them to you." She got to her feet. "Let me assure you I am no child. As you are aware I'm carrying a child of my own and it seemed to me from your correspondence that the baby was of more importance than the mother. As for shipping me back home, much as I wish that were possible, if I go back there'll be no place for me in Da's house, or probably anywhere in the village. So much as it pains me to say this, you bought me body and soul, and unfortunately, here I stay." Bella tossed her head, glared at him and stormed out of the room.

Slamming doors brought Red out of the kitchen, he took one look at her and ducked back inside. *Wise man.* Bella took the stairs two at a time and stomped the short distance to her room. She paused for a moment to catch her breath, annoyed her condition was already beginning to slow her down. Papers clutched in her fist, she went back to D'Arcy's room.

"Here!" She threw the birth certificate, along with her baptismal one as well. Glaring, she stood at the end of the bed with her arms crossed. "Since we're being so blunt, it's my turn. What's wrong with you? Are you permanently crippled? If you are, we might both be able to get out of this ridiculous arrangement."

The man in the bed lifted an eyebrow and regarded her over the top of the paper he was holding. "Just how to you propose we do that?"

"Da made Father Boyle sign some paper promising that the man I was supposed to marry was of sound mind and body. If you're crippled…" She tilted her head to one side and let him fill in the blanks.

He flung the papers at her and she jumped back in surprise. For a swift second he reminded her of Daniel in one of his fits of rage. The realization shocked her to the core. Before she could gather her wits about her, D'Arcy's mug smashed against the wall, the contents flying everywhere and staining the wall.

"Get out," he roared. "Insolent witch. You're right about the one thing. If it weren't for the child I would send you packing. Get out!"

Bella scooped up the papers from the floor and fled the room. Half way down the hall she ran smack into Red. Tears blurred her vision and she didn't see him until it was too late.

"Whoa, hold up there, missy." He caught her arm and peered at her face. "Got the wrong side of D's tongue, didn't ye."

She nodded, not trusting herself to speak.

"Don't worry, his bark is worse than his bite. This dang accident's got him riled up, that's all. You'll see." Red patted her arm.

"Red! In here! Now!"

The imperious summons echoed in the narrow hall. Bella imagined the floor shook with

102

the fury behind the words. Red rolled his eyes and gave her a mischievous grin. "I'll jes' run along and see what's bitin' his ass. Why don't ye go make yerself some tea and calm down a bit."

"He hates me," she whispered. "How am I supposed to marry a man who hates me?"

"Aw, he don't hate ye. He don't know you well enough to hate ye. 'Sides, it's the pain talkin' right now. Ye'll see, it'll all come right."

"Red!"

"Gotta go." The little cowboy gave her arm a squeeze and trotted off with a grin.

She didn't have the heart to go and make a pot of tea. Tea made her think of home, and that set off a crying jag. Smoothing the rumpled papers and folding them, Bella bypassed the kitchen and took the stairs up to her room. Moving without thinking about it, she put the papers back in locked box where she kept important things. Bella sank onto the bed and stared blankly out the dormer window opposite her. Some large bird described lazy circles in the intense blue sky, her gaze followed it and she found it somehow soothing. It was bigger than the buzzards she was used to, but the movements were similar.

The future looked pretty bleak from where she sat right now. The man she was to marry disliked her, and truth be told, she wasn't exactly enamoured with him either. Some form of demon dog roamed the ranch, ready to pounce at any second and Lord only knew what other evil things lurked in the barren countryside. She moved to stand by the window, looking out over thousands of acres. Her heart ached for the green fields of home, the roar of the sea on the rocks, and the soaring dizzying heights of her Cornish cliffs.

Outside the window, the undulating landscape was brown and sere. Here and there a faint blush of green showed, the towering mountains looming over the prairie were still frosted with snow. Almost the end of May and yet no flowers that Bella could see brightened the stark vista. A horse whinnied in the pens near the barn, the sound a stab to her heart. The sorrow of leaving Raven that she'd managed to push to the back of her mind returned in full force. Sarie would look after the mare and care for her, but it wouldn't be the same. Bella might never see the horse again.

Her thoughts turned to the horses in the pens. She could just see the outermost pens before the house blocked her view. Maybe she'd go down to the barns to day and visit the horses. What harm could there be in that? The few she could see were far different than the ones she was used to. The coat patterns on some intrigued her. The bay with huge white splashes reminded her of the gypsy horses back home, only much smaller. But the one who looked like a white spotted blanket was thrown over its hind end was different than anything she'd ever seen. On the spur of the moment, Bella decided she'd go and visit the pens this morning. Maybe there would be one who looked like Raven. She glanced down at her skirt and blouse and grimaced.

It took almost no time to change into more suitable clothing and boots. Bella left by the front door and stood for a moment with her face upturned to the warm sun. She inhaled deeply, rather than the sweet moist smell of moss and earth mixed with the tang of the sea, her nose stung with the sharp tang of some wiry plant covering the hillside, and dry dust. The wind sang in the hydro wires overhead and sent whirlwinds of dust and debris spinning across the space between house and corrals. It seemed to suck the moisture right out of her skin.

Shaking her head, she moved toward the pens, corrals, Rad called them. A few short coupled horses stood eating hay out of large metal feeder. A bay, two chestnuts, and a buckskin ignored her when she called to them. Bella leaned on the rough poles of the pen and watched them for a while, the smell and familiar sound as they ate soothed her. A shout from near the barn caught her attention. Bella shoved away from the pen and went to investigate. Two men in western hats were doing something with a dark coloured horse in a large round pen.

She stopped a few yards from the rails and watched. The horse stood in the centre of the pen, head high, nostrils flared with the white showing in his eyes. It was a male, she noticed when the animal shied and leaped forward in response to one of the cowboys swinging a rope at it. The other man attempted to drive it forward, but the horse spun and faced him, striking out with his front feet. While the animal's attention was riveted on the man in front of him, the other made a graceful throw and dropped a loop over its head.

Bella stepped back involuntarily at the horse's reaction. Rearing and squealing it fought like a demon while the man at the end of the rope snubbed it around a stout post set into the ground and began to winch it in. Another loop dropped over the first and for the first time, Bella realized there was a second post. Soon, the black coat shone with sweat and white foam lathered the neck and flanks. Heaving and blowing the horse kept fighting even when it was secured tightly between the two posts. To Bella's surprise, the two men removed their leather gloves and slapped them on their thighs, raising puffs of dust before they left the pen. She waited to see what they planned to do next. The men disappeared into the barn and reappeared with tack for two horses slung over their shoulders.

One of them nodded to her as they passed. She turned to follow their progress with her eyes, they saddled two horses Bella hadn't noticed before that were tied to a hitching rail. She shook her head in disbelief when they mounted up and loped out of the yard. Her gaze turned to the black horse still tied in the round pen with no shelter from the sun. The ranch house and out buildings were in a hollow and protected from the worst of the wind, Bella was too warm even in just a light jacket. She found herself by the rails of the pen without realizing how she got there.

The big horse stamped a hind foot at the flies buzzing around his sweaty flanks. Surely, they weren't going to just leave him there, tied up like that? There didn't seem to be any other people around, do Bella hurried back to the house, calling for Red as she came through the door.

"Red? Where are you? I need you to fix something." She didn't bother to remove her boots or coat, but continued on into the kitchen.

"Red's gone to town," D'Arcy's voice came faintly down the hall.

Bella marched through the kitchen and carried on to his room. Pushing the door open, she burst in and halted by the bed. The man was dressed today, for a change, sitting upright on the side of the bed. "Your men have gone off and forgotten to untie a horse in one of the pens." She waited for him to get up and come with her.

"Is that what all this belly aching is about? I thought for sure the house was on fire or something." D'Arcy got to his feet very carefully, grasping the high post at the end of the bed frame for support.

"You're not going to leave him like that are you?" Bella demanded, glaring at him with her hands on her hips.

"The horse is fine. It's just part of breakin' him in. Things are different her, Arabella. You're just going to have to get used to it. Now how about handing me that damned walking stick and makin' a sick man a cup of coffee and rustlin' up some lunch?"

"That's not how you gentle a horse," she declared.

"It's how we do it here in the west. The stock isn't any of your business, keep your nose out of it. Now hand me the damn cane."

"Just exactly what is my business?" Bella glared at him, her voice dangerously quiet.

D'Arcy must have mistaken it for submission because he limped a few steps toward her and patted her on the shoulder. "That's better, girl. I know our ways are different, but as long as you just worry your pretty little head about caring for that baby you're carrying and looking after me and the house, we'll get on just fine. You haven't got any call to be out by the corrals flirting with the hired hands, your place is in the house."

Bella stepped away from him, shock at his assumptions warring with outrage. "Are you totally barking mad? I have no intention of spending all my time waiting on you hand and foot and cleaning your house. I love horses and I love riding. What you're doing to that horse is wrong—"

"That's enough," the man thundered. "You'll do what you're told and stay out of trouble. Father Boyle said I might have to use a hard hand with you. Warned me you were head strong and flighty, and he questioned your moral character. Now, go make yourself useful and rustle up some grub and a pot of coffee. I can fill you in on the wedding details while we eat." He retrieved the cane from beside the door and gestured with it for Bella to precede him out the door.

Speechless with rage, Bella stomped toward the kitchen. The bleeder should consider himself lucky if she didn't put rat poison in his coffee. For good measure she cursed Father Boyle as well, questioned her morals did he? The self-righteous git! The momentum carried her into the kitchen where she slammed a thick pottery mug on the pine table and filled it from the pot on the stove. Unsure where to find the plates she flung open cupboards and left them ajar in her wake until she found what she needed. The makings for a sandwich were in the icebox. In short order she slapped the finished product down in front of her husband-to-be.

"Aren't you having something?" D'Arcy indicated the space across the table from him.

She snorted. "I'd rather starve than share a meal with you," she spat the words.

He regarded her for a long moment before shrugging his broad shoulders. "Suit yourself then, woman." He picked up the sandwich and then paused with it half-way to his mouth. "You stay away from the corrals and the livestock, you hear?"

"What if I don't want to?"

"I'm not asking, I'm telling you. Come Saturday, you'll be my wife, and you will do as you're told."

"What if I want to go riding?" She refused to back down.

The big man sighed and set the sandwich back on the plate. "If you really need to go riding, either Red or I will take you. You stay away from the hired hands and the stock." He waved a hand dismissive hand and turned back to his lunch.

Bella whirled on her heel and stalked out of the room. Her fury carried her all the way through the living room and up to her room. She slammed the door hard enough to shake the pictures hanging on the wall. *How dare he?* She paced back and forth across the small room. *He's almost as bad as Da, thinks I should be barefoot and pregnant and happy with my lot.* She paused in mid-stride when the high pitched whinny from the corrals reached her ears. Opening the dormer window and leaning out, the black horse tied in the corrals was just visible. Poor creature, how could they treat such a magnificent animal like that? She sucked in a breath at the realization she was as much a prisoner as the horse down below.

A rooster tail of dust announced the arrival of a car coming toward the ranch. The car that had brought her to the ranch stopped by the front entrance and Red emerged. The door closed loudly below and the rumble of male voices filtered up the stairs. Curious, Bella crept to the top of the stair case and strained to listen in on the conversation. She could only catch a few words, but what she did made it clear Red was to be her keeper, ensuring she behaved and didn't stray into forbidden territory. *Huh, like that's going to stop me if I really want to do something.*

"Arabella," D'Arcy bellowed from below. "Red needs your help, get down here this instant."

Without bothering to answer, she flounced down the stairs and into the kitchen. Refusing to speak to either man, she set about discovering where the various items belonged. The ice box was bigger and more spacious than what Bella was used to. When the last of the groceries were put away, she turned to leave.

"I'd like steak, potatoes, and biscuits for supper, Arabella. I trust you can manage that?" D'Arcy said.

She halted and stepped back into the room. "How do you like your meat cooked?" she managed to say between lips stiff with rage. "What time do you wish your meal served?"

""Six-thirty will be fine. That should give you plenty of time to get the grub ready for the ranch hands beforehand. Red can tell you what he usually fixes for them."

Bella was stuck speechless. He expected her to cook and clean for him and the hired help? The spark of an idea gleamed for an instant. One of the cowboys might be willing to aid in her escape, because she was certainly planning to escape in the very near future. D'Arcy squashed her hopes a moment later.

"Red will be taking the grub out to the bunk house when it's ready, so don't be getting any ideas into that head of yours." He limped out of the room, leaning heavily on the cane.

"Bloody bastard," she hissed under her breath.

"Aw, he ain't that bad, missy. For some reason, ye jes' seem to rub him the wrong way. I ain't niver seen 'im so ornery. I guess ye gotta take inta account he's in a lotta pain. Jes' give 'im a chance, missy."

Bella glared at the little cowboy. "What am I supposed to make for the hands?"

"Them boys ain't picky. Beef stew, chili, jes' 'bout anythin' ye can make with beef. Sometimes we git some pork, and not very often lamb. Sheep and cattle don't mix well on the range. Ye'll find a big stew pot at the back of the pantry. Knives and other utensils are in this drawer. Vegetables in the root cellar out back, just outside the door. I'll leave ye to it, then. Got me some chores that need doin'."

"Fine." Bella found a surprisingly clean apron hanging on the back of the pantry door and slipped it over her head. Lugging the stew pot out of the depths of the narrow room, she wrestled it up onto the wood stove. Opening the fire box, she added wood and stoked up the fire. She checked the oven and the warming oven to familiarize herself with it. There was a large crock of beef in the ice box, she pulled it out and set it down on the counter. Finding a butcher knife she cut the meat into good sized chunks. She added water and the beef to the pot along with a couple of Oxo cubes. While it heated, she located the root cellar and filled a basket with carrots, potatoes, some onions, and to her surprise some withered stalks of celery. She added enough potatoes for D'Arcy and Red's steak dinner as well. Returning to the kitchen, in no time she had the stew bubbling on the stove. A further search turned up some lidded pots to carry the finished product out to the bunk house.

Bella debated on whether to fry the steak or try to broil in in the oven. In the end she decided on the fry pan. Biscuits weren't her strong suit, Bella was far more used to scones or bannock. A daunting thought occurred to her—did he expect her produce dessert as well? Bloody hell! Among the papers shoved into the side of shelf she found a recipe for biscuits and assembled the ingredients. While she racked her brains for a suitable dessert, she kept the stew from burning and peeled the remaining potatoes.

"That's a mighty fine lookin' stew, if ye ask me, missy," Red commented when he returned to the kitchen. "I see ye found the carryin' pots." Without further ado, Red ladled the fragrant stew into the containers, grabbed two loaves of bread from a box Bella hadn't noticed earlier, and left the room.

Lifting the almost empty stew pot off the stove she set it in the large porcelain sink and pumped water into it. Parts of the house seemed to have a running water supply, but the kitchen was still serviced by a hand pump beside the sink. She greased the cast iron fry pan with bacon drippings and seared the thick steaks she pulled from the ice box. Moving the pan to reduce the heat, she set the pot of potatoes over the hottest part of the stove top. The matter of a dessert still tormented her. There wasn't time to bake a cake or pie, muffins perhaps? Bother and damn! She'd forgotten the biscuits! Bella whipped the ingredients together and using an upside down glass cut round shapes out of the rolled dough. She placed them on a cookie sheet she discovered and slid it into the oven box. Checking the time on the clock by the door, she made a mental note of when to take them out.

The steak in the fry pan demanded her attention, by the time Red came back from the bunk house with the pots emptied of stew but filled to the brim with dirty dishes, Bella was frazzled with trying to get everything ready at the same time without under or over cooking any of it. The old cowboy stepped in and took care of draining and mashing the potatoes. The biscuits almost came to grief but she remembered them in the nick of time and whisked them out of the oven.

"D likes his meat still pink inside, but not mooing," Red remarked. "Ye might wanta take his steak outta the pan and put 'er in the warming oven."

114

"Sure, wouldn't want the boss to have to eat over done steak," Bella groused. She pulled plates out of the warming oven and moved to set them on the kitchen table.

"D' eats his supper in the dining room. Ye best take them plates in there." Red nodded toward the door.

"Oh for the love of God!" She burst out and stalked into the dining room. She set two places at the table and returned for the silverware and napkins. Once the table was set she stood back and then with a fiendish grin she set two candlesticks on the table and lit them. There, she surveyed her handiwork, let *D* and Red enjoy their dinner.

Back in the kitchen, she took the bowl of stew she'd kept back from the ranch hands' dinner and carried it out of the kitchen.

"What're ye doin', missy?" Red called after her.

"Going to my room to eat. You and the boss enjoy your supper." She turned in the doorway. "Or do you need me to go and inform him his meal is ready?"

Red gave her an odd look and shook his head. If Bella hadn't known better she would have thought he looked sad and worried.

"Ye run along then, I'll let D know the supper's on the table in the dining room."

"Good, then." Bella went up to her room, feeling like she'd somehow managed to win a small victory. She sat by the window watching the darkness deepen while she ate. Loneliness swept over her, along with a major case of homesickness. Maybe it would have been better to swallow her pride and eat with the men. The moon rose in the sky while she gazed blankly out at the night. A shrill whinny caught her attention. Setting the bowl aside, she unlatched the window and leaned out. In the pale light of the moon, the black horse tried to toss his head, still bound between the two posts.

"Poor man, he's as much a prisoner as I am, and just as miserable." The night air was chilly after the warmth of the day. Bella closed the window and settled back in the chair. The horse whinnied again, twisting her heart with sympathy. She waited until all sound below faded before venturing downstairs to return the bowl to the kitchen. The sight that met her made her blood boil anew. Dishes and pots were piled in the sink and on the sideboard. A note propped on the table informed her that the dishes were her business. By the bold strokes she recognized D'Arcy's handwriting, underneath in a less educated hand, Red had scrawled a short apology.

Rolling up her sleeves, Bella set to work. A good two hours later, she put the last pot away. Wiping her hands on the wet apron, she placed her hands on her lower back and stretched. She removed the apron and stood with it in her hand wondering where the laundry basket was. That, she supposed bitterly, was her business too. Laying the apron over the back of the chair, Bella was seized by an urgent restlessness. In spite of the physical exhaustion weighing her down, she needed to move, to do something. Picking a jacket from the hook by the back door, she let herself out into the night. It was pitch dark in the shadow of the house, once clear of the structure, the faint moonlight allowed her to pick her way across the yard. It was a relief no demon dogs seemed to be in evidence.

A plan formed in her rebellious mind, Sarie would talk her out of it if she was here, but she wasn't. Grinning triumphantly, Bella approached the round pen where the black horse waited. He raised his head, the whites of his eyes gleaming in the moonlight, when she unlatched the gate. Speaking softly, she moved toward him. A bucket of water stood just inside the gate, she picked it up out of the dust and held it in front of her. The big horse snorted and shifted his hooves restlessly.

"Hey big horse, you're thirsty aren't you? This is purely a stupid way to gentle a horse," she spoke in a soothing voice and halted a few steps from his head. "Here, want some of this?" The water in the bucket looked all black and silver in the night. The horse leaned back against the ropes which tightened around his neck. The nostrils bulged and he was forced to come forward again. She continued to stand still and croon to him softly. After a time, when she thought her arms would fall off from holding the heavy bucket, he stretched his nose toward her. He snorted loudly and Bella glanced toward the house fearful one of the men might hear and come out to investigate.

"Shush, now. Shush. Come get a drink, that's a good boy," she crooned. Bracing the bucket against her hip she dipped the fingers of one hand into the water and splashed it around a bit. The big ears swivelled forward and back. "C'mon, boy. There's a good fellow." She shifted the bucket back to both hands. The horse moved forward a few steps and dipped his nose into the water. Bella stood as still as she could until he finished, watching the ripple of the muscles in his neck as he drank. When he raised his head, she set the pail down at her feet and moved toward the post on the left.

The big horses shifted nervously and eyed her with a wary expression. She took care to make her actions smooth and unhurried, though her heart was hammering in her chest. Her fingers fumbled on the stiff rope snugged around the post, the few moments it took to free it seemed like hours. With one ear she listened for any movement from the house or the bunk house, while she kept a close eye on the horse. She counted herself lucky that the animal didn't seem to realize it was partially free. With an economy of movement she stepped over to the far post and released that tie as well. The black horse shifted forward and snorted, apparently realizing for the first time he was free. In one swift motion, Bella stepped in and pulled the loosened ropes off over his head. She jumped out of the way at he lunged forward and then trotted around the pen, head high and tail flagging over his back. She ran to the gate and opened it wide, then spread her arms and hissing between her teeth she herded him out the opening. It took the animal a moment to understand the implications and then he bolted for freedom.

"Bother and damn," Bella cursed. Sure enough the horses in the nearby corrals whinnied and whirled. Lights came on in the bunk house and the main house. She slunk into the deep shadows on the far side of the round pen. Red came out of the house on the run, D'Arcy stood in the open doorway leaning on the frame. Only seconds later the hired hands come pouring out of the bunkhouse in various stages of dress. Red reached the round pen first.

"I'll be damned! How'n the hell did that black bastard git hisself lose?" He stomped into the pen where the coiled ropes lay on the moonlit sand.

"I shut the gate. Curly checked it too," a sock footed cow hand declared.

"Ayup, ain't no way it opened on its own," the other man said, tucking his shirt tails into jeans hung low on his hips.

A third hand bent down and picked up the end of the rope by the post. "Dang rope ain't broke, someone untied it."

"What!" D'Arcy Rowan limped across the pen. "Which one of you let that spawn of Satan loose?"

Bella shrank further back into the shadows and began slipping away from the round pen, scurrying across the patches of silver moonlight. She circled behind the barn and peered around the corner. There was no cover between her and the house. The wind picked up a bit, sending chilly fingers over her skin. Bella shivered and pulled the light jacket closer around her shoulders. D'Arcy's furious voice carried clearly in the night air, the fury and violence in his tones scared her just as much as Daniel Treliving ever had. Curses and threats of retribution against whoever freed the expensive piece of horseflesh continued. Red was attempting to calm his boss down, when Bella peeked at the men from her hiding place he was limping back and forth in front of the hands who stood quietly waiting for the rage to blow itself out.

"Holy Mother of God," she whispered. "He's going to figure out it was me. If he's anything like Da, he'll scald me arse so I won't sit down for a month. The magnitude of her transgression was greater than she had ever imagined. At the very worst she had thought there would be a bit of grief, but nothing of any consequence. For heaven's sake all she did was free the poor thing so it could stretch its neck and eat something. What was all the fuss about? Another outburst from D'Arcy decided her that she didn't want to stick around and find out. Taking her courage in her hand, Bella prepared to race across the open ground toward the back of the house.

"Arabella! Where the hell is that girl?"

D'Arcy's bellow stopped her with a foot raised to bolt. She shrank back against the rough barn boards. The murmur of Red's voice reached her but she couldn't make out the words. The two men crossed the yard toward the house, the larger man leaning on the wiry little cowboy for support. Bella spared him a moment of sympathy when he stumbled and went down on one knee. He staggered to his feet again, cursing. The cow hands silently went back to the bunk house averting their gaze from the boss man's painful progress in the opposite direction.

"Arabella! Get your ass down here. And I mean right now!" D'Arcy bellowed when they two men gained the front door of the main house.

Well, this was a fine kettle of fish, wasn't it? There was no way she could get back in the house without them seeing her, and no way she could make it before they discovered she wasn't in her room. Her toes curled inside her boots and she chewed on a thumb nail while she reviewed her options. And came to the conclusion she really didn't have any. Lights appeared in the upper story of the main house, shadows moving across the windows. Panic bloomed in her chest and despite the coolness of the evening an internal heat burned under her skin.

Sarie! Sarie would know what to do. But her best friend and voice of reason wasn't here. Bella was on her own, and she found the experience overwhelming and daunting. Maybe she could sneak in the house and get the keys for the car off the hook by the back door. But, what then? She didn't know how to drive, and these barbarians drove on the wrong side of the road, just to complicate matters. Besides, it would be just like Red to lurk in the dark waiting to catch her when she tried to sneak back in. No, the house was out. For more than one reason. It would take a stronger woman than her to face D'Arcy Rowan considering the rage she'd seen him in earlier. So what did that leave? *I can't stay here, I just can't. I don't care what Da promised the man. I guess to be fair, I promised too, but that was before I met the bloke and discovered he's meaner than a polecat. I think there was a rail station in that town we went through on the way here. If I can get there, I can go back east. I don't know what I'm gonna do once I get away, or how I'm gonna get home. I'll think about that once I'm free of here. Something will work out, it always does.*

The upper level of the house was dark again. The slamming of the house door sent her heart hammering in her throat. Bella slipped into the barn through an unlatched door she found in the back and hid behind a feed bin. Outside, Red called her name and his boots scrunched on the gravel outside the barn. She held her breath when he gave the inside of the building a cursory search. When he finally left, Bella was lightheaded. She crawled out of the narrow space she'd managed to cram herself into and sat for a moment to regain her equilibrium. It would take way too long to walk all the way to town, they'd find her for sure once the sun came up. One of the horses in the pens whinnied and Bella smiled.

She found where the hands stored the tack. The bridle look easy enough but the saddles were bigger and heavier than what she was used to. Panting with the effort she lugged a saddle out to the pen that sat in the deepest shadows. Another trip and she had bridle and blanket. Now, all she needed to do was catch one of the horses. It was easier than she anticipated. No sooner did she slip into the pen than three horses ambled over to inspect the intruder. Bella looped a piece of binder twine around a dark coloured horse who seemed the friendliest. She stroked the soft nose and led it over to where she dumped the tack on the outside of the pen. In short order she had the animal bridled and managed to get it out of the pen without turning the other horses loose. While she heaved the heavy saddle unto the horse and figured out how to secure it, she also determined the horse was a gelding. All the better, if he ran truc to form, he would be less likely to give her trouble than a mare.

Satisfied the saddle wouldn't slip, she mounted with only a bit of difficulty. The high cantle of the saddle caught her thigh for a second as she swung aboard. Once settled, Bella decided she liked the western saddle, the high back and rounded swells on either side of the knob that stuck up in the middle of the front made her feel secure. She was very conscious of the baby she carried, the thought of falling and hurting Vear's child made her cold and sick. Touching a heel to the gelding she turned him up the small gully that cut across the back of the pens. If she remembered rightly, she should be able to come out of the ravine and find the road back to Pincher Creek. She hoped.

It wasn't really horse stealing, she could leave the horse at the railway station with a note saying to return it to D'Arcy Rowan. Come to that, the animal had some kind of identifying mark on it, a brand Red called it. She leaned down and stroked the diamond with the initials DR under it. The last thing she needed was the law looking for her. She gave the horse his head and he seemed content to follow the path that wound away from the ranch buildings. The moon was on the far side of the sky now and the light was fainter than before.

Bella halted after checking her watch and realizing she'd been riding for twenty minutes. It should be safe to leave the gully and follow the road for bit. Once the sun came up, if she hadn't made it to town yet, she'd have to find a way to stay near the road but out of sight. Turning the gelding's head, she urged him off the track and up the side of the hill. Gaining the crest, she expected to see the dirt road shining in what was left of the moonlight. Only grey and silver prairie met her gaze. No matter, the gully must have veered further to the south than she realized. She sent the horse down the shallow grade and up the next rise. The damn land looked flat from the car when Red brought her here, but in reality she discovered it was a series of rolling hills that folded in on each other.

Doggedly, she kept going, heading north toward where she was sure the road and freedom lay. Finally, as she topped the fourth small hill, a silver track gleamed in the distance. "Not too much further now, old boy." She patted the horse and gave him his head as they began to descend. The next hill was steeper than it looked and Bella was forced to skirt the edges of it adding miles and taking far more time than she was comfortable with. Another hour and she halted the horse. Uncertainty taking root in her heart. There was no way she could have gotten this far from the road, just by cutting up the gully behind the barn. Where was the bloody road?

High pitched yipping erupted to her right and she jumped, squinting into the dark. The gelding picked up on her fear and shifted nervously beneath her. Another pack of the demon dogs answered the first from the other side. Totally spooked now, Bella slapped the horse with the ends of the long split reins and sent gelding racing across the prairie. She hung on for all she was worth when he leaped a brush filled ditch and stumbled on the far side. If she fell off the demon dogs would kill her for sure. Hampered by the small bump of her belly, she leaned forward and urged the horse faster.

Wind whistled in her ears and the cold brought tears to her eyes. A jack rabbit burst from the bushes under the gelding's feet, Bella clutched the knob of the saddle hard when the horse shied violently, but kept going. She was out of breath as her mount when the horse came to a plunging halt, snorting and pawing. It was dark, she opened her eyes, only then realizing she'd squeezed them tightly closed during the flight across the prairie.

"Oh, no," she moaned. The gelding stood on the bank of a huge river gleaming silver in the last light of the moon. The ribbon she'd believed was the road to Pincher Creek was the bleeding river. The horse danced beneath her, unwilling to enter the swift current. She wheeled him away and up the shallow bank, where she halted him. Once away from the river, the horse settled and Bella wrapped one arm across her belly. Breath rattled in her chest and her throat ached from the cold. The moon was gone, only the stars gave any illumination. The wind had dropped, the night was dark and still. Far away the demon dogs were yipping again, sending fresh shivers down her spine.

"Now what am I supposed to do?" The horse ignored her and used her inattention to take the opportunity to snatch a few mouthfuls of the short prairie grass. She leaned her forearms on the saddle, resting her head on them and let the tears come. It was all too much, the strange angry man she was expected to marry, the dry arid countryside… "I want to go home," she wailed. Eventually, the tears spent themselves and she raised her head. The sky was lightening ever so slightly to her left, the river flowing as if to meet it. *That must be east.* She needed to go east, the town and the railway was east. "Okay, horse. Enough eating, let's go." Bella pulled his head up and turned him down river. As she rode the light grew brighter, black and silver, faded to shades of grey. Finally, the sun crested the horizon in a brilliant ball of fire that hurt her eyes. The faint track she was following, curled away from the course of the river and up a steep bank to higher ground. Bella hesitated, the river gave her a sense of comfort, a compass in the alien environment. She pushed on, breaking a new trail through the coarse bushes that gave off a sharp scent. A few hundred feet further and she had to admit defeat. The river bank dwindled away to nothing where the water cut a steep sided channel through a rocky outcrop.

Tears of frustration pricked the back of her eyes. The short coupled gelding managed to turn himself around and Bella was forced to retrace her steps. The horse scrambled up the rock studded incline unto flatter ground. At least she could tell which way was east now the sun was up. *Is anyone looking for me? I need to avoid high ground just in case.* She kept riding, trying to ignore her thirst and the hunger pains gripping her complaining stomach. It was pretty stupid of her to go running off without any supplies. It was also far too late to think about that. Even the breeze skimming over the brush and short grass was hot and dry. Bella licked her cracked lips and gave the horse his head. He must be thirsty too, so hopefully he would find them some water. The river was far behind them now.

Bella slipped into a daze, lack of sleep and hunger was catching up with her. She almost toppled out of the saddle when the gelding stopped and dropped his head. Shaking herself awake, she blinked and rubbed her eyes. The stream of clear water didn't disappear. Scrambling out of the saddle she fell to her knees and crawled to the edge, not caring if the mud squished up between her fingers or wet her jeans. After drinking her fill, she sat back on her knees and looked at her watch. Ten in the morning, she'd been riding for hours and finally had to admit she was totally and completely lost. Getting to her feet and shading her eyes with her hand, Bella surveyed her surroundings. No sign of the river she followed earlier, around her the prairie rolled away endlessly to the horizon, no matter what direction she looked.

The gelding threw his head up and whinnied. Bella grabbed for the reins she'd left looped over his neck and missed. He shied away from her and then trotted off across the short coarse grass, breaking into a gallop and leaping a depression in the ground. Running after him, she tripped over a stone and fell head long into a bunch of brush. By the time she picked herself up, the gelding was out of sight, only the dust hanging in the air told her which direction he'd gone.

"Bother and damn," she cursed, slapping dirt from her pants. A tall pile of rocks a little ways off promised some shelter from the sun, so she struck off toward it.

Chapter Eight

The stupid pile of rocks was farther away than it looked. Bella was dusty and prickly with heat by the time she reached them. She collapsed on a convenient stone, her knees folding by their own accord. Leaning forward she rested her elbows on her thighs and hung her head forward. Her tongue was thick and stuck to the roof of her mouth. *Water, I need water. What kind of idiot am I to run away without food or water?* The kind of idiot who depends on Sarie to think of those things for her, a cynical part of her brain answered.

She raised her weary head and gazed across the rolling hills. Somewhere over there was the river, but there was no way she could walk that far, and besides, she's probably bloody well get lost again. A harsh croak of wry amusement forced its way up her throat. *Again? I'm still lost from the first time.* The heat shimmered and wavered over the scrubby brush and coarse grass. The hills were starting to show a pale green and a haze of short purple flowers peeked out from the grasses in places.

The sun was directly overhead so the sheltering pile of stones provided little shade at the moment. Bella slid off her rock and tucked herself under a small overhang. Her cheeks and nose were stiff and sore. Sun burn, great. Just what she needed to add to the misery. *I can't die out here. Someone will come and find me. Who's going to find you? Nobody knows where you are. Maybe he won't even care, he'll be glad he's rid of you*, the detached part of her mind argued. "Oh, shut up!" Bella hissed. She crossed her arms over her stomach and closed her eyes against the wave of nausea rolling over her. Her throat contracted and she retched, but nothing came. The effort of remaining upright was too much effort, she rolled to her side and curled up with her back to the rocks. Hot sand scraped her cheek, the dry dusty scent of sage and earth stung her nose. Bella opened her eyes and followed the heat waves shimmering over the prairie upward. She floated above the pathetic figure lying in the scant shade of the rocks, turning away from it, she soared on the thermals. How wonderful it was to be a bird, free of the earth. She spiralled higher.

"Bella! Bella! Wake up!"

It must be raining. She paused in the exhilarating dance with the heated thermals rising from the arid land below. Her sky was still a clear intense blue, so where was the disturbing sensation of cold moisture coming from. She dipped her wings and circled downward toward an oddly familiar pile of stones.

"Bella! That's a good girl, open your mouth."

A flood of water filled her mouth, choked her. With a great reluctance, Bella gave up her sun stroked wings and struggled to open her eyes. Blessed coolness soaked her face and hair. Gentle hands wiped cool water on her throat and arms. Deep within, she felt the new life she carried stir giving her the impetus to open her eyes.

"She's awake," the voice sounded relieved and oddly triumphant.

"Vear, is that you? Love you, miss you," her thick tongue struggled to form the words.

"Hush, girl." Strong arms moved her body upright.

"Vear? The baby's alright..." *Oh no, he doesn't know about the baby, he can't know...*Bella struggled back to consciousness. "No, that's not right, Vear. I'm talking nonsense, there's no baby."

"Hush, Arabella. Yer talkin' gibberish. Do ya think ye can stand?"

She strained to recognize the speaker. Her brow wrinkled with the effort and her head pounded unbearably. Breath left her in a rush when she was bodily lifted from the sandy hollow, the world spun in crazy circles. Her fingers clutched the rough fabric covering the hard muscles beneath her cheek.

"Hot. Too hot. Put me down," she mumbled. Somewhere the urge to struggle against the arms holding her made itself known, but the effort was too much. Bella drifted back into the dream where Vear held her close, while outside the cave the waves beat on the rocky cliffs. His lips caressed her forehead and she gave herself up to the comfort of his touch.

* * *

Birds singing far too loudly forced Bella back to reality. Pushing up on her elbows, she opened her eyes and blinked at the overly bright rectangle of light. A lance of agony threatened to split her head in two. "Bloody hell," she muttered, throwing back the quilts. Through slitted eyes she groped her way across the room and yanked the curtains shut. "Shut up, you annoying birds," she said a bit louder. The irritating things took no notice of her distress and if anything sang louder.

Somehow she made it to the bed before her legs gave out. *What the hell happened? Why is my head splitting?* She closed her eyes and the pounding lessened a bit. Slowly, pieces of memory came flitting back. The last thing she remembered was a pile of rocks and being terribly thirsty. So how did she get here, wherever here was? Bella sat bolt upright and then wished she hadn't. Breath hissed between her teeth while she waited for the pain to subside.

Here, had to be the ranch. She was back at the ranch, right back where she started. Damn it. Boots scraped on the stairs setting her heart racing. "Probably Red coming to check up on the prisoner." For a minute she considered faking sleep, but decided against it. She was going to have to face the music at some point, it might as well be sooner than later. Wrapping a quilt around her shoulders, she turned to the door. *Wait a minute! Who undressed me and put this nightie on?* The door swung open just as heat flushed her face.

"About time you decided to rejoin the living."

Bella's head flew up to meet D'Arcy Rowan's gaze. "What are you doing up here? I thought you were too injured to come up the stairs?"

His face clouded and a muscle jumped in his jaw. She waited while he inhaled sharply. He hobbled another few steps into the room and sank into the one chair in the room. "Arabella, let's not bandy words with each other. Like I said before, we need to talk, you and I. Sit down." He gestured toward the rumpled blankets on the bed.

"I can stand," she lied while her legs trembled.

The big man sighed loudly. "Suit yourself. Arabella, we need to come to an understanding about all this." D'Arcy waved a hand vaguely between them.

"What's to understand?" Bella stuck her chin out in belligerence. "You've bought yourself a wife and a ready-made family. Something I never really had any say in. The agreement is between you, Da, and the damn priest." She laughed harshly. "Now there's an unholy trinity if I ever saw one. More like a deal with the devil."

"Is that how you see this, Arabella? That I've bought and paid for you with no thought to your feelings?" his voice was soft.

"How else could I see it?"

She wavered on her feet in spite of her determination to not give in and sit on the bed. The room began to tilt sideways. The big man lurched to his feet and caught her as he stumbled and half-carried her to the bed. She sank onto the soft surface, keeping her feet firmly on the floor. The mattress shifted when D'Arcy sat beside her. He poured a glass of water from the pitcher by the bed and handed it to her.

"Drink this. It'll help with the sun stroke. Better?" he asked as she swallowed half the glass and handed it back to him. "If this arrangement is going to work we can't be trading harsh words all the time. Why do you hate me so much? I offered you a way out of the situation you got yourself into and I thought you agreed to take me up on that offer."

"You haven't said a civil word to me since I got here. All you've done is yell and be teasy as an adder. I know you're disappointed in me. You were expecting some beautiful English lady, and then you got me. You bought a pig in a poke, but that's not my fault. I don't hate you, but from what I've seen so far, I don't like you

135

much either." Bella pulled the quilt closer and leaned away from his bulk at her side.

"I reckon I should apologize for acting like a bear with a sore paw. The dang accident has got me down, and I admit I'm not good at bein' patient waiting for things to heal up. I don't think I bought a pig in a poke, as you so quaintly put it." He reached out, caught her chin in his large hand and turned her head toward him. "You're a very attractive woman, Arabella. You may find this hard to believe, but I am glad you're here."

She regarded him with wary eyes. He looked sincere, but then so could Daniel before you got to know him. It was too much of switch from the scowling angry man he'd been up til now. Was he just trying to sweet talk her into his bed? The thought of anyone touching her in those intimate places curdled her stomach. Bella scrambled up from the bed and whipped around to glare at him.

"I'm here because I had no other place to go. According to Da I'm your property, bought and paid for. Just for the record, how much did you pay my father? Enough for him to drink himself stupid, I'm sure."

"Arabella, it was my understanding that you agreed to the arrangements. Your letter said you would marry me and let me raise your unborn child as my own. Are you telling me now that isn't true?" A line appeared in his forehead above troubled blue eyes.

She was very tempted to lie and say Da forced her into writing the letter, maybe then D'Arcy would send her back home. *Home to Vear!* The thought sobered her and scuppered the half formed plan. She couldn't go home again, ever. "No, I did agree to marry you. To be very honest, I'm not thrilled about the idea but I really didn't have any other options. I didn't realize it was going to be so hard to leave home. Everything here is so different and strange." Bella paced back and forth in front of the window. "My baby needs a father, and I have no prospects back home, none at all." Her voice broke slightly on her last words.

"What about the father?" the big man's voice was soft again. "Is he not willing to take responsibility?"

"He can't, he isn't in a position to take care of us." She shook her head so the hair swished about her shoulders.

"Is he a convict, then? The voice hardened.

"Not at all," she protested. "He just...we can't...it just isn't possible. I don't want to talk about it anymore." She turned her back to him.

The hand on her shoulder startled her. "Fine then, Arabella. Let's talk about our situation." He pulled her resisting body back against him and wrapped both arms around her. "We are supposed to be married on Saturday, if you are still willing. I would very much like it if we go ahead with the plans." One hand dropped lower and rested on the swell of her abdomen. "It will be harder to save your reputation if we wait

137

much longer. For now, only Red and I know about your delicate condition."

"But everyone will figure it out when the baby arrives in four months," she protested, afraid to move within the steel trap of his arms.

"I've taken measures to prevent that. I went to Winnipeg just after the arrangements were made with your father. Red told everyone I had gone to England, so the story is that we met while I was there and fell in love. We married, but it took time for all the necessary paperwork to be taken care of. To our great joy, you became with child on our wedding night." He sounded quite pleased with himself.

"You think people will really buy that load of nonsense?" She turned in his arms to glare up at him.

"If they don't, they will at least give the appearance of believing it. I'm a powerful man in this part of the world, money helps to convince many people of many things, and no one will dare to call me a liar." He looked solemnly down at her.

"What's today? How long before I'm supposed to sell my soul to you?"

"It's Thursday. Day after tomorrow you will become my wife. All the arrangements are made, you don't have to worry your pretty little head about anything. I understand you brought your wedding dress with you? If not, I'm sure Sara could rustle something up that would be suitable."

"Who is Sara?" Quite unexpectedly, Bella experienced a pang of jealousy.

He grinned. "Sara is an old friend and a very talented dressmaker. You'll meet her on Saturday, I'm sure."

"So let's get things straight between us. What exactly are your expectations for this marriage?" she said, the words sounding bolder than she felt.

He frowned down at her, his arms pulled her infinitesimally closer. "I thought the terms were very plain. I expect you to be my wife, in every way. That includes sharing my bed and pulling your fair share of the weight around the ranch. Obviously, you aren't expected to do the work the hired hands do, but I do insist you keep the house clean, cook meals, tend to the milk cow, make butter and cheese. There is a seamstress in town, and the general store has a supply of ready-made pants and shirts, but I do expect you to mend and darn. I'm sure I'm forgetting things, but you get the idea."

"I can do all that. Except maybe sharing your bed...I'm not sure...I don't know..." Bella dropped her gaze and her body heated with embarrassment.

D'Arcy lifted her chin with one hand. "I think you'll find sharing my bed will not be the chore you seem to imagine it will be. I am a fair bit older than you, my dear. Over the years I have not been, shall we say a monk, and the ladies who have shared their charms with me have gone away quite happy and well satisfied."

"But I don't love you," she burst out.

"Love doesn't have much to do with our arrangement, I'm afraid. Let's not argue over this right now. Concentrate on our wedding, I'm sure there are things you will need to prepare and things you may have forgotten. If you reckon you need to run into town for anything Red will take you. But, please Arabella, don't go running off on your own again. It's far too dangerous for a green horn like you. I love this country, but it can be harsh and unforgiving." The tall man bent forward and kissed her cheek before letting her go. He limped to the door, but paused after he opened. He caught her gaze and held it. "Make no mistake, Arabella. I have no intention of spending my wedding night alone."

Before she could protest, he was gone. Bella collapsed into the chair and buried her face in her hands. As Sarie would no doubt tell her if she was here, she'd made her bed and now she had to lie in it. If only it didn't mean also lying with D'Arcy Rowan. There was no sense protesting and carrying on. In her heart, she knew this was what she agreed to. Vear Du was lost to her forever and there was the baby to worry about. With any luck the man would be kind to her and far more gentle than Daniel Treliving ever would be, given the situation.

By the time Red knocked on the door, she was dressed and composed. She opened the door and he brought a tray with some soup and a teapot into the room.

"I thought ye might like some lunch, seein's how yer awake now. What possessed ye to go hightailin' it off like that?"

She hung her head. "I let the black horse go free. Everyone was so mad and D'Arcy was roaring like Da when he's in a killing mood. I was too scairt to do anything, but run," Bella confessed.

"Wal, it was plumb stupid. Ye almost got yerself kilt. D's bark is a lot worse'n his bite. He hollers and carries on, but once he calms down the man wouldn't hurt a fly. He was right upset when we found out ye were missin'. I was too, tell ye the truth. I've grown mighty fond of ye, missy. Don't go givin' an old man a scare like thet again."

"I didn't know. I thought he'd scald my arse like Da would'a done. And then, I was scairt he'd be like Daniel and..." she faltered.

"And what?" Red prodded her.

"Daniel, well...he'd take great pleasure in hurting me and in the most humiliating way possible. If he owned me like your man does...Lord, I'd be black and blue and tied naked to his bed..."

"Are you tellin' me ye Da would let someone treat ye like that?" The little man's face was dark with anger. "Just who is this Daniel?"

"He's the bloke Da promised me to. Daniel got Da corned and then got him to promise he could have me."

141

"Surely, your pa changed his mind once he sobered up?"

Bella shook her head. "Once Da gives his word, it's law. No matter what."

"Reckon I can kinda see that, but still..." Red set the tray down on a small table. "Eat this while it's still hot." He waited until she finished the soup and poured two mugs of tea. "I 'spect you and D worked things out? There weren't too much hullabaloo comin' from up here. The boys had a heck of a time catchin' that black bastard. Pardon my English, m'am. Man was well within his rights to be angry."

"You can't treat a horse like that," Bella flared at him. "All it does is teach them to be afraid."

"I want that hellion to be afraid of me. Otherwise he'll kill me dead. He's an outlaw, a bad'un," Red declared.

"Horses are what humans make them," she insisted. "Give me a month with him and I could settle him down."

Red snorted and spewed tea out his nose. "Ya stay away from that hoss, ya hear me? Woman in yer condition ain't got no business foolin' around with a critter that ornery."

Bella refused to argue with the pig-headed cowboy. Besides her head was aching again. She jumped and spilled what was left of her tea when a horn blared outside.

"Thet'll be Doc, come to check on ye and the young'un," Red announced getting to his feet.

"Doc?" She didn't remember seeing a doctor.

"Doc was waiting when we got ye home yesterday. D was fit to be tied when we couldn't find you and then Gus showed up all saddled and draggin' his reins. Ain't never seen 'im quite that upset afore."

"He was worried about the baby. I'm just the broodmare he bought and paid for, already in foal. Wouldn't want to lose out on his investment," Bella said sullenly.

Red looked at her with an odd expression on his weathered face. "Don't undersell yerself, missy. D sets a store by ye too. Mark my words. I gotta go let Doc in and get him to check on D afore he comes up here." Red picked up the tray and left, leaving the door open behind him.

She couldn't resist eavesdropping when the murmur of voices drifted up from the front hall. Standing in the shadows at the top of the stairs she was fairly certain no one could see her.

"Blame fool idiot, getting on a horse in his condition. What did he do that sent the poor girl running off into the hills anyway?" That must be Doc, she didn't recognize the voice.

"You try and stop D when he has the bit in his teeth." That was Red speaking. "I told him I'd find her, just had to foller the tracks back to where she lost the horse. He's only been out of bed to go and check on the girl. Came back down looking white as a sheet and disappeared back into the back bedroom."

"I'll just go have a word with him. If he doesn't give that leg and his ribs the rest they need he's gonna end up with permanent damage. Shouldn't even be going up the stairs at all."

The voices faded as the men moved toward the kitchen and down the back hall. Bella slipped back into her room and curled up in the chair as much as her growing belly would allow. She stroked the bump, marvelling at how hard and taut it felt. A flutter under her hand brought a gasp of surprise to her lips. She pressed a bit harder and was rewarded with another tiny movement like butterfly wings inside her. "Holy mother of God! The baby moved."

For the first time it really hit home that there was another life inside her. Up til now, it had been an abstract thing. She knew she was pregnant, and she loved the baby because it was Vear Du's, but there had been no real connection to reality for her. She'd read all the clap trap in the novels about women being all sappy and sickeningly eloquent about their offspring. Right up until this second she had never understood what all the nonsense was about.

Thank goodness no harm came to the little thing because of her impetuous behaviour. It was a stupid thing to do, she forced herself to admit. Now she had more than just herself to think about and take into account before she acted. "Sorry baby." She rubbed her belly. "Mummy will try not to be so dumb in the future." *Mummy, that's me. I sure plan to be a better mother than my mum.*

Voices floated up from below followed by the sound of boots on the steps. She was glad she'd taken the time to get dressed after D'Arcy left. Bella smoothed her skirt and twisted her unruly hair into a loose knot and skewered it with a pencil off the dresser.

"Hello, young lady. I'm happy to see you up and about. I'm Doctor Philips." A middle aged man with thinning hair entered the room and extended his hand.

"Pleased to meet you, Doctor Philips. I'm sorry if I've been a bother." Bella shook his hand.

"If ye need anything jes' holler." Red stuck his head in the door and disappeared after delivering his message.

"Now, if you'd just lie down on the bed, Miss Angarrick, I'd like to examine you and make sure everything is okay. You gave us quite a scare yesterday. Can't say as I've seen D'Arcy that upset over anything."

Bella closed her eyes and endured the embarrassing examination, answering the doctor's questions with monosyllabic responses. She bit her lip to keep from squirming when he checked on the baby. Why couldn't there be women doctors? There were a few in London, but it was more than she could expect our here in the back of beyond.

"Everything seems to be fine. You're a lucky girl. D'Arcy will be pleased to know everything is in order with the baby." The doctor moved away from the bed and washed his hands in the pitcher and basin by the window.

Bella straightened her clothing and got off the bed as fast as she could. There was something way too intimate having even a doctor touch her in those private places in her own bedroom. She moved to look out the window, hoping he would take the hint and leave her alone.

"I'll leave you now and pop in and give D'Arcy the good news before I go on my way. I'll see you in a month unless you feel the need to see me before that. Just have D'Arcy or Red give me a call. I'll see you on Saturday at any rate. Congratulations on your upcoming marriage."

"Thanks," she mumbled not turning from the window. The door snicked closed behind him and his boots sounded hollow on the steps as he descended to the main level.

Chapter Nine

Saturday Bella was awake before the sun. She sat up and leaned against the headboard waiting for the darkness outside the window to begin to fade into shades of grey. Small bumps and bangs filtered up from below telling her Red and his army of volunteers were already turning the living room into flower be-decked background for the wedding.

Her dress hung from a hook on the wall, ephemeral and fragile. In the dim light it looked like a ghost hovering in the corner. Sara showed up yesterday, exclaiming over the workmanship of the dress and fussing about with pins and things. To Bella's embarrassment, the woman had to let out the side seams to accommodate her expanding waistline. Fortunately, the overskirt along with the trailing bouquet of flowers would hide it from the guests. Her lips twisted in a grimace, of course there was no guarantee Sara wouldn't gossip about it all over town. The woman was D'Arcy's age, wouldn't she have made a better match for him than Bella? Their reactions to each other in the short time she'd seen them together made her suspect there was once more than friendship between them.

"I wouldn't mind in the least if he took his pleasure with her and left me to myself," Bella whispered. The morning chorus of bird song rose outside. As the sky lightened, the raucous shouts of the magpies brought a smile to her lips. A discreet knock sounded at her door.

"Are you awake, missy?" Red waited for her response.

"Come on it, Red. I'm decent, sort of."

The door pushed open and he backed into the room carrying a breakfast tray. He hooked a foot around the leg of the small table and pulled it nearer the bed. Averting his eyes from her, he set the tray down and crossed the room to open her curtains.

"Looks like a beautiful day for a wedding," he announced. "When yer finished yer breakfast, Sara'll be up to help you git ready."

"Thanks, Red. I am decent you know, you can quit looking at the floor or the wall," she teased him.

The cowboy shook his head. "No, m'am. It jes' ain't right fer a man to see ya in yer night clothes on yer weddin' day. Jes' ain't right."

"I've got the quilts up to my nose." She laughed.

"Time enuf fer this old goat ta see ye when ye're ready to walk down the aisle." He headed for the door.

A sudden thought struck Bella. "Red, wait. Who's giving me away? Da isn't here to do it, and I don't know anyone. I can't believe I didn't think of it before now."

"Didn't ye and D discuss them things? Lord, sometimes I don't know what gits inta that man."

"The topic never came up," she muttered. "Do you know?"

"I do believe D asked Doc to do the honours," Red confessed.

"Doc? Well, I suppose…"

"If ye don't need anything else, I'll jus' be goin."

"Can't you do it, Red? Please?" Bella swung her legs over the side of the bed and clutched the quilt around her.

"I'm right proud yer asking, but I cain't. I'm standing up for D as his best man."

"Oh." For some reason she felt betrayed and hollow inside. *Foolish, foolish. Of course he has more loyalty to him than to me.*

"I'll send Sara up in half an hour." Red made his escape and left her to her own devices.

"Great, can't wait," she muttered mutinously. An overwhelming urge to run swept through her. Clenching her fists and squeezing her eyes tight shut, Bella struggled to control the impulse. "Think of the baby. You can't afford another disaster."

Throwing off the covers she picked at the eggs and biscuits on the tray. The food stuck in her throat, but she forced some down. Seemed like she was always hungry lately, though when she ate anything it sat like a ton of bricks in her stomach. Taking a cup of tea cradled between her palms Bella wandered over to the window and leaned against the side of the dormer, staring unseeing out over the hills. Sarie would have a fit when she saw the photos of the day. All those lean hipped men in wide brimmed hats. Bella wished she could be there to share in the laughter. Resting her head, she sighed and gave into a bout of self-pity. A tear slipped down her nose and landed with a plot in the rapidly cooling tea.

"Miss Angarrick, come along, time to get ready!" Sara, the blasted woman, carolled as she came through the door.

Bella turned from the window and used the excuse of setting the tea cup down to surreptitiously wipe her cheek. It was just as well she'd set the cup down, the perky expression on the woman's face made Bella want to throw something. She forced her stiff lips into a semblance of a smile, or at least she hoped so.

Since there was no point in protesting, Bella allowed herself to be chivvied off to the bathroom. Apparently, D'Arcy had spared no expense in the upstairs waterworks. The room was equipped with a large bathtub and hot and cold running water. The tub was already filled to the brim with water, steam rising gently from the surface. The room smelled of roses and violets. She choked back a scream of frustration. Obviously, she wasn't even to be allowed to draw her own bath water on what was

150

supposedly the happiest day of her life. The lack of control over her destiny galled her and this was just another cut at her independence. For a moment she considered draining the bloody thing and refilling it. The baby curled in her belly and the fight went out of her. *What's the point? It doesn't matter. Nothing matters anymore. This time tomorrow I'll be signed, sealed, and delivered. Property of a man I hardly know, his to do with as he wishes.*

Bella stepped out of her nightgown, letting it pool on the floor before she kicked it aside. She slipped into the tub and immersed herself to her chin, laying her head against the high back and attempting to let the hot water relax her. Her eyes closed, the sleepless night catching up with her.

"Bella, sweetling. Don't despair. They can part us, but they can never destroy our love."

"Vear?" She reached for him.

"Hush, my love. Don't disturb the dream. Let me look at you, all swollen with our love. I wish—"

"Miss Angarrick. I thought I'd just come and help you wash your hair," Sara announced, jarring Bella from her dream.

She jumped and water sloshed over the rim of the tub. "Bloody hell," she muttered under her breath. "I'd just as soon drown the witch."

"Oh, I apologize for startling you, dear. I hope you approve of the scented bath oils, rose and violet are D'Arcy's favorites, you know."

151

"No, I didn't know, thank you." Bella gritted her teeth.

"Oh how silly of me, of course you couldn't know, could you?"

Bella stared at the woman for a long moment trying to decide if she was sincere or if there was some hidden message behind the seemingly innocent words.

Sara picked up a small pitcher and dipped it into the bath water. "Here now, let's get that hair of yours washed, and then I'll arrange it for you. That lace in your veil is lovely, you're so lucky. Things like that are hard to come by here." She prattled on while she dumped water over Bella and soaped her hair with a rose scented shampoo. Bella endured the ordeal in silence, wishing herself miles away.

"There we go, dear." Sara dumped a last jug of clean water over Bella's head and wrapped a towel around it. "Now, if you'll just stand up and step out onto the mat, I'll get you dried off and into the wrapper."

The very last thing in the world Bella wanted to do was stand naked in front of this woman she hardly knew. She was acutely conscious of the pronounced swell of her belly, it was a private matter between her and Vear, and she was protective of it. She acknowledged it was weird, but she couldn't change how she felt.

"C'mon, Miss Angarrick. You need to get out now or we'll never get you ready in time."

"For God's sake, call me Bella. Or Arabella if you choose." She heaved herself upright, water running off her in sheets. It took a great effort of will not to cross her arms over her belly and breasts. Closing her eyes she stood stoically and let the woman wipe her dry. When it came to her private parts, Bella snatched the towel from Sara with a glare and turning her back, dried her breasts, belly and upper legs. Tonight she would have to let a stranger take liberties with her body, but not yet.

Bella was oddly detached from the proceedings. She moved like an automaton, allowing the woman to dry her hair and apply the hot tongs of a curling iron. The smell of scorched hair wrinkled her nose, but it was as if it was all happening to someone else. She stood on command and allowed Sara and another woman—*When did she come in?*—to pull the wedding dress up her body once she stepped into the folds. She must have smiled at their exclamations of delight when it was finally in place, all button hooked and laced.

"You look lovely, Arabella." Sara stood back and admired her handiwork.

"A right pretty picture, for sure," the other woman remarked.

"Now, we just need the veil for the finishing touch. Vera, will you hand it to me, please."

Sara stood on a stool and fastened the lacy froth to Bella's hair. It fell in a cascade of lace and seed pearls like a cape around her. It reached almost to her knees. Sara stepped off the stool and came around in front of Bella.

"If you'd just bend down a bit, dear. Vera, if you'd help on your side, please. There."

The two women flipped the last bit of veil forward over Bella's face. Her sense of detachment increased, it was like looking at the world through a wavy piece of glass. Numb, she was numb, and hoped the sensation would last long enough to get her through the day.

She was astonished to notice the sun was sliding toward the west. *How can it be afternoon already?* The clarity of the thought jarred her out of her detachment. Sara was speaking to her and Bella tried to concentrate on what she was blethering on about.

"I guess you don't really need me to explain what to expect on the wedding night, now do I?" She smiled archly and glanced at Bella's stomach. "It's plain you've already lain with a man, so you'll know just what to do when your new husband claims his marriage rights."

Bella stared at her blankly. *Whatever is she going on about?*

"Let me tell you, Arabella. D'Arcy Rowan is a fine man, there's many a lady whose heart broke when they heard he was getting hitched. He's a man any woman would be glad to call her husband."

"You'll never have to worry about the almighty dollar like a lot of us," Vera chimed in.

"And, he's a most wonderful dancer. The man surely fills out his jeans in all the right places."

Vera and Sara broke into gales of laughter. Bella stood and let the conversation flow over her. She refused to think about anything past the ceremony and reception. *I will not think about afterward. I will not.* Her stomach curled in protest at the thought of lying in the man's bed, his to take and do with as he pleased. *A woman should have some rights! She should be able to say no if she wants to.* Bella heaved a sigh and looked about for a place to sit. Her knees threatened to buckle under her.

"Oh, no, dear. You can't sit down. Think how wrinkled your beautiful dress would get." Sara caught her arm.

"Oh yes, you'll be wanting to look your very best for your new husband." Vera giggled behind her hand. "If it were me marrying that fine specimen of a man, I'd be hard put to keep my clothes on til after the reception. Remember what happened with Ray and Elvira?"

"Oh my Lord. That was purely scandalous!" Sara waved a handkerchief in front of her face.

Vera leaned close to Bella and whispered, "Someone walked in on the wedding couple outside the kitchen door and they were…caught in the act. It was quite the disgrace, I can tell you."

"Oh my stars, look at the time," Vera exclaimed. "I've got to go start the music." She whirled out the door in a flurry of lilac skirts.

155

"Just one last thing." Sara dabbed rose scented perfume behind Bella's ears, on her wrists and in the hollow at the base of her throat. She handed the tiny bottle to Bella. "If you'd like you could put some in your decollate. I've heard men seem to like that."

How would you know what D'Arcy likes? The thought swam to the surface of her mind. *It should be her marrying the man, not me.*

Piano chords thundered from below them, followed by the murmur of voices and the scraping of chairs. Vera sent the strains of the Wedding March soaring through the living room. Bella gathered her long skirts and moved toward the door. Sara picked up the train that trailed behind her. She hesitated at the top of the stairs and looked down to where Doc waited to escort her to the altar. *Like a lamb to slaughter.* She put one satin pump on the top stair and proceeded down. The material of the dress was slick in the grip of her sweating hands. Reaching the bottom, she gravely placed her hand on the arm Doc extended to her.

Sara spread the long train out behind Bella and fussed with it until she thought she'd scream. Finally, the woman was satisfied and nodded to Vera who struck up the Wedding March again. Slowly and sedately, Bella went up the flower petal strewn aisle to where D'Arcy Rowan waited. His eyes never left her as she came toward him. When she came even with him, Doc placed her hand on the groom's arm and left her to take a seat in a front row.

Bella kept her eyes downcast, but didn't miss the way D'Arcy's gaze lingered on the exposed swell of her breasts above the lace of her bodice.

The ceremony was a blur, Bella repeated the words the reverend gave her and stood stupidly while D'Arcy said his vows in a voice that reached everyone in the room. When he raised the veil off her face and let it fall behind her, she lifted her head, startled. His mouth descended on hers before she had the presence of mind to turn her head. His right hand tightened on her left one where the wedding band pinched her fingers. The left hand held her jaw, effectively stopping her from avoiding his kiss. It was over in a moment, his thumb rubbed over her bottom lip before he released her. She closed her eyes as something twisted in her lower gut and heat pooled between her thighs.

Before she knew it, her signature was on the licence and her husband was taking her arm and walking her down the aisle to the cheers of his friends. Showers of rice and rose petals rained down on them, grains of rice finding their way into her bodice, petals sticking to the rounded curve of her breasts. As they left the living room, and were alone in the hall for a brief moment, D'Arcy reached over and ran his forefinger over her exposed skin on the pretence of removing the petals. The expression on his face and the hungry light in his eyes told her it was far more than that. A band of steel encircled her waist and she was pulled tight against his body for an instant. His other hand closed on her breast, kneading the fullness with supple fingers. His excitement pressed hard against her belly igniting a fire she tried hard to ignore and harder to conceal from him. It reminded her of the time in Vear's cave when she first discovered what exquisite pleasure her body could produce.

Vear, think of him. I love him. Anything else is just dirty sex, shagging, not making love.

Her husband took possession of her lips, running his tongue along the inner side of her lower lip and forcing itself inside when her mouth opened of its own accord. He raised his head for a moment to look at her while his thumb brushed her nipple through the lacy dress. He smiled at her indrawn breath and lowered his head to nuzzle her ear, sucking the lobe into his mouth. "Roses, you smell like lovely roses, Arabella. Do you smell like that everywhere?" He pressed his hips more firmly against her, wandering fingers slipping inside the wispy material covering her breast. Involuntarily, she arched toward him when his long forefinger grazed her aching nipple. He laughed against her neck.

"Save it til later, ye two." Red slapped the groom on the back. "Ye got guests waitin' on ye. The canoodlin' will have ta wait."
She was thankful D'Arcy shielded her from view while he removed his hand and released

her breast. Keeping her head down she walked at his side out onto the side yard where a long trestle table was waiting. The waiting guests clapped and cheered, shouting their congratulations. Her husband sat her at the head of the table and stood beside her. He made a brief speech and then encouraged everyone to help themselves from the side tables laden with food. The canvas awning stretched over the area flapped in the breeze, sheltering the merry makers from the last heat of the day. To Bella's surprise the sun was almost gone and the sky was darkening to the luminescent blue she loved. If only the sea was nearby, throwing itself at the cliffs. A plate of food appeared in front of her.

"You should eat something, Arabella," Sara said.

"You'll need to keep your strength up for later." Vera giggled and set a tall glass of champagne beside the plate. "The Rowan men are lusty buggers."

Bella nodded and pushed the food around the plate with her fork. She was saved from having to eat anything by the steady stream of people coming by to congratulate her and wish her happiness. She smiled and murmured her thanks, thinking she'd never be happy again. She sipped the champagne and nodded. When the glass was empty it seemed to magically fill again. After the second glass she was feeling decidedly muddle headed, and sleepy.

The band D'Arcy hired began to strike up some lively music and guests gathered around the planks laid for a dance floor. Her husband materialized at her side and drew her to her feet. "They're playing our song, Mrs. Rowan." He smiled at her and took her in his arms, whirling her out onto the floor.

Chapter Ten

Apparently, her new husband was a very good dancer. Bella was hard put to follow him through the intricate steps and turns of the totally unfamiliar patterns. The music switched to a slower waltz, D'Arcy pulled her closer, tucking her head under his chin. She was uncomfortably aware of his hips pressing against her. Leaning her head back in order to look at him, she inadvertently moved against him and shied away when his penis twitched, pushing against her belly.

D'Arcy laughed and dropped his hand lower on her back, strong fingers caressing her lower back just above the buttocks. The liquor on his breath registered a moment before his mouth claimed hers. Whiskey tasted sharp on her tongue was he pressed deeper into her, the unexpected flavour triggered vivid reminders of Daniel. Panic engulfed her and Bella squealed in protest under his lips. His arms tightened while his hips pushed harder against her. He lifted his head for a moment.

"Don't be afraid, Arabella. I promise you'll like what comes later." His lips brushed the sensitive skin by her temples. "I'm no green youngster when it comes to lovemaking." He swung her out and away as the music changed, drawing her back hard against him.

"Oh? Am I supposed to ask for references from your former lovers? Sara, for instance?" Bella hissed the words at him, but kept a smile pasted on her lips.

Hoots and well intentioned cat calls reached her ears as his common cowboy friends made ribald remarks, only to be shussed by their women.

"What happened in my past is none of your concern. You'll be polite to the nice people of this community, and not air our dirty laundry in public. Right now every one of them is politely not noticing you're up the post. I'm not asking you to love me, but you will be my wife in every sense. You seemed scared and I was only trying to reassure you."

Dark lights flickered in his eyes and a muscle jumped in his cheek. Fear gathered in her stomach, memories of another man with whiskey on his breath and hard hands make her drop her gaze and stumble. D'Arcy caught her and whirled her faster across the floor, steering around other couples. *When did other people start dancing?* Bella had been so absorbed in the interchange with her new husband everything else faded into the background.

Her feet hurt and she was out of breath. It seemed every man in the place wanted to dance with the bride, and she was obligated to oblige them. Numerous breaks to ease her thirst with champagne dulled the sense of doom colouring the day for her. *Oh Vear, where are you? It should be you I'm marrying, not some stranger I hardly know. I should never, never agreed to this. Never!*

"C'mon, wife. These boys have had you long enough. Come dance with your husband." D'Arcy took the glass from her hand and set it on a table. His face was slightly flushed and a hungry light flashed in his dark eyes under the shadow of his hat. He winced as he spun her around, the injury to his leg making itself known. Bella's head spun while the room tilted around her. She clung to D'Arcy's shoulders to stay upright and leaned her head on his chest as he stopped in the middle of the floor. "Come sit down. Too much champagne in your condition, I think." D'Arcy steered her to a chair at the edge of the dance floor but still under the canvas canopy.

Bella closed her eyes. The lanterns hung to illuminate the party danced in the winds and made her head ache. For one humiliating moment she feared she might be ill, but a few deep breaths helped the nausea pass. She took the handkerchief from her husband's large hand and wiped her hot face. The evening was cooling now the sun was down, but Bella was sure there was a furnace somewhere inside her. Her skin was cool under her fingers but her internal combustion felt like she was going to explode.

"Are you alright, Bella?" D'Arcy's face swam in her vision, replaced intermittently with Vear Du's features.

She reached a hand up to cup his cheek and drew it back when Vear's face disappeared at her touch. "Don't call me that," she managed to say.

"Call you what?" A frown furrowed his forehead.

"Bella, don't call me Bella." A tear streaked down her face. "I miss him so much," she whispered.

D'Arcy reared back as if she'd struck him. "What should I call you then?" his voice was cold.

She blinked at his sudden change of demeanour. "Arabella, you can call me Arabella."

"That's very formal and I don't like it. If you insist I don't call you Bella, then it will be Ari."

"Whatever you like, as long as it isn't Bella."

"Are you feeling better? Shall I go and get Sara to help you with anything?" D'Arcy stood and looked down at her.

"No," she spat vehemently. "I don't want any help from your fancy lady."

"She's not mine, or a fancy lady," he ground out the words between his teeth. "Suit yourself then, if you're fine I'll leave you now. I have guests to attend to." He spun on his heel and strode off to join a group of men, accepting a bottle of beer from one of them.

Bella sat where he left her feeling suddenly bereft and alone in the throng of people. Wasn't this just grand? She'd just annoyed the bloke she was married to and who expected her to warm his sheets this night. A shudder rippled over her. Would he exact revenge for her words? According to the law she was his possession now, a chattel, just like a broodmare. *What have I done?* The effort to stand left her light headed and swaying, the baby kicked hard and she sat back down. Thoughts of stowing away in one of the vehicles and making her way to town fled. She was in no condition to run away and look how that worked out for her last time. Better to stay put and face the music, she supposed.

The crowd of revellers was gathering by the musicians. Bella looked up in surprise when D'Arcy strode across the now empty dance floor toward her. His lips were smiling but the eyes were cold and dark. He took her hand and drew her to her feet, tucking it into the crook of his arm he led his bride across to the stage. Sara appeared on her left and pressed her bouquet into her hand. D'Arcy released her hand and helped her step up onto the musician's stand. She realized they were waiting for her to throw the flowers to the young women gathered in front of her.

"Throw the bouquet, throw the bouquet!" The crowd chanted.

Bella looked down at the flowers quivering in her shaking hands. D'Arcy appeared in her line of vision. "Smile for God's sake, and throw the damned thing," he said for her ears alone. She nodded and managed to twist her face into a semblance of a smile. The young women were a blur in the wavering light. Drawing her arm back she flung the bouquet of daisies and wild roses violently over their heads. Squeals and laughter ensued as the girls vied to catch the prize. A shout of approval went up when a pretty girl of about seventeen held the bedraggled bouquet aloft in victory. Bella heaved a sigh of relief and went to step down from the stand.

D'Arcy climbed up beside her and took the chair one of the fiddlers pushed forward. "Sit down," her husband ordered softly. Her face heated when she realized everyone was waiting for him to remove her garter. "Now, Ari." D'Arcy frowned and raised an eyebrow.

She sat down, finding her legs no longer wished to hold her at any rate. Cowboys in their Sunday best pushed and shoved good naturedly in front of the band stand. A waft of cold air brushed over her lower body when D'Arcy raised her skirts, exposing her silk clad legs. She blushed harder at some of the comments from the men.

His fingers on her skin were cool as D'Arcy made a show of sliding his hands up her leg. He started at her foot, removing her satin slipper, then up her leg, bending to kiss her knee. He

166

used the opportunity to fondle her inner thigh above the garter, coming close to the bits of lace covering her privates. He smiled darkly at her when he raised his head. Moving to one side, he took her foot in one hand and extended her leg. His hand was sure and steady as he slid the beribboned garter down and off her foot. Before turning to face the crowd, he settled her skirts around her. "Later," he promised. Bella stomach's curdled with fear or some strange excitement. She wasn't sure which. The champagne she'd drank made it hard to think.

D'Arcy turned to the rowdy single cowboys clamouring for him to throw the bit of lace. He played to the crowd, much to her dismay. Her husband held the garter to his nose and made extravagant gestures of bliss and rubbed it over his cheek. While Bella burned with embarrassment, he kissed the tiny bow on the garter. Turning his back to the men, he held it over his head and shot the garter over his head. Dark eyes burned into Bella's, promising her things she'd rather not think about.

The young men swarmed each other, fighting good naturedly for the prize. Finally a youngster of no more than fifteen by her estimation emerged victorious. He waved it over his head, then jumped up on the band stand, bowed to Bella and took her hand to kiss it.

"Yer a right lucky man, Mr. Rowan," he said before he leaped back down. He was carried away by his friends to the bar for a celebratory drink or two.

D'Arcy assisted Bella off the raised platform. He turned her into his arms and joined the couples on the floor. The song was plaintive and slow, she couldn't quite make out the words, but it really didn't matter. She was so tired, tears of defeat threatened to make an appearance. All the fight seemed to have drained out of her and all she was left with was the dread acceptance of her fate. Vear was lost to her forever. She would never set foot in her native Cornwall again. It was over, somehow she had to find a way to start her life over. Without Vear, without Sarie.

The music ended, the couples milled on the plank floor around them. "Midnight supper is on the tables! Come an' get it before it's gone," Sara's voice cut through the murmur of conversation. "Lots of strong black coffee, too." Bella raised her head and stepped away from D'Arcy, shivering as the cold night air touched her where his body had warmed her. Her husband took her hand and led her toward the laden tables where he filled a plate with sandwiches and date squares.

Perched on a chair out of the wind, Bella nibbled at a date square unable to stomach anything more substantial. D'Arcy stood nearby, another glass of whiskey in his hand. Sara settled into the chair beside her.

"He's a handsome man, Arabella. There's more than a few broken hearts here tonight."

"So you've said. Is yours one of them?" The words were out before she could stop them.

168

Sara regarded her with a solemn expression for a moment. "There was a time when that would have been true, I admit. But not now. Whatever it was between us is long past and water under the bridge." She changed the subject abruptly. "Those are Emma's matrimonial squares, she makes the best in the area."

Bella looked at the date square and then up at Sara? "Matrimonial square?"

"What better thing to eat tonight of all nights." She laughed and patted Bella's hand. "I expect there are a lot of things you're finding hard to understand. You'll get used to it." She stood and moved off into the crowd.

Bella wrapped what was left of her square in a napkin and set it on the plate of sandwiches. Her appetite deserted her. She wished she could just get stinking bladdered, but the buzz of the champagne was still making her dizzy. There was no way she wanted to make a fool of herself by falling on her face trying to get to the house. A roar of laughter caught her attention. A fancy enclosed carriage drawn by a white horse waited at the edge of the gathering. It was all decked out with ribbons and flowers, even the horse had flowers braided into its mane and tail.

"My stars, you scared me half to death!" Caught up in wondering what was going on she didn't notice D'Arcy until he put his arm around her waist. She glanced up at him, the lantern lights glittered in his dark eyes and there was an unreadable expression on her face.

169

"Your buggy awaits, Mrs. Rowan." He walked her down the path that opened through the crowd in front of them. His dark head dipped toward her. "For the love of God, would you smile, woman?"

Raising her chin Bella pasted a fake smile on her face and moved as slowly as possible. It was childish, she realized, but she wanted to postpone whatever was coming for as long as she could. Reaching the buggy she hesitated and started to gather the long skirts of her wedding gown in shaking hands. A squeak of protest elicited more laughter when her husband picked her up and deposited her in the shadowed interior. He climbed in beside her and shut the half door. Red was perched on the drivers box, he waited for D'Arcy's signal before clucking to the horse and setting the buggy in motion. D'Arcy waved out the window and then sank back with a sigh.

"Thank God that's over with," he said. One hand rubbed his injured leg stuck out in front of him. "I don't think *every* one of our guests realized you're the most unhappy bride ever seen in the MD of Pincher Creek."

Bella started to have a bit of sympathy for him, but his last words killed the emotion before it manifested. "I'm very sorry if I've disappointed you," she said stiffly and moved as far away from him as she could in the close confines. From the corner of her eye she was aware of the movement of his head as he turned to look at her. She held her breath afraid of what

170

his next move would be. To her relief he removed his hat and leaned his head back against the canopy.

They rode in silence for a time, the only sound the creak of the buggy and the horse's hooves in the dirt.

"Ho, whoa." Red's voice penetrated her thoughts. The buggy creaked to a halt. Startled, Bella peered out the window. There was nothing but star lit prairie as far as she could make out. A waft of cooler air swirled through the interior when Red opened the door. D'Arcy unfolded his long frame and got out. He turned and offered her a hand. Bella huddled in the far corner, too gob smacked to move.

"Where are we?" Her voice was reedy and thin. Why are we stopping here?

"Oh for the love of Mike," her husband muttered. He reached in and pulled her across the smooth leather seat toward him.

The hand on her arm was firm, she had no choice but to scrambled ungracefully out of the buggy. Even when she stood beside him D'Arcy kept a firm hold on her. As if she could bolt in the stupid dancing slippers still on her feet. Although the idea did hold some merit…

"See ya at the ranch in the mornin'," Red called from the drivers box. He turned the horse and trotted back the way they'd come, the buggy rattling along the dirt road.

"Wait. What? Come back," Bella called. She rounded on D'Arcy. "What are we doing out here in the middle of nowhere? It's dark,

171

and I'm cold and tired." She shivered violently in the light wind.

"I can take care of that little problem." He wrapped an arm around her and snugged her against him. "Quit fighting me, Ari. I didn't marry you to bring you out here just to murder you." White teeth glinted in the ghost of a smile.

Unwillingly she allowed herself to be propelled along with him. To her surprise over a low rise the big ranch car came into view. When they reached it he opened the door for her and waited until she was settled then tucked in her skirts and closed the door. When he joined her the scent of his aftershave seemed to fill the interior. The car growled into life at the turn of the key. D'Arcy manoeuvered the vehicle back onto the road but drove in the opposite direction of civilization. Or at least Bella thought that was the case.

Her suspicions were proved correct as they travelled over the rough road up into the foothills. Presently, he turned off into shallow valley, the land rose a bit and the engine growled as it slipped into a lower gear. They crested the brow of a low rise and entered a grove of tall trees, their leaves whispering in the night breeze from the mountains. D'Arcy stopped beside a small cabin where the wavering yellow light of a lantern shone through the window.

"Who lives here?" Bella asked.

"We do for tonight," he answered and shut off the car.

No one will hear me if I scream. It was the first thought that sprang into her mind. Which was silly of her, but she was all sixes and sevens. Her door opened and she allowed D'Arcy to help her out. To be truthful, her legs were unsteady and the effects of the champagne hadn't worn off yet. He lifted her up the two steps onto the porch and opened the door with one hand, the other not relinquishing his hold on her. *Like he thinks I'm going to bolt.* Given her earlier thoughts, she acknowledged he was probably right.

The tall man swung her up into his arms and carried her through the door into the cabin. It was one room affair, but cozy in a rugged sort of way. Red must have been up to see to things beforehand because a fire blazed in the fireplace, a plate of sandwiches was on the table and a bottle of something sat in a bucket of ice beside it. He set her on her feet near the fire and she sank into the willow wood chair thick with cushions. Footsteps sounded hollow when he crossed the floor to the door, the scrape of a key in the lock set her heart pounding again. The pop of the champagne cork startled her, but she refused to look around. The room was far too small and the rustic double bed with its fluffy quilts and pillows seemed to dominate her vision.

She took the glass filled with amber bubbly wine automatically. D'Arcy stood behind her and began pulling the pins that held the long veil in place. How it had managed to survive this long was a minor miracle. More pins followed the first, the net and lace fluttered to the floor, his fingers still busy in her hair. Embarrassed by the intimacy of his actions and not knowing quite how to deal with her conflicting emotions, Bella drank half the wine in a single swallow.

His breath tickled the curls by her temple a second before his tongue traced the outline of her ear. In spite of herself the breath quickened in her chest. Her fingers tightened on the stem of the glass when he moved from her ear and kissed the length of her neck and across her collar bone, his hands still playing with her hair, sending erotic thrills over her body. She downed the rest of the glass in two gulps.

"Is there any more?" her voice was breathless.

D'Arcy chuckled and took the glass from her, setting it on a low table behind her. "Slow down, Ari. I don't want you to pass out before we consummate the marriage." He stepped in front of her and taking both hands pulled her upright. "Your hair looks like spun gold in the fire light," he said with a husky rasp in his voice. A large hand cupped the back of her head and then his mouth was on hers. Asking, demanding—taking. Bella stood in his grasp, fingers clenched in the folds of her satin dress. She closed her eyes and quivered as his attentions transferred lower, his mouth kissing and licking her collar bones and the hollow of her throat.

Vear! Oh, Vear, it should be you. She bit her lip to keep from crying his name aloud. Whiskers prickled the soft skin on the upper curve of her breasts, D'Arcy's hands held their fullness in his palms. Releasing his grip, he turned her in his arms and fumbled with the row of tiny buttons down the back of her dress. The fabric gave way with a soft tearing sound when his patience wore thin. Bella thought it echoed the sound of her heart breaking. A swift tug and the tiny pearl buttons pinged on the floor.

"You'll ruin it! Those buttons cost a fortune," she protested.

A last tug and the yards of material pooled at her feet. "I paid your pa for it, besides you're never gonna wear it again." His hands roamed over her exposed flesh.

A stab of betrayal gave her the impetus to briefly summon anger. "Da didn't pay for it, I did."

He lifted his head to look at her, eyes bright with something besides the liquor. "Then its mine anyway, isn't it wife?"

Bella stood in the lacy petticoat and bra, the latter which exposed more than it covered. She resisted the urge to cover herself with her hands. She closed her eyes and clenched her teeth when the pads of his thumbs rubbed over the sensitive nubs straining against the silk and lace. Her body had a mind of its own and responded to his touch. The alcohol she'd foolishly indulged in made matters worse, it was impossible to concentrate or ignore the liquid fire pooling in her groin, while the champagne muddled her head.

The rustle and slither of clothing made her open her eyes. Firelight flickered over the hard planes of D'Arcy's chest. His jacket, shirt and tie were flung over the second chair by the hearth. She stilled the movement before her hands could reach up and feel the hard corded muscle sliding beneath the tanned skin. Silvery lines of old scars shone as he moved. A shock of dark hair hung over his forehead, he'd removed the ever present hat at some point, of its own volition, one hand smoothed the wayward hair back. D'Arcy caught her hand and pressed a kiss into the palm. Bella's breath left her in a rush.

She drew in a deep breath when the confining long line bra sprang open, freed by her husband's expert fingers. She spared a thought as to how he gained that particular talent, but his mouth sucking and nuzzling the exposed flesh drove it away in short order. He knelt in front of her, one hand still playing with a nipple, while the other roamed lower. A sharp tug and the petticoat and crinoline disappeared, leaving her in only the scrap of lacy underwear, garter and stockings. The taut skin of her belly shone in the firelight.

She jumped and he tightened his hold, the hand leaving her breast and grasping her hip. Large fingers pushed the bit of underwear aside and dipped into her most private parts. A part of her wanted to protest, but the fissions of electricity rocketing through her chased the thought away. She didn't remember him removing her panties, but he must have at some point, he parted the soft folds at the apex of her thighs, wet tongue probing. Bella's knees buckled when the pointed tip swirled around and pressed on the pleasure knob hidden there.

"That's it, Ari. Come to me." D'Arcy lowered her to the thick rug in front of the fire place. She lay still catching her breath while he removed the garter and stockings. When he came to lay over her, the curly hair on his thighs was rough on her skin. He rose over her, penis bumping on his lean belly. Lips claimed her mouth and she opened it to him. He moved down her body, pausing to kiss the mound of her pregnancy. Kneeling between her thighs he took her hand and pressed it to his hot hard erection. "Touch me, Ari. You've done this before, surely you know what to do."

She wanted to tell him it wasn't like that, but he slipped a finger inside her and pressed on her special place with his thumb. Her fingers closed on satiny shaft in her hand and squeezed in response to the electric pleasure thrumming through her. He pushed against her hand and she squeezed harder as his hips moved in time with his fingers. The pressure built in her belly and she swallowed convulsively. His body trembled against her, his hips thrust and then he pulled away.

"Not yet, Ari. Not yet." Fingers caressed the skin high up on her inner thighs.

Bella wanted to scream and weep in frustration. She sucked in a shuddering breath when he leaned forward and drew the clitoris into his mouth, sucking hard, the point of his tongue titillated her. Bella's hips lifted off the rug, his thumbs parted her inner folds and rubbed the wetness over her opening. "You're not a virgin, Ari. But I promise to be careful of the baby." His mouth disappeared to be replaced by the tip of his penis poking at her. D'Arcy loomed over her, his belly rubbing on her own, mouth kissing her breasts, the side of her neck, nipping her collar bone. She was acutely aware of the slip and slide of his erection as it probed, the head entering and withdrawing, leaving her wanting more. His mouth suddenly clamped down on hers and he thrust himself into her, pubic bone connecting with the sensitive area at the apex of her thighs.

D'Arcy leaned on his elbows, his hips advancing and retreating while long fingers pinched her nipples lightly. His face above her flickered in and out of shadow. Vear's features came and went, superimposed over the face of the man who was now her husband. She wanted to cry at her sense of loss, but the waves of the impending orgasm swept her away.

"Vear, sweet mother of God, Vear. I love you." She wasn't aware she'd spoken aloud until D'Arcy muttered a curse even while his penis throbbed and twitched in its own release inside her.

"What did you say?" He withdrew and sat up with his back to her looking into the fire. He looked very young and vulnerable in the red gold light, dark hair streaked with bits of silver hanging over his forehead. Bella reached out a hand to stroke his thigh. "Don't touch me," he growled, his voice low and tense.

"I don't know what's wrong. Wasn't it good for you? Did I do something?" Bella was confused, the effects of the champagne faded to insignificance. *Does he think I'm a dolly mop acting like that? Maybe he's used to whores, but he thinks a wife shouldn't act like that?*

"Don't you know, Arabella? It wasn't your husband's name you called out on your wedding night, even though it was my prick in your slit."

The harsh words made her recoil. "I'm sorry…sorry. It'll never happen again." She got to her knees and reached a hand out. "I'm truly sorry, D'Arcy."

The large body uncoiled in one motion and he stood looking down at her upturned face, his still hard penis twitching against his flat belly. "You're right about one thing, Mrs. Rowan. It will never happen again. I won't have three people in my bed, or be a stand in for bastard who screwed you and then left you holding the bag." He shook his head. "And yet you still love him."

He gathered his discarded clothes with barely controlled savagery and moved into the shadows at the far side of the cabin. A pump squealed in protest before the rush of water splashing into a pail sounded. Bella knelt where she was, trying to make sense of the situation. Her mind was still full of the passion of the lovemaking. The final moments came back to her, Vear's face superimposed over D'Arcy's. *Bloody hell, I called out for Vear. No wonder he's angry. Daniel would have beat me half to death for less than that.* D'Arcy stalked across the floor, fully dressed now in a shirt and jeans he must have had stored in the cabin. He flung the wedding finery into the fire and then threw a long night gown at Bella. She caught it and held it pressed to her chest, staring up at him. *Oh God, what's he going to do? What comes next?*

Her husband kicked the wedding dress into a heap and shoved it toward her. The underwear joined his clothes in the fire. "I never want to see those things again. You do what you want with that mockery of a dress, but I never want to set eyes on it again. Am I clear?" A muscle leaped in his temple and in his jaw.

Bella nodded, making no move to touch the pile of shimmering satin and lace. D'Arcy threw more wood on the fire before disappearing into the shadows at the back of the cabin again. Bella pulled the flannel nightie over her head, glad for the dubious concealment. She shivered even though the cabin was warm. Not trusting her legs to hold her, she pulled herself up into cushioned chair she'd vacated earlier. The clink of glass and the gurgle of liquid pouring send shudders over her skin.

180

The sharp smell of whiskey stung her nose. *He's getting bladdered, just like Da, just like fecking Daniel. Maybe I can sneak out, say I need to use the bathroom, before he decides to smack me around. I don't even have Sarie to run to.* D'Arcy stalked across the room, coming to stand by the chair and look down at her. The large glass of amber liquor in his hand shone in the fire light. Bella focussed on it and waited.

"Go to bed, Mrs. Rowan." He turned his back on her and stared into the flames.

"What?" she whispered.

"I said go to bed, I'm certainly not going to use it tonight." His fingers tightened on the glass.

"You're not going to beat me? Da would tell you to skin my arse for not obeying my husband. Daniel would just tie me up, beat me and rape me senseless, then wait til I woke up to do it all over again." She curled her toes under the hem of the long gown and gripped the arms of the chair.

"What are you talking about?" D'Arcy turned to look at her with an incredulous expression on his face. "I've never raised a hand to a woman in my life, and I don't intend to start now." He shook his head. "If what you say is true, your pa needs to be horsewhipped and your other lover should be in jail. There's some whores that like it rough, but I didn't peg you as the type." He turned his back on her.

"It isn't like that!" she protested. "Da would tell you to beat some sense into me, I've

181

felt the back end of his hand often enough. Daniel was never my lover, not ever." She stamped her foot. "But I heard enough around town to know what he's like, and he made it very plain to me what my life would be like once I was married to him. I don't like it rough, as you so crudely put it."

"So this Daniel character isn't the father of the child I've promised to claim as my own? The poor child isn't a result of a rape?" He took a long swallow of the straight whiskey.

Bella got to her feet and stepped between him and the fire. "I can promise you, the child I'm carrying is not Daniel's."

"Whose is it then? I got the impression from Father Boyle you were basically a good child, but a little wild. Too wild for Penzance. There were other men, even though you were promised to another?" His eyes bored into her and she flinched at the distain she saw there.

"It isn't like that. There was only one man, and only one time we ever made love."

"That's the guy you called for while I made love to you? What sort of name is Vear, anyway?"

Bella hung her head. "Yes, his name is Vear Du. It's old Cornish for Great Black. I can't explain anything more about him, but we can't be together. Ever."

"Did he dump you when he found out you were up the stump," he asked crudely.

"No, he doesn't even know. I couldn't tell him, and well, we just can't…it would never be allowed."

"Great Black, this man of yours is a person of colour. Is that the problem? Are you telling me this baby I've claimed as mine could be coloured?" He slumped into the chair behind him and drained the whiskey in one gulp. "God dammit, won't the town gossips just love that, the old bitches. You, or your Father Boyle, might have mentioned this when the arrangements were being made."

"The priest has no idea, and you can quit worrying about your wounded pride. The father isn't a man of colour." She crossed her fingers and prayed the child would be more mortal than selkie. *What if it's born in selkie form, how the bloody hell do I explain that?* Her eyes widened in fear. D'Arcy must have misinterpreted her reaction because he waved a hand at her and went to refill his glass.

"Go to bed, Arabella. What's done is done. I'll keep my end of the bargain and give you the shelter of my name and my house. You keep my house in order and deliver me a healthy heir. Let's leave it at that for now." He returned to the chair by the fire. "Go on, woman. I'm through talking for tonight."

Bella slunk away from the warmth and slid between the cold sheets on the bed. It seemed very big and empty. She shoved the pillows behind her and reclined half-sitting which seemed to be the only way she could sleep at the moment. But sleep refused to come, she lay staring at the back of the large man drinking himself silly by the hearth. The empty glass eventually slipped from his hand and thudded to the rug, D'Arcy's head leaned to the side and Bella finally fell asleep listening to him snore.

Chapter Eleven

The smell of coffee woke her. D'Arcy was busy preparing breakfast, but turned when he heard her moving. She pulled the quilt up to her chin and smiled tentatively. After the events of the evening before she was unsure quite how to behave. He crossed the floor and set a cup of coffee on the short table by the bed.

"There's a change of clothes in the trunk. I'll just step out and see a man about a horse while you get dressed." He pointed to a trunk at the end of the bed she hadn't noticed up to this point. The white heap of her wedding gown glimmered in the morning sunlight coming in the window. She averted her gaze, and nodded. The door closed behind him and Bella slid out from under the covers.

Shivering in the cool air she poured water from the pitcher into the large basin and washed quickly. The trunk opened easily, she blessed whoever packed a flannel shirt, study boots and dungarees, along with every day small clothes. The thought of having to wear the lacy nonsense her husband stripped off her the night before curdled her stomach. Belatedly, she remembered he'd burned it. Bella dressed as much as she could while still wearing the voluminous nightie, pulling her arms inside out of the sleeves. Hopping on one leg she pulled the pants into place and fastened them. Only then did she feel safe enough to pull the night gown over her head. Folding it neatly, she placed in in the trunk. Turning, Bella regarded the spill of satin on the rug in front of the cold fire place.

The car door slammed outside the cabin, setting her into motion. In a swift move she gathered the dress in her arms and crammed it into the trunk. No point worrying about folding it since the fastenings were ripped at any rate. Heat flushed over her skin at the sight of the lacy petticoats and garter flung over the chairs and on the rug. He'd missed snatching them up in his fury. She stood for a moment pressing cold hands to her hot face. With trembling hands she scooped the lingerie up and shoved it into the trunk along with the dress. A saucer on the table by the chair caught her attention. On closer inspection it proved to be full with the pearl buttons from her gown. She had to admit it was very thoughtful of D'Arcy to gather them up. Bella wouldn't have bothered, no matter how much they had cost her.

Her back was to the door, bent over closing the clothes trunk when boot heels thumped on the porch announcing her husband's return. Straightening up, she turned and stared at the snaps on his shirt, unable to meet his eyes.

"Should I strip the bed, or just make it up?" She winced inwardly at her choice of words.

Strip brought the events of the wedding night all too close to the surface.

"Just leave it, Sara said she'd take care of it for me later today." He crossed the floor and picked up the trunk along with a rigging bag with what Bella supposed were his good clothes. The cabin door was open behind him, as he passed the chairs near the fireplace he halted and set the things down. Bella caught her breath, what was he planning now? D'Arcy leaned down and fished one of her silk stockings from under the side table. "You forgot something?" Balling it up in his hand he shoved it into his jacket pocket. He picked up the trunk and bag again and walked out the door without looking back.

Bella hesitated by the bed. She hated the idea of Sara coming up to clean up after what was supposed to be a night of romance and marital bliss. She snorted, nothing could be farther from the truth. She blushed again, well, there had been sex...but romance? Not hardly. The powerful roar of the car engine startled her and hurried across to the door. *Is he leaving me to walk home?*

"Arabella," he roared just as she reached the door. "Get your arse out here, woman. Chores aren't gonna wait on you today or any day."

"Coming," she replied with as much dignity as she could muster. Bella crossed the porch after pulling the door shut and descended the steps in what she hoped was a graceful manner.

Refusing to rush, she made her way to the car and got in the passenger side. The door was barely closed before D'Arcy punched the accelerator. The vehicle jumped forward spewing sand and dust into the air in its wake. *Lordy, he can't wait to get away from this place.* For some reason the realization hurt her feelings. Which was totally ludicrous, there was no reason why Bella should feel any affection for the place she spent her wedding night.

* * *

D'Arcy parked the car in front of the house and carried the trunk into the front hall. He slung the rigging bag over his shoulder and instead of going through the kitchen to the ground floor room he'd used since the injury, he sauntered up the stairs. Bella couldn't help being aware of the way his jeans moulded his rear, her mouth suddenly dry. *Where the hell is he going? Surely he doesn't intend to move into my room? I can't...I can't...I just can't*

She fought to control her panicked breathing in vain, pressing one hand over her belly she gripped the newel post with the other. Black spots danced in her vision and she gasped for air.

"Missy, what's ailin' ye?" Red appeared at her elbow, unclenching her fingers from the post, and pushing her unto the third step of the staircase.

"I'm fine," she managed to say. "Just tired."

"Wal, I guess that's to be expected, after yer big day and all." He patted her hand.

To her dismay, she burst into tears and buried her face in her hands.

"What the hell?" D'Arcy's baritone rumbled from above her. "What did she do this time, Red?"

"Ain't nothing, D. Just them baby hormoney things."

Bella managed to reduce her sobs to hiccups. She got to her feet and looked up at her husband towering over her. "I'm just going up to my room." She went to move past him on the stairs, he caught her elbow and assisted her up to the landing and down the hall to her room. He opened the door and stood aside for her to enter. She hesitated on the threshold, afraid to go in and find his things strewn around. He gave her a light push into the room.

"I've got things to take care of," he said shortly and shut the door.

A quick glance showed her the room was empty of anything except her own belongings. She whirled around at a tap on the door. Red shouldered his way in, the trunk in his arms. He set it down by the wardrobe and turned to look at her.

"From the looks of ye, things didn't go that good with the two of ye. It's a cryin' shame, so it is. D is purely excited about that young'un yer carryin'. He's a good man, missy. Ye could do a lot worse."

Bella collapsed onto the bed and looked at the little cowboy beseechingly. "Red, I just can't seem to do anything right. Nothing I do or say seems to please him. I think he hates me..." her voice trailed off.

Red sat on the bed beside her. "Now yer jus' talkin' crazy, girl. D can't hate nobody, especially the woman who's gonna be the mother of his baby."

"But it's not his baby," she wailed. "What if he hates it as much as he hates me?"

"He don't hate you, girl. It ain't in the man to hate a little bitty baby. Ye gotta remember, ain't nobody but you, me, and D, what knows that little'un ain't D's."

"I guess." She sniffed back tears.

"Ye'll see. Things' ll work out. I don't know what went on atween ye two last night and I sure as shootin' don' wanna know. Give it some time, missy. Ye both gotta git used to each other and this bein' married thing."

"Where are his things?"

"Reckon D has decided to park his butt in the master bedroom, he was fixin' to have me move your stuff in there when you got home t'day. But it's lookin' like that's on hold for the time bein'. Ye'll work it out between the two of ye. Wait an' see." He patted her hand and left her alone.

The events of the past twenty-four hours caught up with her. *I'll just lay down for a minute, then I'll see about what's in the kitchen.* Bella swung her legs up onto the bed and curled on her side. Her privates tingled and stung a bit from her husband's attentions the previous night. She resisted the urge to cup her hand over the area. *Will he ever want to touch me again? Do I want him to want to?* She closed her eyes against the sting of tears. Lordy, all she seemed to do anymore was blub. Sniffing loudly, Bella opened her eyes and took a mental inventory of the situation. The only problem was her mind kept straying, the flames casting shadows on D'Arcy's hard body, his face hovering over her, lips on her skin, the hard rhythm of his body joined with hers. "Bloody hell, this is getting me nowhere. I love Vear, not him. It's just hormones, that's it," she whispered between clenched teeth.

Her gaze fell on the trunk, satin and lace spilling over the edge under the half open lid. She heated with shame at the memory of her response to D'Arcy's love making. What kind of woman was she? She loved Vear with all her heart, so how then, could her body respond like that to touch of another man. A man she hardly knew, for heaven sake. *Maybe I am a whore like Daniel and Da said. Like Mum was, to hear Da tell it. It must be bad blood that makes a part of me want to see him naked again. Feel the satiny hardness deep in my cunny.* The direction of her thoughts produced a tightening in her groin and

191

she groaned. *I am a scrubber, a slapper. Just like me mum, get some drink in me and I lift me skirts and waggle me fanny for any Tom, Dick, or Harry.* "I'm not pissed up anymore and just thinking about what he did to me makes my cunny all squidgy," she whispered into hands which were clamped over her face in shame.

She flung herself off the bed and shoved the offending trunk and its contents under the bed. *Think about it later. Think about it later.* Bella lay back down and pulled the quilts over her head. To her surprise, she must have fallen asleep, because somehow she was back in Cornwall walking on the cliff path near Vear's cave. He sauntered along at her side, dark hair flung back in the stiff wind, long legs adjusting their stride to hers. Bella's hand was twined with his and her heart sang with happiness. The selkie halted in the lee of some granite up thrusts and pulled her close. He lowered his head and though his lips were moving she couldn't make out the words. She tipped her head back and wound her arms around his waist, loving the solid safe feel of his body against hers. The realization she didn't seem to be pregnant in this dream caused a moment of startlement, but she dismissed it. The happy thought that perhaps this was real and the nightmare of her journey across the Atlantic as the dream. Vear's mouth tasted of tobacco and an essence that peculiar to him when he brushed his lips over hers. Bella opened her mouth and pressed as close to him as she could. His hand drifted from her shoulder down toward her br...

"Miz Rowan, missy, wake up."

"What the bloody hell?" She surfaced abruptly, sitting bolt upright and staring around the room wildly. "Vear? Vear? Where are you? Where am I?"

Red coughed and she focussed on his face. He looked pointedly down at her and then averted his gaze, a faint blush staining his face under the whiskers. Bella glanced down and snatched her hand away from her breast.

"Ye've slept most of the afternoon. D'll be looking fer 'is dinner shortly. I've got the boys tucker ready and I kin rustle up somethin' fer you and D iffen ye like."

Bella threw back the quilts, glad she hadn't removed any clothing before laying down. She got up and moved to the dresser to try and comb the snarls out of her hair.

"I know it ain't rightly none of my business, missy. But I heered ye call out some odd name, is he the baby's pa? Sounded like the same name D was cussin' about this marnin'. Did ye tell 'im about the lad last night?"

Bella hesitated. She wasn't totally sure she could trust the little man, but dammit she needed to talk to someone, she was so confused. "Not exactly."

"How do ye mean?" Red's forehead furrowed.

She took a deep breath and plunged on. "My husband was exercising his...conjugal

193

rights…and I…well, I…might have called him by the wrong name." Bella's cheeks burned.

"Ye called 'im by yer lover's name while D was…?"

Bella nodded, unable to speak.

"Wal, I kin unnerstan' how that would put a man off his feed. No wonder the man's madder than a wet hen. Reckon ye don' have any idee how that would hurt a man's pride…"

"Pride! A man's pride!" She fisted her hands on her hips. "Oh I understand pride all right. It was Da's pride that sold me like a slapper to that fucking scut Daniel. What about my pride? What about how I feel?"

"What are ye goin' on about? What's a slapper fer God's sake?"

She calmed somewhat. "A slapper is just another name for a whore."

"But yer pa was gonna make the bastard marry ye, wasn't that what ye said?"

"Yes, he was going to make me his legal property by marrying me, then he planned to use me in ways I have no intention of repeating. After he tired of me, he said he expected me to *be nice* to his *friends*. You know what that means as well as I do."

"I'm mighty sorry he had to deal with that, missy. But D ain't like that, not a'tall. But ye gotta unnerstan'…fer a man to be makin' love to his wife, on his wedding night for God's sake, and have her call out fer another man? Ye gotta cut the lad some slack, missy."

"I suppose you've got a point. And I did promise to obey and be his wife in every sense. Which I did I might add, even if it wasn't what I would have chosen. I will make sure it never happens again."

"That's a good girl. Ye've got a good heart, I know ye do. It might take some time fer him to git over it. He's a man with a powerful passel of pride, yer gonna have to be patient."

"I can do that." She nodded. "After all, it's not like I can ever go home. For better or worse, this is my life now."

"I think ye'll find it's not so bad here , missy."

"Right then, let's go rustle up some grub." She giggled at her use of Red's vernacular.

* * *

The days passed. The long June days faded into July, and then August. Arabella threw herself into learning to cook for a 'passel a'boys' as Red termed the hired hands. The old cowboy was kind enough to deliver the heavy pots out to the bunk house at meal times. She marvelled at the amount of food the men could consume. Red showed her the trick of keeping eggs and flapjacks hot during the transfer to the men in the cool mornings before the sun was up.

Bella was relieved the days were shortening as the year turned. Late May and all through

June the grey light of dawn came around four in the morning. By lunchtime she was yawning and wishing for a nap, but there was lunch to be made and then supper to get started. During the long Alberta summer days the men were busy from sun up to sun down. The number of mouths to feed lessened when teams of men went out to the line shacks and disappeared for weeks at a time checking fences and camping out in the rugged cabins dotting D'Arcy's range. She'd made the mistake of referring to the little houses as cottages once. D'Arcy had looked at her like she was a nutter and Red had laughed himself sick. She settled on calling them cabins, not sure why the term shack bothered her so much.

D'Arcy was gone from the house long before the grey light of pre-dawn turned the landscape into sepia tones. Bella often woke to the hollow sound of his boots on the hall floor boards. She made a mental note to see about runner carpets, but then dismissed the idea. It would be just one more thing for hair and dust to cling to. The bare pine floors were so much easier to care for, a quick sweep with a stiff broom did the trick nicely. She never managed to beat him down to the kitchen, finding only a still warm coffee mug on the sideboard. He must eat with the hands, she supposed. Red lingered long enough to take the towel wrapped pans of breakfast out to the bunk house for her.

Bella was strangely adrift, busying herself with laundry and housework along with the never ending production of food. In the still of the late summer afternoons she often felt like she was the only person for miles. It was an oddly disturbing sensation. She was used to the closeness of village life back home where there was always some sort of activity going on unless she chose to wander over the green valleys or the moors. The only reality that kept her grounded was the presence of the life growing in her ever swelling belly. Seven months along, the child kicked and squirmed making life most uncomfortable some days. She wondered how there was room for the baby in there among her own essential organs.

* * *

Bella collapsed onto the cushions of the wicker chair on the wide porch. The sun beat down on the hard baked earth just past the shade of the overhanging roof. She wiped the perspiration from her forehead on the sleeve of her blouse. Her skin was papery thin and dry. Lord, she missed the salty humidity of Penzance. The passing thought surprised her, lately she'd been far too occupied with the immediate demands of life here on the Alberta prairie to even think of anything beyond the next task. Not to mention the demands her body made on her energy. Even her dreams were absent of late, exhaustion overcoming her while light leaked from the western sky. Golden dust hung in the air, and overhead a golden eagle rode the thermals, a dark dot against the intense blue and gold of the sky.

The fabric of her dress rippled as the baby turned over for the hundredth time that day. Bella smoothed a hand over the taut bulge and grimace. "Hey baby, give your mummy a break, would you. My insides must be black and blue."

"Talking to yourself, Ari? They say that's a dangerous sign." D'Arcy sank into the wicker chair beside her, long legs stuck out in front of him, dusty boots crossed at the ankle. He pushed the sweaty Stetson back off his forehead and closed his eyes.

"You scared the life out of me," she exclaimed. "I don't usually see you during the day, I thought I was alone."

"Dreaming of your long lost love?" Her husband's upper lip twitched.

"Not hardly," she replied tartly. "I was begging the scalawag to quit kicking my liver."

"It's only a couple more months, and then you'll be rid of him." D'Arcy uncrossed his legs but didn't move otherwise.

"I hardly think of it that way," she protested. "Well, maybe in the middle of the night when I can't get comfortable." A grin quirked at the corners of her mouth.

"So you're not still carrying a torch for this mystery man who disgraced you, and then for some reason you won't share, dumped you?

You're not pining for him?" He opened the eye nearest her.

Heat flamed up her chest and into her face. "I miss him, yes. I'm far too busy to pine for anyone or anything, but I do love him. I always will." She fanned herself with one hand.

"I see." D'Arcy sat up and turned toward her, an enigmatic expression on his sun tanned face. "Well then, I have a proposition for you, Arabella Angarrick."

"Whatever do you mean?" A cold stab of fear pierced her gut. "Am I not entitled to the protection of your name anymore? I've kept my part of the bargain."

"Have you now?" A lazy grin crossed his features, but there was a darkness behind it that frightened her. "What bargain is it you think you've kept to, Arabella?"

She hated sparring with words and being put on the defensive. Debate had never been her strong point. "I came across the ocean and then out here to the back of beyond. I'm providing you with an heir you apparently can't sire on your own. I'm working my fingers to the bone keeping your house and preparing meals for your hands. What more do you want from me?" She glared at him.

"You've forgotten the other part of the agreement, haven't you?" He raised an arrogant eyebrow at her.

"I've done no such thing!" Bella's anger flared. Between the heat, the baby kicking her ribs, and lack of sleep she was in no mood for whatever game it was D'Arcy thought he was playing.

"Oh, Arabella. Is the memory of our wedding night so far from your mind? You also promised something more, or at least your father and the priest said you did. You were to be my wife in every sense of the word. Your vows were to love, honour, and obey. Keeping only onto me, I believe was the phrase, or something close to that. Yet even while the sham of a marriage was consummated you called out another man's name. Do you have any idea what that does to a man's pride, woman?"

"I apologized for that, more than once." The hands she held to her hot cheeks were freezing cold, all the anger fled from her. "I've hardly seen you since, you're gone before I get up and even after dark you lock yourself away in the office til late into the night."

D'Arcy leaned toward her, a strange light flickering in his dark eyes. Bella stared, mesmerised. *Almost as dark as Vear's.* She chased the thought away and forced herself to concentrate on the man in front of her. "You aren't missing me are you? Looking for a bit of attention?" He ran one finger down her cheek. Bella recoiled before she could stop herself. The big man's expression changed abruptly and he sat back in the chair.

"Well, then. You might be interested in what I have to say. This situation can't continue as it is. I'm a man with needs and I have saddled myself with a wife who doesn't welcome me to her bed. But because I'm married I can no longer ease those needs with someone else. I put great pride in my reputation as an honourable man. So you see, we're at an impasse. Other than the child, I can hire a native woman to take care of the housekeeping and your other chores. So, I propose this solution. Once the baby is born and is off the tit, I'll give you a divorce and pay your way back to where you came from." He sat back and waited.

Cold, she was cold. Clasping her hands in the fold of her skirt to conceal their shaking, she tried to comprehend the words still echoing in her head. "Divorce?" *Christ, wouldn't Daniel love that? I'd never be able to hold my head up in the parish again.* "You want to be rid of me and the baby? I don't understand, and how would we go about getting a divorce?"

"You misunderstand me, Mrs. Rowan. The child stays with me, once it no longer needs to suck at the tit, you can go. A marriage in name only isn't what I paid for."

Bella scrambled to her feet and glared down at him. "That's all this is, isn't it? I'm a broodmare you bought and paid for, once the baby doesn't need this anymore," she cupped one swollen breast and thrust it toward him, "I'm expendable." He didn't reply, his gaze riveted to her chest. Bella glanced down and was mortified to see a dark ring visible to him through the material over the tip of her breast. She crossed her arms over her embarrassment and stamped her foot.

"It wasn't how I wanted it. I truly thought I was making a contract with someone who was committed to living up to the terms. I didn't realize how young you were at the time." He tore his gaze away from her breasts back to her face.

"You're the one who hasn't come near me since our wedding night. I let you have your way then, I didn't make a fuss or protest when you put your hands on me." Her voice quivered.

"I put more than my hands on you, and in you, as I recall." A derisive grin creased his face. "I hoped there was a chance for us to have a proper marriage when you responded to me. Imagine my surprise when I realized I was only a stand in for your absent lover. I'll not have three people in my bed, Arabella. So, I'm asking you to help me make the best of a bad situation. I will support you and put a roof over your head for the rest of the pregnancy, and until the child is weaned. Then, you'll leave. The child stays here at the ranch."

"How is a divorce even possible?" She said the first thing that came into her mind. It was the last thing she wanted, but somehow the words fell from her lips.

"Good, I'm glad you're being sensible. I've talked to my lawyer and the easiest thing will be for me to give you grounds. It might blacken my reputation for a while, but then the story will be spread about how loveless my marriage to the odd English girl was and how I needed to seek companionship elsewhere. I'm not sure I like that idea. The lawyer advises, that since you will be leaving the country anyway that the blame should rest with you. It would be easy enough to get the boys to sign an affidavit that you had relations with one or more of them."

"You'd make me out to be a whore?" The words were flat and emotionless.

"Better you than me who has to keep on living here." He glanced up at her. "Oh for God's sake, woman. Don't look like I'm sending you to the fires of hell. You can tell them whatever story you want back home, make yourself out to be the injured party."

"I'm not leaving my baby. Ever. You do what you want, whatever you think you need to, but I will never give up my child." Bella left him on the porch and went up to her room to lie down. *What a bloody mess. I can't go home.* She rubbed her belly. *I won't leave you ever, little one. No matter what Mr. High and Mighty thinks. It's a big country, I could go back east...Oh, I don't know...* Tears of frustration and exhaustion soaked the pillow. Sometime later, she got to her feet and peered out the window. The yard was empty so she crept down the stairs. Relief weakened her knees as she took in the vacant chairs on the porch. Going through into the kitchen she fixed two cold beef sandwiches and took a crock of cold milk from the icebox. *Damn, the cow needs milking. To hell with it, let Red or D'Arcy take care of it, and dinner too.* Bella scurried back upstairs and locked herself in.

Chapter Twelve

Bella looked out the big window in the living room. Red and a bunch of the hands were stringing lights around the pavilion erected on the side yard. The same one she remembered with a pang they'd used for her wedding celebration. The end of August and the first weekend in September marked Labour Day. The Diamond DR Ranch also intended to hold the fall branding at the same time. She'd barely seen her husband since the disastrous discussion on the porch two weeks ago. It was just as well, she supposed. What was there to say to him? Could he make her give him a divorce even if she didn't want to? She shook her head and went downstairs, there was far too much to do today. Worry about the future would have to wait. Bella paused partway down to ease a cramp in her leg. Her shoes were uncommonly tight this morning, she continued down and kicked off the offending items, shoving them into a corner of the kitchen. For the past few days her legs had started aching and her ankles were puffy by the end of the day. This morning Bella eschewed stockings and now wriggled her bare toes on the floor planking, glad of the freedom.

It was promising to be a long few days and being any more uncomfortable than was necessary wasn't an option. The ground beef sizzled in the large cast iron fry pan while she cut onions and fresh tomatoes from her carefully tended garden into it. Another large pot waited nearby. Chili and stew could be stretched to go a long way. Bella wasn't sure how many were coming to the branding, but Red seemed to think it would be a large continent. The little cowboy was outside at the BBQ pit keeping an eye on the cherry red coals and turning the spitted hog he'd started roasting the night before.

The whole procedure seemed to Bella like branding was just an excuse for a big party. She wasn't even sure what branding actually entailed and be damned if she was going to show how ignorant she was by asking. *Sara would know*. The bitter thought galled her. No doubt that paragon of virtue would show up at some point today. *Why didn't D'Arcy just marry her instead of me?* "Because she's probably too old to give him his precious heir," she muttered. "And it'd be harder to dispose of her afterward." Only maybe he wouldn't want to be rid of Sara, maybe he'd want to grow old with her. For some reason that bothered her like a stone in her shoe.

Growling with frustration, Bella transferred the browned beef into the pot and added the sauce she'd made the night before and the beans that had soaked overnight. The knife blade flashed in the sunlight while she made short work of the potatoes, carrots, onions and turnips, readying them for the stew pot. She retrieved the chunk of beef from the ice box to chop for stewing beef and almost dropped it as Sara sailed into the room.

"Oh." She stopped and took in the bubbling pots and other preparations Bella was in the midst of. "Looks like you've got things well in hand here." With a familiarity that irked Bella no end, the other woman opened a drawer and removed a flowered apron. Tying it around her waist, she turned back to Bella. "Now, what can I do to help?"

"You can peel those, I guess." She nodded toward a bushel basket of apples sitting on the floor by the table. "I was planning to start the pie crusts once I got the stew going."

"Would you like me to take a hand with the pastry? D does say as I make a mighty fine pie." Sara reached for the flour bin.

"No, really, I'd much rather you peeled the apples, if you don't mind." Bella stopped her. "I'm a dab hand at pastry if I do have to say so myself."

"That's the God's honest truth," Red remarked from where he leaned in the doorway. "I was just comin' to see how ye were getting' on, missy. Didn't know ye was expectin' Sara here ta help."

"Thanks, Red. Actually, I had no idea she was planning on showing up." Bella smiled at the little cowboy.

"Didn't D tell you? I offered to help when I saw him in town the other day." Sara seemed to be watching Bella's expression closely.

"It must have slipped his mind," she said through gritted teeth.

"Sara, whyn't ye come on out ta the yard and see if them trestle tables are in the best place," Red took the escalating situation in hand. "Ye can let D know yer here, an' I'll help Mis Rowan with them apples."

"Oh, of course. Is D'Arcy looking for me then?" Sara untied the apron strings and tossed it over the back of a chair. She left without waiting for an answer.

Bella exhaled loudly through her nose and poked viciously at the haunch of beef waiting to be cubed. Red settled himself at the table and long strings of red peel began to fill a tin pail by his feet.

"Don't ye fret none about that Sara, missy. She done set her hat for D years ago and she ain't never figured out he ain't interested in her in that way."

"She said they were sweethearts once." Bella bit her lip, annoyed at the jealous note in her voice.

"That was a very long time ago, they weren't no more'n young'uns. She made no bones about how she felt and D was flattered at the attention."

"So they were going steady? Were they lovers?"

"Wal, missy. I cain't say fer sure. Ain't my place to say any road, even iffen I knowed. But if yer askin' fer my two bits I'd say D weren't so foolish. He weren't never in love with her, but he shore were in lust fer a bit. Come to his senses purty quick once she started hintin' around fer a ring."

"Do you mean he led her on and then dumped her?" Bella quit chopping meat and turned to look at Red. "He'd be running true to form, I guess. It's not much different than what he wants to do with me."

"Weren't D doing the leading, let me tell ye. And what're ye jawing about? What's he wanting to do with ye?"

"He didn't tell you? I thought he would have discussed it with you. Maybe he shared his plans with Sara, maybe that's why she's buzzing around like fly to honey."

"Tell me what? What in tarnation has that boy done now?"

Bella dumped handfuls of chopped beef into the huge stew pot and after washing her hands at the pump came and sat by the apple basket. Picking up a paring knife she began to peel. "Your precious D came to me about a fortnight ago and offered to give me a divorce—"

"He did what?" The little cowboy's eyes bugged out and he dropped the apple he was holding. "Ye shore ye didn't get it wrong?"

"He was pretty plain about what he wanted. He'll set me free and pay my way home, in exchange for my baby." Bella rubbed a hand over the mound under the flowered apron. She sniffed back the tears that pricked at her eyes.

"Blame fool idiot." Red cursed and picked up the dropped fruit. "What'd ye tell 'im?"

"I told him no. There's no way in hell I'm ever going to give up my baby. He's barking mad if he thinks otherwise. I know you swear by him, but honestly, what kind of man would ask a mother to hand over her first born, once it's off the tit, as he so crudely put it?"

"I purely don' rightly know what ta say, missy. That don't sound like D a'tall." He paused and studied her face for a long moment. "Now, ye can tell me mind me own beeswax, but maybe iffen I understood the situation better, I could help. What in tarnation happened up at that cabin on yer wedding night? D come back looking like a whipped pup, but putting up a good front. Man fooled everyone but me, cause I've knowed him since he was knee high to a grasshopper. He didn't…do somethin' agin yer will like?"

Bella's hands stilled on the apple and she struggled with the urge to understand the stranger who was her husband of just over two months and the embarrassment of the night in question. Making up her mind she laid the knife down and wiped her hands on the apron. "No, he didn't force me. I made an agreement and I meant to stand by it. I had more champagne than I should have, and I think he was corned too, but that isn't any excuse." She stopped, throat working as she swallowed hard.

"What'd he do?" Red frowned. "He better' ve acted like a gentleman or I'll be having a word with 'im."

"It wasn't like that, Red. I let him...make love to me...but while he was doing what he did...you know I called him by someone else's name. Oh, God. I'm so stupid. I promised myself I'd never say his name out loud once I got here. But I did...And now my husband hates me and can't wait to get rid of me. What am I supposed to do? I can't go home, and I don't want to at any rate..."

"Wal, that do explain a lot." Red rubbed the stubble on his chin. "The Rowan men are some prideful. Ain't no man wants to hear the woman he's pirooting on his weddin' night callin' some other tin horn's handle, let alone one as all fired splendiferously full of honour like D."

"I didn't do it on purpose," she said quietly. "I really want this arrangement to work out."

"Pardon me sayin' so, but even iffen it means movin' inta his bed?"

She lifted her chin and met his gaze. "It's what I agreed to. I knew what I was getting into."

"There might be hope fer ye two yet, then. Just bide yer time till the nipper's finished cookin'. Things'll look different fer both of ye once yer back to normal."

Bella glanced down at her distended belly and grimaced at the sight of her pendulous breasts. She'd always been well endowed, but pregnancy had made it hard to fit into her blouses, let along brassieres. "I can't say as I blame him for not wanting to touch me. I look like a Jersey cow waiting to be milked. Not anything to make a man think about a little slap and tickle."

"Now, missy. Thet's just silly talk. Fact is, a breedin' woman is mighty attractive to some men. Means ye can provide 'im with strong young'uns, and God's honest truth, there's somethin' about a woman wearing a backward bustle that sets a man's blood to stirrin'"

"Oh, Red. That's the nicest thing anyone's said to me in a long time." She got up and hugged him awkwardly. "Why couldn't I have married you instead?"

"Once you drop that load you're carrying and you're free, you can marry whoever you want," D'Arcy's harsh voice growled from the outer door. "Sara said you wanted me?" He glared at Red.

Bella stepped back and turned to stir the stew, heart thumping in her chest. *Why does he always think the worst of me? God damn that Sara!*

"Hold yer horses, D. Ain't nothin' goin' on that shouldn't be. Miz Sara is just aimin' to cause trouble 'tween you and the missus. She were in here earlier, all nice on the surface and catty underneath. Lookin' to give Miz Rowan here reason to think you're still chasin' her tail like ye was in school. Time ye got off yer high horse and unbent a little, iffen ye ask me." Red jammed his hat further down on his forehead, nodded to Bella and stomped past D'Arcy out the back door.

Bella gave the stew one last stir, checked on the chili, and crossed to the table, one hand pressed to the small of her back. Once seated she took up the paring knife and continued peeling apples, being careful not to look at her husband.

"Are you feeling up to snuff?" His voice was gruff. "Day's hardly started yet. I'll have one of the boys come and carry the grub out to the tables when it's time. Sara and some of the other ladies brought enough sandwiches for lunch, so you don't need to worry about that."

She looked up to find him frowning at her with an odd expression on his face. Too tired to try and figure out what it meant, she kept peeling. "I'm fine. Don't bother your head about me. I'm sure you have more pressing things to worry about."

"You'll let me know if you feel poorly, or any pain, you hear?"

"Don't worry, husband mine. If your precious heir is in any danger I'll be sure to let you know. Maybe you'll get lucky and I'll die in childbirth. Then you won't have to put up with me anymore."

He took a step toward her, hand outstretched. "Ari, I didn't mean it like that. I'm just purely concerned for you, you're looking mighty peaked lately."

Anger flared but she was just too exhausted to fight. "Get out. Go and do whatever it is all this fuss is about. I'll stay out of way. I don't need to hear all the catty gossip about why my newlywed husband prefers to spend time in town with his old flame."

"I don't know where you heard that clap trap, Ari. But it's not true. As God is my witness."

"Just go, D'Arcy. Go to hell."

Rising, she crossed to the bakers table and began putting the ingredients for the pie crusts together. She was keenly aware of him standing uncertainly in the doorway. Clenching her jaw she cursed the tears threatening to fall. *Bloody hormones, all I do is blub anymore.* His boots thumped on the step when he left by the back door. She let out a huge breath, unsure whether she was relieved or upset that he'd gone.

Much later that afternoon, Red came and cajoled her into sitting in the shade of the canvas over the long trestle tables. She rested with a glass of cold lemonade in one hand. The sun was still high and heat rippled over the prairie hills like a distorted mirror. In the corrals, cattle bawled and men grunted. The scent of burnt hair and flesh curdled her stomach, but it was too much effort to go back in the house. There seemed to be four or five teams of men working in the pens. Two cowboys on horseback separated the calf from its momma then roped the head and the hind legs. Once the calf was caught it was laid down, another cowboy holding it still while the last man wielded the hot iron. She understood enough from what Red explained to know each rancher had a unique brand and it was applied to a specific section of the animal. All the brands were registered in a brand book kept by the government.

D'Arcy's Diamond DR shone red and smoking on the left shoulder of each newly branded calf. The cows all were marked with the same brand, but the older symbols were filled in with white hair. The red, white faced cattle were Herefords, originally from Herefordshire, England. Bella felt a kinship with them, even though these were born and bred here, their genetics reached back to her home land. Unlike the small herd of Longhorn D'Arcy kept almost as a hobby, the stocky beef cattle were polled. The wicked deadly reach of the Longhorns sent chills down Bella's spine. It was all noise and organized confusion around her. She sat while the sun slid down the sky, casting long shadows across the rolling hills. The temperature dropped and her skin rose in goosebumps. Getting carefully to her feet, Bella wandered back to the kitchen to check on the pots simmering on the cook stove and make sure the pies were still cooling in the pie safe by the back door.

She jerked back in surprise at the sight of D'Arcy and Sara standing in the middle of the kitchen floor. Sara's face was flushed and her hands were busy straightening her hair. Her husband had his thumbs stuck behind the large silver buckle of his belt. Sara giggled like a young girl and swept past Bella, sending her a triumphant glance as she did. D'Arcy glowered at the door.

"Really?" Bella spat. "You can't keep your hands off the randy bitch? Sorry, if I interrupted your love making." She stomped to the stove. "I don't know why I care," she muttered.

"Ari, it's not what you're thinking. Will you let me explain, at least?" His boots scuffed the floor.

"Explain what, D'Arcy? You can't expect me to believe she didn't have her hands all over you. Your shirt's pulled out of your jeans. Maybe she thinks cow shit and man sweat is a turn on. There's no accounting for taste."

"What do you think you saw?"

"Enough to know she was all over you and you didn't seem to be protesting. Are you going to deny it?"

"Arabella, Sara seems to be under the impression I'm still interested in her. I just finished telling her she's mistaken. She was trying to convince me I was wrong."

"Looked like she was successful." Bella piled tin plates on a large tray, along with cutlery.

"I'm a married man, and I told her so. That carries an obligation in my books. Regardless of what you think of me, I have no intention of shaming you in that way."

Bella whirled toward him and gripped the counter for support. "You honestly think that woman isn't out there right now whispering behind her hand about how you and her are sparking, and it's only a matter of time til you dump the English tart and come back to her. I've heard the gossip, D'Arcy."

He scrubbed his hands hard over his face. "Ari, I can't control what others say. I can only assure you there's no truth to the talk. If it will make you more comfortable, I'll go out there right now and announce it to all and sundry, Sara in particular."

"I'll not tell you what's right or wrong. You do what you think you must." She turned back and picked up the tray.

"I'll take that out for you." D'Arcy brushed her fingers as he took the laden tray from her.

"Fine then. I'll just bring the pies." She retrieved another large tray from the rack over the baking table. Setting the platter on the small table just outside the back door she proceeded to load the pies. It would take two trips to get them all out, maybe three. The tray was heavier than anticipated, but she didn't want to take the time to unload it. Her foot caught on a root as she rounded the corner of the house, she bumped into the side to steady herself. Straightening, she stepped out into the front yard and moved toward tables under the canvas awning. The scent of roast hog made her mouth water. Bless Red for taking care of that heavy task for her. A knot of people were gathered by the bonfire in the middle of the yard, D'Arcy's tall form silhouetted against the flames.

She set the tray of apple pies down on the end of a table under the lights dancing in the evening wind sweeping down through the hills. Red caught her arm when she turned to go back for rest.

"There's somethin' ye should hear, missy." He pulled her closer to the fire. Puzzled, Bella allowed him to tow her closer to the gathering. Her stomach clenched at the sight of Sara's upturned face gazing adoringly at D'Arcy, her hand on his arm. She pulled away from Red and turned to leave. He put an arm around her waist and kept her still. "Trust me, missy. This is somethin' yer gonna want to hear." Frowning, she stood and waited. She was tired and her legs hurt, what was a little more humiliation?

D'Arcy looked over the heads of the crowd and met Bella's gaze. He nodded and Red shoved her forward through the throng to her husband's side. Sara moved to make room and glared at Bella with her back to D'Arcy. Red patted her hand and grinned. He stepped between the two women, forcing Sara a little further away. He frowned when D'Arcy beckoned her back to his side. Smiling triumphantly the hateful woman took her place.

"I want to thank all of you for coming today. Branding is always a good time, getting together with family and friends. In two weeks we'll be over at the N Bar Y, branding Maisy and Caleb's stock. Afore we get down to packing away the grub waiting for us, I have something I'd like to share with you all. Most of you were here a few months ago to celebrate my good fortune in being lucky enough to marry this little lady." He smiled down at Bella and wrapped his arm around her shoulder, drawing her close to his side.

She panicked and sought out Red in the crowd, he grinned and nodded. To hide her confusion she glanced up at her husband. He tipped his head and whispered in her ear. "Just keep smilin', don't throw a monkey wrench into the works." Mystified, she remained silent and waited.

"As you all know, Arabella here hails from England, same as those cattle." He nodded at the corrals. "And I'm right happy and looking forward to being a dad in a couple of months. There's been some talk goin' around that I want to set straight. This here young'un that my wife is carrying, is my child. I'm saying it straight out here in front of all of you, so let's put the gossip to rest. It's upsetting my wife in her delicate condition and I won't stand for it. I know there's some out there who expected something different, but Arabella Rowan is my wife, she's having my kid, and I aim to stand by her. I don't expect to hear anything to the contrary." He bent down and kissed Bella full on the mouth to her surprise and the cheers of the cowboys. "Now let's put on the feed bag, my belly thinks my throat is cut!" The crowd parted to let them through and D'Arcy led her to the head of one of the long tables near the warmth of the fire. Red brought her a plate of BBQ, potatoes and salad. He grinned as he set it down.

"Told ye ye'd want to stick around and hear what he had to say."

D'Arcy appeared at her side, sliding his tall frame into the chair at her side, plunking a laden plate down in front of him. He glanced over at her. "I hope that makes things a bit easier for you, Ari. I promised you the protection of my name and my body and I meant it. We'll let sleeping dogs lie until after the nipper's born, then we'll figure out where to go from there. Deal?"

She nodded, not trusting herself to speak. Emotions chased each other through her mind, he'd stood up for her, basically said she was under his protection and made it pretty plain to Sara, and any other female, that he was taken. *Sara! Where did she go?* Keeping her head down she looked through her lashes trying to locate the dratted woman. She finally spied her at the end of the next table over, sitting between two of her cronies and across from some of the mature cowboys. *At least she's not robbing the cradle, going after some of the younger boys.* She hissed sharply when the baby kicked hard into her ribs.

"Ari?" D'Arcy bent toward her. "Something wrong?"

"No, I'm fine." She shook her head.

"It's not too much longer now. I reckon you'll feel a might more comfortable once the little bugger decides to make an appearance."

"Little bastard, don't you mean?" She couldn't help saying.

He gripped her hand hard where it lay on the table. "Don't ever say that again. The baby is a Rowan, girl or boy, it'll carry my name. Don't ever think I'd let anyone change that. The guy you left behind isn't likely to show up is he?"

"No, and you've got nothing to worry over on that score. I'm sorry I said what I said." She ducked her head.

"Eat up, Ari. It's bin a long day. Time to cut loose a bit and have some fun." D'Arcy tucked into the huge plate of food.

Bella managed to get some of the tangy BBQ pork down, and then picked at the stew. There didn't seem to be enough room for her stomach and the baby. Let alone her bladder or other essential organs. Over by the fire someone broke out a guitar and began to sing. People drifted over, pulling chairs and stumps up to sit on. Out in the hills the coyotes joined their voices to the hootenanny. Bella wished her back didn't hurt so much. Another couple of cowboys produced fiddles and soon there was impromptu dancing, boots kicking up dust. Her ankles were cold, and she suddenly became aware her feet were still bare. She swung them back and forth trying to warm them up and ease the ache at the same time.

D'Arcy stood up and moved over by the fire. Bella took the opportunity to get up as well and stretch her back. The sky above was a limitless ebony bowl, the cold light of the stars seeming to flicker in the vastness. A crescent moon rose over the shoulder of the hill behind the house. She wanted to linger on the outskirts of the gathering feeling somehow a part of the community. Her thoughts turned to the huge amount of clean up that still needed to be done and she sighed. Might as well get at it if she wanted to see her bed before sun up. Red's clear tenor voice was in full cry by the fire, singing about a strawberry roan. A Wilf Carter song, whoever that was. Moving unobtrusively through the shadows thrown by the strings of lights over the tables, she set about gathering up the tin plates and utensils. She piled them on trays and shoved them in empty bucket. With a load in her arms she started for the kitchen door at the back of the house. The overhead light made her blink as she came in the door. Her faint hope that there might be some of the women already there up to their elbows in soap suds died a death. The clang of the plates on the porcelain sink echoed in the empty room. Sighing, she poured hot water into the sink and added soap. Immersing what she'd already collected to soak, she went back for another load. Two more trips and there was no more room, so she started in to washing. Spreading thick toweling on the long kitchen table she set the clean dishes out to air dry while she kept

221

going. There were still dishes in the water by the time the table was full.

She had just started to wipe the plates when a draft curled around her ankles. Thinking the wind had just changed direction, Bella didn't turn around.

"You think you've won, don't' you?" Sara hissed the words.

"Won what?" Bella turned, dish cloth in hand. The slave lottery?"

The woman laughed cruelly. "Barefoot and pregnant in the kitchen, like the little slut that you are. He won't stay with you, he loves me, always has." Her eyes were glassy and her gait unsteady as she advanced further into the room.

"Time will tell." Bella was too tired to wrangle with her. "Go find him then, he sure as hell isn't here." She turned back to the table.

"You bitch!"

The unexpected attack took Bella by surprise. She turned as quickly as her bulk would allow in time to put an arm up to block the wild swing. Too stunned to fight back, Bella stood gaping at the wild eyed woman. Sara snatched the butcher knife from the counter where it had been left earlier and advanced. Bella eyed her warily, putting the table between them.

"The only hold you have on him is that damn brat in your belly. I think I'll just take care of that little problem right now. Don't worry, it won't hurt...much." Sara moved

222

unsteadily around the table, waving the blade in front of her.

Thoroughly frightened now, Bella looked frantically for some weapon to defend herself while trying to keep an eye on the unpredictable foe. "Sara, you don't want to do this. If he loves you, then you have nothing to worry about. Once I'm gone he'll come back to you."

The other woman hesitated and Bella prayed someone would think to come in the house looking for her. "What do you mean, once you're gone?"

"I'm leaving when the baby's old enough. You'll never see me again." She fought to control her panicked breathing, her head was starting to swim and her knees felt weak.

"He'll never let that happen. You're lying! D'Arcy would never let that brat of yours go. No, if I have any chance, I need to finish this now." Sara lunged, knocking into the table. Bella lurched backward, banging a bare heel on a chair leg. She lost her balance and fell to her knees. The woman loomed over her, the glint of the overhead light on the blade capturing Bella's gaze. She closed her eyes.

"What the holy hell is goin' on in here?" Red burst into the room, tossing the load of plates to the floor as he tackled Sara. "D, hurry up!"

Bella folded over, supporting herself on hands and throbbing knees. She took great shaking breaths and gave in to the sobs of terror ripping through her. "Oh, baby. Baby, I'm so

223

sorry. We should never have come here." The words came out in gasps between the sobs. Hands gripped her upper arms and she struggled against them. "No, no, you can't hurt the baby. Get away from me," she wailed.

"Ari, Ari. Listen to me. It's over, you're safe. You're safe." D'Arcy set her on a kitchen chair and supported her with his body, his hands stroking her hair, gentling her like he would one of the horses. "What happened?" He spoke over her head to Red who came in the back door when Bella looked up through her tangled hair.

"That crazy woman was attacking Miz Bella with a knife. Iffen I hadn't come in when I did…well, I reckon I don't want to think what might have happened. She was raving about getting rid of the nipper."

"Who? Arabella?" D'Arcy's voice hardened.

"No, you dad-blamed idiot. Sara was aimin' to cut that young'un outa Miz Bella like a stuck calf. She's plumb loco that piece of calico."

"Is that true? She tried to kill you and the baby?" he addressed Bella.

She nodded, her teeth chattering so hard she couldn't manage any words. Cursing under his breath, D'Arcy took the wool blanket Red handed him and wrapped it around her. He kept murmuring comforting words which only made her cry harder. "Where's that woman?" he growled at Red.

"Out by the fire somewheres. I drug her out and left her with them old crows she hangs with.

Told the boys to keep an eye on her and keep them away from the house until you went out to deal with her," Red replied.

"Stay with Ari, will you?" The solid heat of his body removed itself, but was replaced immediately by Red.

"It's okay now, missy. You don't have nothin' to worry about. You and the nipper are safe and sound. Jus' calm down now. Carryin' on like this ain't good fer you or the baby."

"What is wrong with that woman?" Bella managed to get some words out. "What did I ever do to her?" Fresh tears welled in her eyes.

"Ain't nothin' you did, missy. That girl set her cap for D way back when they was kids. She just ain't never accepted he weren't interested. Land sakes, D is over forty, and Sara ain't no spring chicken either. Iffen the man was gonna put a ring on it he would'a done it long ago."

The door opened and shut before boots echoed on the plank floor. "The stupid bitch is drunker'n a skunk." D'Arcy spat on the floor. "A couple of her cronies are takin' her home now. I made it plain, loud and clear, that she isn't welcome here. Ever." Large callused hands cupped Bella's face and tilted her head toward him. His thumbs wiped the moisture from her cheeks. One hand moved to tuck tangled curls behind her ear. "I am so sorry, Arabella. I had no idea the woman was that obsessed with me. If I thought there was any danger to you or the baby from her I wouldn't have let her within a country mile of this place." He knelt at her feet

225

so his head was level with hers. She was vaguely aware of Red going out to put out the bonfire and take care of things in the yard. Her attention was captured by the luminous sheen in her husband's eyes. "Can you ever forgive me for putting you in danger, Ari?"

"Not your fault," Bella muttered. "Sweet mother of God, she's a nutter." She crossed her arms over the bulge of her belly. "She said she was going to kill the baby." More shivers coursed through her.

D'Arcy's arms closed around her and held her close. His forehead resting on hers. "God, I'm sorry, Ari. I can't tell you how much. Are you okay? Do you need the doc?"

She shook her head. The last thing in the world she wanted was someone else prodding at her. It was safe here right now, with strong arms shielding her from harm. When had anyone ever protected her? "I'm fine. I just want to go lie down." She made to get up.

He pressed her back into the chair. "Take a minute. Let me get you some water." D'Arcy stood up and she heard water running. A cold glass was pressed into her hand and she managed to sip some without spilling too much. "Ready?" He steadied her as she got to her feet.

Her head spun and it was taking a lot of effort to stay upright. Bella sagged against his tall frame feeling him jump when the baby kicked out where their bodies touched.

"Whoa now, girl. I'm not so sure you are okay."

"I just need to lie down. Really." She pushed away from him, meaning to move toward the stairs. Instead she swayed back against his strength.

"That's it, darlin'." He picked her up, and against her protests, carried her up the stairs. He kicked open a door and laid her on the wonderful softness of the mattress. "You stay put, I'll be right back. I mean it, Ari. Stay put."

She flipped her hand at him, already half asleep. Lordy, it felt good to just lie down and let the ache in her legs ease a bit. She opened her eyes when the bed sagged at her side.

"Ari? Doc's on his way out. I really think it's best he takes a look at you. Did you hit your head at all?"

"No, my knees hurt though." She moved restlessly. D'Arcy shifted and pulled her skirt up to her thighs, cursing softly.

"I guess they do, darlin'. You've got some good bruises and they're pretty scraped up. Long way from your heart though. Doc'll have ye fixed up in no time." He drew a quilt up over her and she reached for his hand as he moved away a bit. His fingers twined with hers and she held tight.

Light blinded her and she blinked while the bed creaked as D'Arcy stood up.

"Doc's here," Red announced.

The whole process was a blur to Bella. Finally, they left her alone and shut out the lights. She rolled carefully onto her side and tried to find a softer spot. Sometime later the door opened and soft steps crossed the floor. The bed sagged as D'Arcy joined her in the bed. He snugged himself against her back, one long arm wrapping around her just under her breasts. She thought he nuzzled her neck, but decided she must be mistaken.

"D'Arcy?"

"What Ari?" Breath stirred the curls near her ear.

"You can't be comfortable, my bed isn't big enough for two." She wriggled against him, trying to find a better spot.

"Don't worry your head about it. We're in my room. There's no way I'm leaving you tonight. It made more sense to have you here. Now close your eyes and go to sleep. We'll figure the rest of this out in the morning. Red's sleeping at the foot of the stairs. Nobody's getting anywhere near you. You're safe, Ari." His arm tightened around her.

There were things she wanted to say to him. Questions that needed answers, but somehow they slipped away. D'Arcy pressed kisses on her shoulder and the back of her neck before he heaved a big sigh and the tension went out of the big body lying so close to her.

Chapter Thirteen

Bella was alone in the big bed when she woke up. The unfamiliar surroundings were confusing. *Where am I?* The everyday sounds of cattle being moved and rumble of the hands calling to each other was reassuring to a degree. Rolling over, she went to sit up, hissing at the stab of pain in her knees. She piled the pillows up and lay back against them. This must be D'Arcy's bedroom, what was she doing here, and in his bed?

The thought brought her fully awake. Yesterday's events coming clear in her mind. Her hands caressed the hard mound of her pregnancy. *The baby, the baby's safe. Everything's okay. Well, as okay as it can be, I guess.* A shudder ran through her at the memory of Sara's crazed face leering over her, knife waving in her drunken grasp. *Thank God for Red. What if he hadn't decided to come help with the cleanup?* And D'Arcy...Never in a million years would Bella have thought he would take her side over Sara. He'd certainly proved her wrong on that front.

"He loves you, little one. Even if he doesn't love your mummy." She believed her husband when he vowed that no harm would ever come to her child. "Time to get up, it must be eight at least." Bella threw back the quilts. The morning air chilled her body. "What the hell?" She was dressed in only her small clothes, where were her clothes? And more importantly, who took them off of her? Wriggling to the side of the wide mattress, she got to her feet and cast around for her skirt and blouse. The garments were nowhere to be found and she stood uncertainly in the middle of the sunlit room. An oak armoire stood between the two large windows overlooking the yard, inside she found one of D'Arcy's flannel shirts and pulled it on. The sleeves hung way down over her hands while the tails brushed the top of her calves. At least it hid the ugly scrapes on her knees. The urgency in her bladder moved her toward the door.

She was within a few steps when the latch rattled and her husband came into the room. Bella stepped back a few paces, heat flooding her face. There was no way she could bring herself to look at him.

"What are you doing out of bed?" His voice was gruff.

Is he mad at me? "I have to use the loo," she whispered. "Why are you angry with me? I can't take the agro this morning, I just can't…"

He put a hand under her elbow, the musky scent of soap filling her senses. His fingers tilted her chin up so he could see her face. "I'm not mad, Ari. Not at you, anyway. I was just coming up to check on you. Doc says you need to stay in bed for a few days. No running up and down stairs and no cooking or cleaning."

"I can't do that," she protested. "Who's going to cook for the boys? I need to earn my keep—"

"You don't need to do anything, Arabella Rowan, except stay in bed and keep our baby safe. You hear? Red and I made out just fine before you came, we can the same now."

"Are you saying you don't need me? That I'm only good as a...a...broodmare?" To her disgust, she sniffed and tears pricked at her eyes.

In a swift movement, he pulled her into his arms, the material of his shirt rough on her cheek. "That is not what I said, Ari. I've kinda gotten used to having you around, you're way easier on the eyes than Red." A chuckle rumbled through his chest. "I was trying to set your mind at ease. Your job right now is to rest and let that young'un stay put for a while longer. Me and Red can take care of everything else. Okay?" He held her away from him to look into her face.

Bella nodded, unsure how to respond to his unexpected attitude. She could deal with his indifference and orneriness, but D'Arcy as a caring husband made her feel all at sea. Her bare feet shifted uneasily, bumping against his boots. "I...um...I need to..."

"Sorry. Of course."

D'Arcy released her but kept an arm around her shoulder. Staying beside her, he ushered her to the bathroom and waited outside the door while she relieved herself and did a quick wash up. She leaned on the counter and stared at her reflection in the mirror. *What is happening to me? Why is he being so nice to me all of a sudden? Why do I want him to keep being that way?*

"Ari? Are you okay? Do you need me?" His voice startled her.

Do I need him? I'm starting to think I do. I want him to like me, respect me. Is that being unfaithful to Vear? Lord, I wish I could figure things out.

"Ari?" The bathroom door inched open. "You decent? Answer me or I'm coming in."

"I'm fine, okay? Though I'm hardly decent." Bella pulled the door the rest of the way open.

He grinned down at her, a piece of dark hair falling over his forehead. "You do look prettier than a picture in my shirt."

She dropped her gaze and tried to move past him. Her protruding belly made it impossible, she halted and glanced up. Heat flooded her body and she was acutely aware she was wearing almost nothing. "Could you move?"

"I could," he replied without giving an inch. His dark gaze roamed over her face sending tremors of tension through her. The baby moved and the shirt rippled over her belly. D'Arcy's large hand was warm through the material where he placed it over the bump of what Bella was sure must be a knee or elbow. "Strong little bugger, isn't he?" A proud smile spread over his features. "He's gonna make a good cowboy, this little guy."

"What if it's a girl," her voice was breathless.

"Then she'll be as pretty as her momma."

Her eyes widened when the dark head bent closer and his lips brushed hers. Too stunned to do more than stand there, she stiffened as the kiss deepened, his tongue slipping between her lips. A hand cupped the back of her head, the other played with the hair by her ear sending delightful thrills through her body. His gentleness was her undoing. With a sigh of surrender, Bella reached for her husband. She splayed on hand on his hard chest, the other snaked around his neck, holding him closer.

"Ari," he whispered against her lips. "If you want me to stop…"

In answer, Bella pressed closer to him. Sensitive breasts rubbing against him, making her knees weak.

"Do you want me to stop? Ari?" He lifted his lips from hers and gazed at her, unreadable expression in his dark eyes.

"No. God help me, no." She raised her face inviting his caresses. The over-sized shirt slid off one shoulder, the bra strap slipping down as well. D'Arcy's mouth rained kissed over the exposed flesh, tongue flicking over her collarbone. "D'Arcy…"

"Say it again. Say my name, Arabella." The voice was husky and low in her ear. Callused fingertips traced circles on the upper swell of her breast.

"D'Arcy, oh my!" Breath left her in a rush when his thumb skimmed over the distended nipple.

He guided her out of the bathroom and across the hall. The back of her knees bumped into the bed and she allowed him to ease her onto the mattress. He lay down with her, touching her with infinite care as if she would break. She looked down at the dark head nuzzling at her breast and wondered when the bra disappeared. D'Arcy's shirt hung open and she reached inside to run her hands over his chest. Crisp curly hair twined around her fingers, one hand followed the line of hair down over the flat planes of his stomach. He lifted his head to gaze at her, a hand holding her full breast up for his attention.

"Arabella, you are so beautiful." He dropped his head and flicked the tip of his tongue over the engorged nub.

"I'm fat," she protested.

"You're full of new life. A pregnant woman is the most beautiful thing in the world." His hands continued to ignite intense sensations in her body.

"Any pregnant woman would do then?" She teased, bold fingers stroking the bulge in his jeans.

"Just you, Arabella. From the minute I saw your photo from that priest, I knew you were the most beautiful woman in the world."

"Seriously?" She turned her head toward his lips and was rewarded with a kiss.

"I've dreamed of having you like this, all full and open under me. I can make you happy, Arabella. Are you willing to give me the chance? Are you ready to let go of the past and make a future with me?"

"I thought you hated me. I thought you didn't want me and regretted marrying me." Bella lifted his head from her breast and made him meet her gaze.

"I never hated you, Ari. I hate that you still love the man who abandoned you and the baby. I hate you called his name while I made love to you. Can you understand that?"

"I am sorry, D'Arcy. I never intended to hurt you and I certainly didn't intend to call out another man's name on my wedding night."

"Can we start over, do you think? Make today the first day of our marriage and go forward from here?"

"Is that possible? Can you forgive me for being pregnant with some other man's child? That I didn't come to you a virgin? According to Da a man sets a huge importance on that. He said I was ruined, a disgrace…he called me a light skirt, a dolly mop…and he let Daniel call me a slut and a whore…" She turned her face away from him.

"Arabella, you're none of those things. I'd like to take a horse whip to your father, and beat the tar out of that two bit skunk you call Daniel. Listen to me." His hand tucked under her chin and made her look at him.

"What," she muttered. "Why would you want me, I'm a fat whore carrying a bastard."

"Don't ever talk about yourself like that again. You're my wife and for all anyone knows that baby is mine."

"But you know, and I know. I can't expect you to overlook that," she persisted, even though her flesh yearned for his touch.

"But I can, Ari. I'm asking you to give us a chance, to start over from today. Why are you throwing it away?" He sat up and moved away from her.

"I'm afraid," she whispered, drawing the shirt up over her shoulder.

"Afraid of what?" his voice was gentle.

"I don't rightly know. Afraid of what I'm feeling, afraid I'm not tough enough to survive out here. I'm afraid to have this baby, and I know I can't run away from that…"

"You never have to be afraid of me, never. Don't be so hard on yourself, you've worked like an injun all summer." He laid back down and pulled her close. "I can't help you're afraid of delivering that baby, but I can assure you I'll be with you every step of the way. And Doc can be here in pretty quick time. Red and I have birthed more calves and foals than I can count—"

"Are you saying I'm on the same level as a cow or a horse?" She twisted to look into his face.

D'Arcy grinned at her, white teeth flashing in his tanned face. "Well, it isn't that much different."

Bella smacked him on the chest. He caught her hand and brought it to his lips, kissing the palm. "I'll keep you safe, I promise, Arabella. You and the baby. So, can we start over then? You, me, and the child?"

"If you're sure you really want to, then yes. I will do my very best to be a good wife to you."

Her husband rolled as much on top of her as her belly would allow, pushing the flannel off her shoulder and down her arm. Her body arched into his embrace, her hands touching and stroking as the passion flared between them.

"Do you want to…um…you know…to kind of make it official like? I'm not sure how good it'll be…"

"Hush, Ari. Doc would have my head if I took you up on that. He cautioned me about marital relations until after the baby is born. I can make it good for you, though. If you'd like…" His hand closed on the bare skin of her breast, tweaking the still hard nipple gently. Her hips bucked in response and he smiled. "I take that as a yes?" Without waiting for her answer, his mouth replaced his hand, licking and suckling.

Bella squirmed and twisted under his ministrations. One hand pressing his head closer. "Like that, do you?" He slid lower down her body, careful of her bulk. "I'll be gently, Ari. I promise you'll like this."

"Oh, oh my stars!" She gasped when his fingers thrust aside her panties and stroked her most private parts.

The sensations rolled over her, between his hands and his mouth on her body she was oblivious to anything else. When it was over and her breathing settled, she turned toward the man lying beside her. It didn't seem fair he had given her such pleasure and asked for nothing in return. "Is there something I can do for you? I mean…" She wriggled a hand between their bodies, finding the bulge beneath the denim jeans. The look of surprise on his face made her laugh.

"Arabella? Are you sure, do you know what to do?" He shifted under her caresses.

"I think I have an idea. You could tell me if I do something wrong…" She fumbled with his belt and then slid the zipper down. His hard length filled her hand. He rolled onto his back as she stroked the hot satin skin. "Is that okay?" Bella thrilled at the strength of the emotions chasing across his face.

"Oh, Ari…" His hips undulated against her hand.

"D! Hey, D. You here?" The kitchen door slammed and Red's boots echoed in the downstairs hall as he came to the foot of steps. "D, are you up there?" Boot heels thumped on the lower treads.

"Damn it all to hell," D'Arcy cursed, softly. "Keep your pants on, Red. I'm coming. Be down in a minute, coffee's on in the kitchen," he shouted through the closed door. Leaning on his elbow, he smiled down at Bella. He removed her hand from his pants, gently squeezing her fingers. "Sorry, Ari. Duty calls. Maybe we can finish this later." He kissed her and ran a hand down her breast. "You get some rest, Mrs. Rowan. If you need anything just holler, either me or Red will be around." He got up off the bed, buttoned his shirt and tucked it into his jeans. Snugging his belt, he picked up his hat from the bed post and pulled it on.

Bella watched the sway of his hips as he sauntered across the room. Now she knew what the denim hid, the sight sent thrills through her. *Is this what love feels like? Or is it just sex? How the bloody hell am I supposed to know?* She pulled his shirt closed, wrapping her fist in the folds. The fabric was full of his scent, the sharpness of his shaving soap mingling with the musk of their love making. Rolling over, she curled around her belly and slept.

* * *

Two months was way too long to spend in bed. Bella sighed and watched the sun beam crawl across the floor the bedroom. She stretched and yawned. The baby rolled as well and she swore his feet were going to come out her ribs. D'Arcy had taken to referring to the unborn child as a boy and Bella went along with him. It really didn't matter what sex the child was as long it got here soon. She adjusted the pillows under her swollen legs and wondered if she'd ever have ankles again.

Red assured her she would, but what did he know? Wasn't like the little Irishman had ever delivered a baby. Another problem worried her. It wasn't something she really wanted to talk to her husband about either. He was being so gentle and careful with her and Bella had developed a genuine affection for him in spite of their rough beginning. It seemed the dust up with Sara had begun a new phase in their relationship. She looked forward to lying in the dark beside D'Arcy listening to him tell her about the ranch and his plans for the baby's room.

Since the branding, Bella had moved into the master bedroom, so D'Arcy was making some changes to her old room. Even though the baby wasn't even born yet, there was a small desk and chairs along with a 'grown up bed', as he called it. Her gaze fell on the cradle under the big windows of the bedroom. Red and D'Arcy had argued over the making of it. The thought brought a smile to her face. Pine or cedar, Red was partial to oak. He claimed it would protect the child from the fairies. Her smile faded, if he only knew...

A chill of dread twisted her stomach. What if the baby looked like...well...less than human when it finally got here? What if he looked like a seal? How was she supposed to explain that? D'Arcy had been fine with marrying a pregnant bride, but how would he react when he found out the child was less than human. Or maybe, it was more than human? Bella shook her head and leaned back into the pillows propped behind her.

"Ready for lunch, missy?" Red backed in the door carrying a tray. He set it down beside the bed before parking himself in a chair drawn up close by. "What's troublin' you, Bella? An' don't tell me nothing, me mum was fey so she was. Sometimes, I know things..."

She bolted upright, arms crossed over her belly. "What?" her voice came out thin and reedy. "What do you mean by that?"

The old cowboy reached out and took one of her hands. "I've what me Scottish friend calls the second sight. I can see you've been touched by the fairies, and that childer D is so all fired proud of already has a sense of otherness to it as well. Don't look so scairt, woman. I'm trying to tell you I'm on your side. I'll do whatever I can to help you."

Bella gulped and took a deep breath. The baby kicked hard and she rubbed her side. "Do you mean it? Oh, Red. I'm right frightened the baby will look...odd...when it's born. What will D'Arcy think?"

"I don't think you've got anything to worry about as far as D is concerned. I ain't never seen him so happy as he's been since the brandin'. Why are you so worried about what the nipper will look like? All babies look like sin when they're first born. Or is it somethin' else?" He waited for her speak, a knowing look on his face.

"The father isn't...well...he wasn't mortal," she whispered.

"It was one of the fey? The Good Neighbors?" Red crossed himself.

"No, not exactly. He's an immortal."

"For the love of God, girl. What did you lie with?" Red burst out.

"Nothing evil, so don't look at me like that! The father is a selkie, a shape—"

"I know what a selkie is. What were you doing in Scotland?"

She shook her head. "I wasn't. Vear Du was living in a cave near Lands End, in Cornwall. He...he saved me from being raped by the man my father said I had to marry. I ran away and hid in his sea cave and well...one thing led to another..." she trailed off, afraid to look at the little cowboy.

"Took advantage of your innocence, did he?" Anger lit his face.

"It wasn't like that, not at all. It was me, all my fault. Oh, Red. I love him so much, and I figured if I was going to have to marry some scut like Daniel Treliving I wanted something good to remember. And I wanted to lose my

242

virginity to someone I loved. Vear refused to lie with me. So...so...I bespelled him." She looked up at his astounded face.

"You did what?"

"I know, I know. It was stupid and selfish and I knew better. It was like something was pushing me and I just had to have him. He loves me too, but I ruined everything. We can never be together."

"Did the priest of your parish know all this when he contacted D'Arcy?" He fixed her with a hard stare.

Bella shook her head. "Lordy, no! Da would have murdered me dead if he knew I had relations with an immortal. Don't look like that, he would have! You don't know him. He was teasy as an adder when he found out I was up the spout, and then even Daniel wouldn't have me. Da was happy enough to be shot of me, anyway he could. The damn priest would have forced an exorcism on me and probably killed the baby in the process. The deception is all mine, I'm afraid."

"I knew there was something strange about you and the sense I was getting from the baby." Red scratched his head. "You have to tell your husband, girl. It ain't fair to the man not to, or to you and the child."

"What if he throws me out?"

"I'd stake my life he won't. Near as I can tell that man has plumb fell in love with you, and the baby. But he hates a liar, so you need to come clean. If I don't miss my guess, he'll do everything in his power to protect you and the baby."

"What if it's born looking like a seal? What do we do?"

"For what it's worth, I don't think you need to worry." He paused and actually flushed red. "When you...err...when you conceived...was the...the sire in human form?"

"Red!" She was aghast at the implications. "I certainly did not have sex with an animal! My stars."

"Don't get yer feathers all ruffled, missy. I had to ask. From all the stories me old granny told me, I think you have nothing to worry about. The trouble might come when the child grows up."

Bella lay back against the pillows. "That does ease my mind a bit, Red. Thank you." A sudden thought occurred to her. "I can't have a mid-wife when I deliver. Promise me, you'll help me. If anything goes sideways I won't be able to hide it from a mid-wife."

Red patted her hand. "I've birthed enough foals and calves to know what to do. Don't you worry your head. And after you explain things to D, he'll be on side too. He already sets a great store on the young'un."

"After you explain what to me?" D'Arcy leaned in the doorway. Crossing to the bed, he hooked another chair with his toe and pulled it beside Red's. "What secrets are you two keeping from me now?"

Bella swallowed and glanced at Red. He shrugged and nodded. "It's your tale, missy. And you need to be the one to tell it." The old cowboy leaned back and crossed his arms over his chest.

"For God's sake, Ari. Quit lookin' like you're on the way to the gallows. I'm not going bite you know. Spit it out," D'Arcy growled.

She wriggled up straighter in bed and looked down at her hands clenched on the quilts. "I'm not sure where to start…"

"The beginning is always a good place," her husband remarked enigmatically.

"I don't know where the beginning is," she wailed. "How much did Father Boyle tell you about my situation?"

"I see your point, Ari. The good father told me you were in a delicate condition and without prospects. He thought you'd jump at the chance to marry me and let me make you an honest woman. For some reason he hinted the baby, or the father of the baby, might be an issue. So why don't you start there?"

"Go on," Red urged her when she turned to him in panic. "Sooner it's out the better."

"I guess you're right." She looked straight at her husband, hoping she wasn't making another huge mistake. "I met a bloke out on the coast path by Lamorna Cove. I thought he was close to my age, and he was ever so good looking. Anyway, he seemed as interested in me as I was in him. He helped me get a stone out of my horse's hoof and then we parted, but agreed to meet on the weekend,' she paused to gauge his reaction

"Innocent enough, so far. How did he become your lover? I'm assuming this guy is the father?"

Bella nodded. "It gets all complicated from here on in. When I got home I found out Da had promised this absolute bastard he could take me to wife. Without so much as a by your leave."

"This is the Daniel guy you were so afraid of?" Red interrupted her.

"Daniel Treliving is a rat of the first water. He's a pervert, if even half the stories in the village are true…" She shivered. "I know for a fact what he did to me, put his hands all over me. He taunted me with the warped things he was going to make me do once he owned me, body and soul. And the things he was going to do *to* me…the bleeder's a depraved bastard, so he is."

"So you ran away with the dark haired fella?" Red prompted her to get on with it.

"In a way. Da locked me in my room but I climbed out the window and crawled along the roof tree of the shed. Sarie helped me get away and I hid out in an old smuggler's cave. I thought I was safe until I could figure out what to do. But…h-h-he found me. Daniel, I mean, and he was some mad. Came at me like a nutter, eyes all cold and glazed…his hands were like talons, I swear."

D'Arcy reached over and took her hand. "Go on, Ari. It's okay, I'm listening."

"I tried to fight him, I really did. He was always stronger than me, and he was that fierce I had no chance. I was on my back, pinned under him. He was slobbering all over me and pinching me so it really hurt. The bastard forced my legs open and I thought it was all over. Then suddenly, he was gone. Just like that. When I opened my eyes and got to my knees, Vear had Daniel by the throat, holding him off the ground. I was never so glad to see anyone in my life. He shook him like the rat he is and dropped him on the sand. I got up and hid behind him, trying to hold my torn clothes shut. I'm not sure how to tell you the rest of this…"

"Just say it, Ari." Her husband's hand tightened on hers.

"Vear Du, he isn't regular folks. He's from Scotland originally, not Cornwall, but he chose to come south. Vear is, well, he's magic kind of."

"Because you love him?" A frown furrowed D'Arcy's brow.

"No, well yes. But no, he's really magic. Oh, I'm telling this all wrong. Do you know what a selkie is, D'Arcy?"

"A what?" He looked at the little Irishman. "Is this some of your nonsense?"

"Not nonsense, D. Them things are as real as you and I are."

"A selkie is a shape shifter, they can be male or female, but not both," she amended at the shocked look on his face. "Vear Du was, is, a bull seal in his selkie form and a young man in

247

human form. There's a bunch of old myths about mortals falling in love with them and hiding their seal pelts from them so they can't change form. I don't know anything about that, I've seen Vear shift, but I never noticed any pelt. I wouldn't hold him that way anyway. But, you see, after he pulled Daniel off me, he took me to his cave and he used magic to do it. I don't know how to explain it, it was like he took a step sideways and then everything was crazy, the next thing I knew we were in his cave by sea cliffs. He shouldn't have done it, of course. The powers that govern the magical folk were angry with him for using magic to aid a mortal. To interfere, they called it."

"So he demanded you lay with him as payment for saving you?" D'Arcy let go of her hand and paced back and forth by the window.

"No, no. It wasn't like that at all. I couldn't go home, I couldn't go back to the smuggler's cave, so I stayed with Vear in his den. I loved him, I wanted him, even though I didn't really know what that meant, and he loved me too." She ducked her head in shame. "I tried to seduce him, but he wouldn't. Said it wasn't fair to me. But in a weak moment on his part, I got what my heart desired. And then all hell broke loose."

"He found out you were knocked up and got shed of you?" D'Arcy growled.

"I wish it were that simple. There's a governing body for the other folks, the selkies, piskies, morgawrs, oh, I don't know what else. Oh yes, the mermen. Anyway, they made Vear stand trial for 'interfering with a daughter of Eve'. They banished him. Even if I was home, I could never see him again. He doesn't even know he's going to be a father." She grimaced and patted her belly. "But here I am. That's what I've kept from you, and everyone else. And I'm dead scared, so I am, that the wean will come out in seal form. Then what will we do? What will I do?" She raised a hand toward him in supplication.

D'Arcy dropped into the chair like he'd been shot. "Red, this calls for a drink. Go fetch the bottle of 80 proof would you."

"Ah yes, the water of life." The Irishman got to his feet and left the room.

"I'm sorry, D'Arcy. I should have told you sooner. I meant to, but things just got so...so...complicated. If you want me to leave..."

"No," the word exploded from him. "That's the last thing I want. We had a rocky start, Ari. But I'm right fond of you. I thought you were coming to care for me too."

"Oh, D'Arcy. I do care for you. More than I can say. You've taken me in and cared for me. You're giving my bastard by-blow your name..."

"Is that all, Ari? Are those your only reasons?" The tension between was tangible as he waited for her response.

Heat flushed her body and she drew back the quilts. Her pulse quickened when his gaze fastened on her breasts straining at the ties of

249

her nightgown. "You're a good kind man, D'Arcy Rowan. I like the way you make me feel, and the things you do when the lights are out. I like your body against mine when I fall asleep and I like waking up with you every morning. I'm not sure if that's love, or not. I am very very fond of you…"

He swooped over her, catching her words in his mouth. "I'm mighty fond of you too, Ari." He breathed the words between kisses. His hand closed possessively over her breast.

"D'Arcy," she squealed softly. "It's the middle of the day!"

"Love makin' don't happen only in the dark, woman. I can see I'm gonna have to show you there's as much pleasure to be had in the sunlight. I'd love to lay you down under a tree naked as a jay bird and watch the shadows and the light play across my wife's skin. Once you're back to normal, we'll have to make sure that happens." He nuzzled the nipple poking against the linen nightie.

"Here now, what's this? I done leave you alone for a second, ya horny devil and you're all over the poor colleen.' Red kicked the door further open and carried the whiskey along with three glasses and a pitcher of milk into the room. "Now behave yerself, D. We need to figger out how we plan to handle this little predicament. He set his burden down on the table by the bed and winked at Bella.

D'Arcy released her and leaned back in his chair. "A selkie, hmmm. Damndest thing. Never knew there was such a critter. You're telling me there's no other half-breeds in the whole world?"

Bella opened her mouth to protest his use of 'half-breed', but subsided as she gave the devil his due. Her baby was a half-breed, just not the variety that usually came to mind. "As far as I know there aren't any others. I wrote Mrs. Waters back home to ask her. She knows about those kinds of things. There are stories of selkies being married to humans and having families, but they stayed because their mate hid their pelts so they couldn't return to the sea. There was no coercion between Vear and I, and I never actually saw his pelt, when he shifted he just...shimmered somehow. I'm not sure this is the same thing at all and neither is she."

"Odds are good the wean will be born a human. We're not even sure he'll be able to shift," D'Arcy mused.

"I gotta agree wi' ye, D. Miz Arabella being his momma and all, I'm thinkin' she'll have more effect on the outcome than the sire..

Bella grinned. "Listen to you two! What if the baby's a girl?"

"She'll be a lovely wee colleen then," Red replied.

"Which brings us to something else. We've never talked about names, heifer or bull calf," D'Arcy changed the subject.

"What are you thinking?" Bella smiled gently.

"Me da's name was George," Red offered.

251

Bella looked at her husband. "I always thought I'd call my daughter Sara, after Sarie, but now…" She shivered and closed her eyes. "Maybe Elizabeth, Lily for short."

"Not Sara, no question." D'Arcy's expression was cold and dark. "I'm fine with Elizabeth if it's a filly, Lizzy for short?" A lopsided grin lit his features.

"And if it's a colt," she teased picking up on his use of filly.

"I'm partial to Colton as a name for our son," he spoke quietly.

"Colton George, then?" Red chimed in.

"I like it, unless of course it's a girl." Bella grinned. She sobered immediately. "We still haven't decided how to handle things when it's time."

"Me and Red'll handle it, Ari. No matter what. We'll deal with it. You trust me don't you?" D'Arcy took her hand.

"No mid-wife?" Bella persisted.

"Agreed, nobody but me and Red."

Bella nodded and his smile lit up the room. "Pour me a shot, Red."

The Irishman sloshed a generous portion into both glasses and handed one to his boss. He passed a tumbler of mile to Bella. The men stood one on either side her bed, facing each other.

"To Colton!" The men saluted each other and Bella before taking a long drink.

"To Elizabeth!" Bella held her glass high.

The three of them drained their glasses.

252

Chapter Fourteen

She realized it was a dream, but Bella didn't care. *D'Arcy's so good to me so why do I still dream about Vear?* It wasn't really fair to the man who'd given her and the unborn child his name, but oh, it was so good to sink her toes in good Cornish soil and lift her face to the salt breeze. She glanced up at the dark haired man with the laughing blue eyes looking down at her. Love shone in his face and he pulled her close. Bella closed her eyes and inhaled the scent that was uniquely his. Pipe tobacco, and the brine of the sea overlaid with Vear's own spicy aroma. Lordy, it was good to be home! Her selkie kissed the tip of her nose and they continued along the windswept coastal path. Below the sea threw itself at the cliffs while the wind bent the purple heather and golden gorse on either side of them. At the top of a steep descent they stopped and Bella recognized Mill Bay far below.

"Nanjizal," she whispered and glanced up at the man beside her.

"Home of the Song of the Sea." He nodded and led her down the steep path. The tide was out and there was sand in the cove. Vear lifted her down the last few steps of the short staircase from the path to the beach proper. His hands warm and strong on her waist.

Bella passed a hand over her flat stomach. This was the best thing about her dreams, things were like they were before everything went to hell in a handbasket. He took her hand and they walked toward the narrow high slot with a shallow pool of sea water still in the hollow at the base.

"The Song of the Sea," Vear's voice was hushed as if in the presence of something holy.

"It's beautiful. I've always loved this place." She leaned into his strength.

"This is a special place, a sacred place. It is where I came through when I travelled from the Orkneys." Vear's gaze was distant and unfocussed. "I come here sometimes to remember what was once."

"What was once?" Bella inquired, frowning up at him.

He shook his head. "No matter, dear one. This is a time for you and I, and the future. The past is over and gone. But remember this place, Bella. You will always find me here."

She turned into him and slid her arms around his waist, turning his face up for his kiss. "I love you so much, Vear. Don't ever forget that."

He kissed her and looked down into her face. "Bella, there is something I must tell—"

The stab of pain in her back and the rush of water startled her. Was the tide coming in? But then why was her back hurting so bad? Vear's face blurred before her and the sand shifted under foot. "Vear?" She reached for him but there was nothing under her hands. "Vear?"

The pain got worse, wrapping around her middle and squeezing. She gasped and tried to double over. The spasm released her and she almost cried with relief. "Vear?" she whispered. Her groping fingers encountered tangled quilts. Sweat bloomed over her body and she threw the coverings off. Her bottom was lying in a large wet patch, she used the skirt of her nightie to wipe the fluid off her thighs, startled at the dark splotches on the white linen.

"Oh my stars, the baby!" The dream forgotten, she placed both hands on the hard curve of her belly just as another spasm hit. She shifted and bit her lip.

"Ari?" Her husband rolled over and propped himself up on an elbow. "What's wrong? Another bad dream?" When she didn't answer, he reached over her and turned on the bedside lamp. "Ari, are you okay? Is it the baby?" He sat up staring down at her wildly.

"I don't know, D'Arcy! Something weird's happening. I'm scared, and I'm bleeding, I think." Her teeth clenched against another wave of pain.

He flung himself out of bed and flung open the door. "Red! Get your ass up here, old man!" Turning back to the bed, he picked up the scattered quilts and dumped them on a chair. "Do you think it's time? Are you sure of the date you caught? It's too early, you should have another three or four weeks…"

"D'Arcy, I'm not a cow. Yes, I'm sure of the date I got pregnant. Caught, as you so bluntly put it. I've never done this before, but I think this is the real thing."

He came closer and placed a hand on her belly. "Can I get you anything? Water?"

"What's up, D? What're ye hollerin' about?" Red stopped just inside the door, night shirt hanging out of his jeans, hair sticking out all over his head.

"The baby's coming. At least I think it is."

The little cowboy smiled and finished tucking in his shirt. "I thought something was wrong. I'll just go boil some water and make us some coffee."

"There is something wrong! I'm gonna split in two. Ohhhh my stars!" Her voice rose to a screech. "I don't want to die." She started to sob.

"Now, Ari. Don't take on so, you're gonna be fine." D'Arcy wiped sweat off her face with a handkerchief.

Red returned with a pitcher of water, some clean towels and a cup of coffee for D. He handed the coffee to his boss, set the water and towels down on the table and approached the bed. "How ya doin', missy? When did these dad blamed pains start? How long ago?" He glanced at D'Arcy standing white faced beside the bed.

"I don't know. I was sleeping and then it was like someone was running me through with a pike, and…and…I'm bleeding…Am I going to die?" She gripped Red's hand.

"Yer water's broke is all. Nothin' out a' the ordinary about that. Means the wean is comin' tonight."

"It's too soon," D'Arcy said between gritted teeth.

"You don't know that, now do you? This ain't no reg'lar nipper, is it? We're just gonna go along thinkin' everythin' is normal, until we know different. Now pass me some of them towels, would ye?" He took the thick wad of towelling and sat on the bed beside Bella. "I gotta lift yer linen, girl. You just close yer eyes iffen ye want to, but I gotta clean ye up a bit and see what's goin' on down there." He hesitated. "Are ye sure ye don't want me to fetch the mid-wife?"

"No mid-wife. Just get on with it." Bella lay back on the pillows, resting before the next pain hit. She cringed a bit when the callused hands plucked the wet material from her thighs. Goosebumps rose on her exposed skin as the cool air hit it. Red's hands were gentle as he swabbed away the sticky fluid and strings of blood. D'Arcy helped Red roll her while they changed the sheets and placed a rubber sheet under her. A thick pad of towels tucked under her rump felt fresh and clean. Another contraction straightened her knees and sent a fresh flood of fluid onto the bed. "How long is this supposed to take?" She got the words out between pants for breath.

"Ain't no way a' knowing. You just keep doin' what yer doin'," Red assured her.

Bella gripped D'Arcy's hand, digging her nails into his skin without meaning to. His features blurred as another contraction gripped her. Panic rose in her throat, she couldn't do this anymore, it was too much. The pain threatened to tear her out of her body and she had more than half a mind to let her soul slip free. The agony eased off and she gasped for breath. "I don't want to do this anymore," she wailed. "I can't, I can't..."

"Now missy, you just hang on. A'course ye can do this." Red passed a cold cloth over her face.

"Ari, Ari, I'm so sorry," D'Arcy whispered. "I wish I could make this easier for you."

"What if something's wrong? What if I can't get the baby out?" Fear sharpened her voice.

"Nothing's wrong, Ari. I promise, everything will be all right." Her husband's voice was strained.

"Don't you worry, Miz Bella. I've put a knife under the bed me old mum says it'll cut the pain in half, so it will.

The process seemed to go on forever, Bella slipped into unconsciousness between the pains. The world narrowed to a long corridor of pain and flashing lights. Bright orbs whirled across her vision. Her entire focus was on the clenching of her belly. Would the bloody child never come out? Her mouth spread in a silent scream as she let herself fall into the black pit where the pain was absent.

* * *

"Ari? Arabella?"

An insistent summons wouldn't allow her to rest. She fought it, clinging to the comforting dark surrounding her. Something niggled at the periphery of her thoughts. A reason she needed to listen to the annoying voice that wouldn't go away. She became aware of coldness on her face and chest, her body choked on the liquid trickling down her throat. Bella spluttered and swam through the treacle thick black sea she seemed to be floating in. One eye opened a hair and she moved toward the light.

"Arabella? Wake up, sweetheart. Please, wake up. Look, your son is here, don't you want to hold him?"

The words penetrated the last of the fog in her mind and Bella opened both eyes. Both men were hovering over the bed, for a moment there were four of them wavering in her vision. She closed her eyes for a second.

"Miz Bella, don't go away again. Stay with me," Red's voice commanded her and she obeyed.

The two men stayed in focus when she looked again. D'Arcy was holding a blanket wrapped bundle in his arms, an unreadable expression on his face. It took her a bit to realize the pain was gone and her belly deflated like a pricked balloon. *The baby! Is the baby okay?* She struggled into an upright position helped by Red who piled pillows behind her.

"She was afraid to ask, but gathering her courage in her hand she looked up at the men. "Is it all right? The baby? It's not making any noise?" She reached a hand out toward D'Arcy.

"The little one is fine, Ari. Just sleeping right now." He dropped down on the edge of the bed. "Do you want to see?" His tired face broke into a smile.

"Filly or colt," she said the first thing that came into her muddled mind.

Red let out a huge guffaw and slapped D on the shoulder. "Told ya she was a fighter."

Bella glanced at him. "What is that supposed to mean?"

The smile faded from her husband's face. "You've been unconscious for a long time, Ari. If you hadn't woke up when you did, Red was gonna go call Doc. You scared ten years off my life."

"How long? I mean how long have I been sleeping?" Her brain still didn't seem to be working properly. Thoughts taking a long time to get from her brain to her mouth.

"Almost twenty-four hours." He shifted the bundle from one arm to the other, drawing her wandering attention back to the new born.

"Filly or colt?" She managed a weak smile.

"The little tyke is a boy. So Colton George Rowan, would you like to meet your mother?" He held the baby up and carefully set him in his mother's arms.

Bella was almost afraid to life the flap covering his head and look. She sought reassurance from Red. "He's...he's...he looks like us?"

D'Arcy nodded before Red could speak. "He looks like a normal baby, ten toes, ten fingers, no flippers," D'Arcy joked.

She let out the breath she hadn't realized was caught in her chest. Lifting the corner of the soft blanket she looked at the tiny face and miniature fists clenched by the little chin. The rush of unconditional love left her dizzy. "He's perfect. Perfect. I can't believe he came out of me." She looked up at both of them to share her wonder.

"It's always hard to believe when the new crop of young'uns come every spring, but this...this was something so much more." D'Arcy laid his large hand on the baby's head and smiled down at her. "His eyes are blue like yours, but they might not stay that way. Most babies have blue eyes."

"Blue like his da's," she murmured. Then she shoved all thought of Vear away. The past was over, it was time to look ahead. Her future was standing beside her and cuddled in her arms. "You're the only da he'll ever know. Unless a reason shows up as he gets older, he'll never know you're not his biological father.

You're his da in every way that counts," she promised the big man who was looking at her like she hung the moon.

"Don' be fergettin' his Uncle Red, now," the little Irishman chimed in.

"Colton, you're the luckiest little boy ever. With a da and an uncle like these two you'll never have to worry about anything." Her son stirred and let out a squawk before he turned his head and rooted at her breast. "I think he's hungry." She looked to D'Arcy for help. "Has he eaten at all yet?"

"You was out of it, so we gave him some goat milk from the nanny out back. But if you're milk has come in it would be better if you could feed him," he told her.

"I'm not sure what to do," she whispered, face hot with shame. "What kind of mother am I going to be?" The sharp cry and the insistent mouth searching at her breast brought an ache and pulling sensation to her chest. Bella bit her lip when the pain intensified. It felt like the engorged lumps on her chest were going to explode. The nightshirt exacerbated the pain in her nipples. "Help me?" She beseeched D'Arcy with her eyes.

He glanced at Red and tipped his head toward the door. The two men moved away from the bed and she panicked. "You're not leaving are you?" Juggling the child with one arm, she managed to get one leg over the side of the bed.

"Ari, for Christ's sake!" D'Arcy closed the distance between them in two long strides. "Get back in bed, woman. I'm not going anywhere, I just need a word with Red here."

She subsided back onto the pillows and shifted her still complaining son to a more comfortable position. The two men conferred by the door and she grew impatient. The child managed to latch onto her breast through the linen. She gasped as a huge wet stain spread across the fabric over both her breasts. "D'Arcy, help! What's happening to me?"

Red left, quietly closing the door behind him. Her husband came and sat beside her, a gentle smile on his face. "Here, Ari. Let me help." His fingers shook a bit as he unlaced the front of her night gown all the way to her waist. He took the baby from her and handed her a wet cloth. "You'll feel better if you clean up a bit first. Your milk just came in a rush when the baby cried. It's normal, don't worry."

She blushed when her engorged teats burst out of the confines of her clothing. They'd become huge during the course of the pregnancy but she never imagined they'd grow larger still. The cool cloth eased the ache a bit, but it seemed strangely intimate and exciting to be washing herself under her husband's gaze. Bella handed the cloth back to him and he tossed it into a basin of water on the floor by the bed. "What do I do now?" She reached for her fussing son.

D'Arcy handed him to her and she put his head near her nipple. The baby rooted and pushed at her with his tiny fists but didn't latch on. She tried again as the child began to cry in frustration and hunger. Milk spurted from her nipples and the baby rubbed his face in it, but couldn't seem to figure out how to get to the source. "What kind of mother am I? Can't even feed my own son," she sniffed and hiccupped between the words."

"Let me help, Ari," D'Arcy offered. He leaned over and stroked her hot flesh, covering the end of his finger with the thin fluid. He rubbed the tiny lips and got some on the searching tongue. Bella quivered at his touch, her belly contracting in response. *What the bloody hell? How can I want him to make love to me when I'm all sore down there?* D'Arcy cupped her heavy breast in his hand, pressing to make milk flood from it.

Bella let her head fall back and closed her eyes. She forgot for a moment about her son and let the delicious feelings he was creating float her away. The sudden pain of the baby finally latching on to her sensitive nipple brought her back to reality with a thump. Her eyes flew open and she looked in wonder at the tiny head pressed against her. How could such a little thing be so strong? Her husband stretched out on the bed beside her, smiling down at them. He held a fresh towel to her other breast catching the milk spouting there. "Is it always going to be like this? I won't be able to go out in public dripping like this."

"You're beautiful, Arabella Rowan." He kissed her nose. "I think once Colton starts eating regular like, that things will settle down. Usually does with the cattle and horses. Not that I'm implying you look like a cow," he qualified.

"I should hope not," she replied with a wink. She switched the baby to the other side and D'Arcy had to hold her breast up for him again. Colton latched on quicker though and before long was sleeping with milk dribbling down his chin. His father lifted him careful not wake him and tucked him into the cradle which Red had moved close to the bed earlier. Bella found her eyes closing in spite of herself.

"You, Mrs. Rowan, are the most beautiful thing I've seen in a month Sundays."

Bella glanced down at her massive chest and laughed. "Not hardly. I'm all huge and sloppy and—"

D'Arcy laid back down beside her, propped up on an elbow. "Seein' you like this, all soft and glowy. Well, it makes a man want to do things he shouldn't" His voice was husky with desire.

She twisted to see him better. "Really? I look like something the cat dragged in," she protested.

He took her hand and pressed it against the bulge in his jeans. "Right there, that's how you make me feel." He lowered his head and nuzzled the soft skin on the upper curve of her

265

breast. She thought she ought to protest, make him stop, but instead she found her hand pressing him closer. His mouth closed over a distended nipple and she arched into him. He suckled gently until she thought she'd scream with the pleasure of it before he lifted his head and kissed her lips. He tasted of sweet milk and tobacco mixed with whiskey.

"How much have you had to drink?" She went cross-eyed trying to look at him looming so close above her.

"Enough, I guess." He sighed. "I wasn't sure you were ever going to wake up. God, Ari. I don't know what I'd do without you now." He kissed her again.

"I wasn't sure I was going to stay, but I heard you calling me, so I came back," she said simply.

"Thank God." The words were whispered against her cheek.

"Everything okay in here?" Red stuck his head in the door. He took in the scene on the bed and winked. "I can see that it is. If you don't need this old uncle for anything I'm goin' to hit the hay." He shut the door and turned off the hall light.

The bed shifted when D'Arcy stood up. Bella followed his movements in the dim light of the bedside lamp. The silver belt buckle caught the light as he unhooked it, and then slid the worn jeans off his narrow hips. The long shirt tails hid his privates and she wondered if he was still hard. *Men! Who knew a woman fresh from her child bed would turn them on? If I live to be a hundred I'll never figure them out.* The shirt slithered to the floor to join the pile of shed clothes. He stood looking down at her. "Do you want to change into something cleaner?" his voice was husky, eyes on her breasts which were still visible in the open neck of her gown.

Bella picked at the material and decided it was pretty mucky. "I need to use the bathroom," she said. He helped her out of bed and down the hall to the necessary, waiting outside until she was finished. "Good thing Red's gone to bed," she teased. "He'd be shocked to see you standing in the hall naked as the day you were born." Her husband chuckled and patted her rear as she preceded him down the corridor.

Once back in their room, she stripped the gown over her head. It felt wonderful to be unencumbered, save for the large pad between her legs. Walking was surprisingly painful and she shuffled toward the bed. D'Arcy stood watching her with hooded eyes. "Do you want a clean gown?" He crossed the room to help her into the bed. She sat on the edge to let the dizziness pass and checked the still sleeping Colton. The heat of his body radiated on her skin. She reached out a tentative finger and stroked the tip of his penis. It stirred and twitched in response and he drew in a sharp breath.

"It's like it has a life of its own." She looked up at him.

"Sometimes," he agreed. "About the gown?"

"Can we sleep like this?" Bella stretched her arms over her head and smiled through her tangled hair.

"Do you want to?" He sounded surprised and unsure.

"Don't you?"

"Hell, yes, woman. But are you sure you think it's proper?"

"Proper be damned, D'Arcy. What about me has ever been proper? I used to lock my door and sleep in my pelt back home. Not that anyone knew that, of course."

Her husband helped her swing her legs onto the bed and pulled the covers up to her waist. He paused on his side before he turned off the lamp. "God, Ari. You're magnificent. I feel like the king of the world standin' here lookin' at you and knowing you're mine."

The room went dark before she could find her voice to respond to his astounding comment. No one, not ever, had spoken to her like that. D'Arcy slid between the sheets beside her, she turned on her side and he spooned around her back. His semi-hard penis pressed into her lower back, a strong arm curled over her waist and a large hand cupped her breast. She held her breath, waiting. *Surely, he doesn't want to do anything? I don't think I can...* Moments later his deep breathing told her he was asleep. In the starlight coming in the windows she looked at her son's peaceful little face in the cradle by the bed and sighed. Vear Du had a son he would never know about and it was probably better that way she decided. What he didn't know he couldn't grieve over. Pulling the quilt over her shoulder, Bella closed her eyes and slept.

Chapter Fifteen

"Happy Birthday, Colt!"

Six immature male voices sang off key in ragged unison. Her son pulled off his wide brimmed hat and blew out the candles to the cheers of his friends. D'Arcy squeezed her hand and she looked up into his dark eyes. She leaned into him and slid an arm around his still narrow waist. Fourteen years had added silver to the nut brown hair and silvery crows' feet in the tan at the corner at the corners of his eyes.

"Hard to believe he's fourteen years old already," she said returning her gaze to the boys crowded around the cake. "I should go and organize the chaos, I suppose."

"They're just boys havin' fun, leave them be for a bit," D'Arcy replied. "Red seems to have them in hand." He laughed at the old cowboy doling out slices of cake and managing to get frosting all over his Sunday-go-to-meeting-shirt. "You can dress that old reprobate up but you can't take him out."

Bella smacked his arm. "Is that anyway to talk about your oldest friend? And our only babysitter?"

"What the ear doesn't hear, the heart can't grieve over," he quipped.

A shadow fell over her happiness for a moment. His words were eerily reminiscent of her own thoughts the night Colton was born, only she'd been thinking about the big selkie who was the boy's natural father. Shaking off the unsettling thought, she stepped away from her husband's side. "I'll go fetch another pitcher of lemonade from the milk house." Earlier, she made a huge batch and left a big stoneware crock of it in the structure built into the side of the hill behind the house. The remains of an old soddy, it served to keep things cold even in the hottest summers and left more room in the fridge in the kitchen.

She returned to find the boys had abandoned the remains of the cake and were engaged in roping a calf dummy set up on the front lawn. Pausing in the shade by the corner of the porch, she admired the fluid motion as Colton whirled the loop overhead and the lariat arched smoothly from his hand to land over the horns of the practice dummy. Grinning, she carried on to the table set up under the canvas canopy. Red and D were lounging in the shade, a tumbler of whiskey in hand. The bottle between them was empty. She set the pitcher down and settled in the chair next to her husband.

"They never seem to run out of energy, do they?" Bella followed the antics in amusement. "I don't ever remember being that full of get up and go."

D snorted. "You were hell on wheels when I first met you, can't imagine what you were like as young filly feeling her oats."

"Lot you know." She sniffed with mock indignation. "I'll have you know I was well mannered and…What?"

Both men wiped tears of laughter from their eyes. "So well behaved your pa had to send ye half way acrost the world," Red choked out the word between gouts of hilarity.

"Well, I never!" Bella was half inclined to be insulted.

"I for one, am very glad he did, and that the benighted priest who contacted me lied through his teeth about what a sweet young thing you were who was led astray through no fault of her own." D leaned over and restored her good humour with a kiss.

"You did kind of buy a pig in a poke, didn't you?" She giggled. "How many of these little heathens did you promise our son could sleep over?"

"Pa, can we practice with the pony?" The birthday boy skidded to a halt, kicking up dust with his boots in the dry grass. "Toby claims he can rope better from the saddle and he says I cain't." Colton glared back at the tallest of his guests.

"Not cain't, Colton. It's can't," Bella broke in.

"I cain't, I mean I can't use the pony?"

"Why don't you go catch old Buck? He's better suited to you hellions than Tumbles. Gang of you would wear that pony's legs to nubs. Buck'll put up with the shenanigans better too." D clapped his son on the shoulder. "He's out in the back corrals."

Whooping, Colton raced off, followed by the others. A flock of magpies rose complaining into the air when they whipped past the granaries. In short order, the boys reappeared with the buckskin gelding, dragging his rig between them. Two boys carried the saddle, another the blankets. Colton had the bridle draped over his shoulder with the reins dragging in the dust, lead rope clutched his hand. The horse ambled along patiently and stopped when the boy dropped the shank on the ground by his parents.

He tossed the blankets on the horse's back. "Hand me the saddle, will ya?" He scowled with annoyance looking very much like his selkie father when the wind flipped the blankets up. He smoothed them back and settled the saddle on the gelding's back. "Damn wind."

"Colt, mind your tongue," Bella scolded him.

"Here," Jared handed him the one ear bridle with the split reins.

The boy slipped the halter off and slid the curb bit into the horse's mouth and passed the headstall over his poll.

"Why don't ya hold onta this bronc while your old pa and I wrestle the gear into the corral?"

"I guess, this old nag ain't goin' nowhere," he muttered.

"Colton Rowan!" his mother exclaimed. "Quit murdering the Queen's English. It's *this horse isn't going anywhere*, and even that's not strictly grammatically correct."

"Aw, Ma! I ain't," he hesitated at the look she gave him and began again. "I'm not going around talking like a dandy. Tell her, Pa. They'll tease me somethin' fierce at school."

The tall man pushed his hat back a bit and looked between his wife and son. "Can we compromise? Colt, when you're around your ma try and remember to speak properly, when you're with your friends you can let it go a bit. But no cuss words, young man. Is that clear?"

"Sure, Pa," he agreed, one eye on his mother in case she decided to object.

Bella smiled and shook her head. "I declare, I don't know what I'm going to do with you, Colt. Take your friends go practice on that roping dummy. Go and have fun."

D and Red were already helping the other boys drag the dummy into the big corral near the house. Once things were set up to the old Irishman's liking he joined them in the shade.

"Tarnation, them young hooligans make me feel old." He removed his hand and scrubbed a hand through his thick hair, now more grey than red.

"We are getting long in the tooth," D agreed.

"Speak for yourself," Bella protested.

"You, my love, are as beautiful as ever. Besides, you're twenty years younger'n me, don't forget." He ducked the playful swipe she made at him.

"I just can't believe he's fourteen already. Where does the time go?" She glanced at the two men. "Have you noticed anything different about him, now he's getting older?"

"Nothing," D assured her. "I reckon if some weird stuff was gonna show up it would'a done it by now."

"I ain't seen nothin' either, missy. Couple more years, once the boy's got hair in 'is pits and down below, I think we can all breathe a bit easier," Red agreed.

"You think if nothings surfaced by the time he's sixteen or seventeen it'll be safe to assume he hasn't inherited anything from that side of the family?" Bella looked from one man to the other.

"Let's not go borrowing trouble, Ari," D said. "So far the boy hasn't shown a sign of being anything but an ordinary kid. Let's just enjoy the day."

"You're right, D. I'm worrying over milk that isn't spilt yet," Bella agreed.

Whoops and shouts from the corral rang in the hot afternoon air. The three adults wandered over to climb up on the top rail with the boys waiting their turn on the buckskin horse. Eventually, the boys tired of the game, hot and sweaty they trooped out of the corral, horse in tow. The gang stopped by the adults who had climbed off the fence. Colt looked hopefully at his dad.

"Can you or Red look after Buck? I'm some hot and thirsty." He held the reins out in a grubby hand.

"You know the rules, son. Your horse's needs come before your own. No real horseman abandons his mount just 'cause he's tired or can't be bothered. The animal worked harder than any of you boys did. Now git." D'Arcy put a hand on the boy's shoulder and squeezed. "We're gonna BBQ on the fire pit for supper."

"Wahooo!" Colt headed for the barn dragging the horse behind him.

When the gang returned half an hour later, Bella was carrying the last of the noon hour picnic toward the house. She smiled at the exchange between the men in her life.

"All done, Pa," Colt announced.

"Did you put the tack away?"

The boy nodded.

"And brush Buck?" Red chimed in.

"Joey did, I made sure the trough was full," Colt replied.

"Pick his feet out?" D'Arcy named the chore the boy usually shirked.

"Yup. Knew you'd ask, Pa. You can go check, if you want." His son tucked his thumbs into his belt and hitched his worn jeans up.

"I'll trust you, son. A man's only as good as his word, you know." He fixed him with his *father stare.*

"I know that, Pa. I always keep my word, just like you and Uncle Red."

The earnest expression on his young face twisted Bella's heart. What a grown-up he was becoming. She wanted to protect him, hide him away on the ranch. Keep him from the pitfalls she imagined waited for him as he grew older. For heaven's sake, the first fourteen years had flown by, before another ten it might be his wedding she was clearing up after. The thought sobered her.

She carried on around the back of the house, kicking the door open with her toe. She deposited the stack of dishes on the sideboard and ran hot water into the sink, adding a dollop of dish soap. Leaning her hands on the edge of the counter, her thoughts drifted back to the night of the branding soon after her own wedding night. She ran a hand over her still smooth stomach. Colton hadn't been born yet and Sara, that crazy bitch, tried to kill her, right here in the kitchen. Thank God, the woman moved away from Pincher soon afterward. In a way though, she owed the woman a debt of gratitude. That was the night she began to realize what a good man she married, even if she hadn't admitted it for a while. In those early days, she'd often wished it was Red she was supposed to get hitched to. The Irishman had always been her champion, even when she acted badly and didn't deserve his regard.

"Whew! We've got a bit of a reprieve." D'Arcy came into the room slapping dust from his hat on the thigh of his jeans.

"What do you mean?" From long practice, she set a mug of coffee on the table by his chair.

"Thanks." He lifted the mug toward her in a salute. "The boys have high tailed it down to the swimming hole by the river."

"Is that safe?" She plunged plates into the wash water.

"Red's going down to keep an eye on them."

"The river's high though, those storms in the mountains…"

"A good thing, too. We could use some moisture around here. 'Sides, them kids know better'n to go in the river when the current's strong."

"I guess. And Red's there to watch out for them." She turned back to the sink, piling steaming dishes on the drying rack. Bella grinned a few minutes later when D put his arms around her and kissed the back of her neck.

"We could go…" He nuzzled her ear and brought his hands up to her breasts.

She wriggled back against him and unslung the tea towel off her shoulder. "You could just help me with the dishes."

"Slave driver." He pulled her tight and she turned her head for his kiss. "Do you think we might have started a brother for Colt up at the cabin on our anniversary?"

Bella hated to destroy the hope in his face. "Sorry, hon. My monthlies started this morning. I know it's silly to hope after fourteen years, but I would so love to give you a son." She turned and held her soapy hands to his cheeks. "I'm so sorry. You should have married a woman who could give you lots of children."

"I keep hoping too, Ari. You've already given me a son. I love him, and I love you. I don't want any other lady in my life but you. So don't go blamin' yourself. Truth is, much as I'd love to make a baby with you, I've never been so scared in all my life as the night Colt came. I thought I'd lost you. Might be just as well I don't have to go through that again." He kissed her forehead while she spluttered.

"You? You don't have to go through it again? Who was it doing all the work?" Bella teased him, a mock scowl on her face. He kissed it away and she lost herself in arms. The tea towel slid off into the sink of soapy water, but she ignored it, giggling when he lifted her and set her butt on the counter. He fit himself between her legs and she rested her chin on his shoulder.

"I do love you, D'Arcy Rowan. Don't you ever forget that."

His arms tightened around her while her fingers fumbled with the snaps on his shirt. "What about the dishes?" he murmured.

"What dishes?" She giggled as he pulled the blouse loose from her jeans.

The shouts of the boys down at the swimming hole came faintly in the open door, honey bees buzzed lazily in the holly hocks along the back walk. Happiness ran through Bella like golden honey. Thick and rich. Another dark haired man crossed the paths of her memory, blue eyes electric in the Cornish sun. A small corner of her heart would always belong to the selkie, but for now he was a part of her past and he needed to stay buried there. She leaned into her husband's embrace.

* * *

"D'Arcy, Arabella!" Red's bellow was accompanied by the thud of his boots on the porch boards. "Where the hell are you?" His red head minus the ever present Stetson appeared in the doorway. "There you are. C'mon, you gotta come down to the river." He paused to gulp some breaths.

D'Arcy kept his hands on her waist to steady her while Bella slipped off the counter to the floor. Her heart leaped with apprehension at the wild look in the little man's eyes. She gripped her husband's hand as he turned to the door.

"What's wrong, Red." He was moving toward the door before the words left his lips. "Where are the boys?"

"Oh my stars," Bella whispered. She followed the men out the door and down the path. "What happened?" she shouted at their backs.

"Damn fool buggers made a raft. They're out on the river and can't get back. The current's got a holt of them," Red answered without slowing his pace.

D'Arcy's long legs took him past the shorter man. "I thought you were supposed to be watching them?"

"I let you down, man. Fell asleep in the sun. The little beggers were in the swimmin' hole and I just closed my eyes for a second..." he ran out of breath.

"They're on the river, all of them?" Bella broke into a run, overtaking him and leaving him behind.

"All of 'em, missy," he wheezed, stopping to bend over with his hands on his knees.

Bella paused and glanced back. "You okay?" She was torn between leaving the old man in the hot sun and reaching her son.

He waved a hand without looking up. "Go on, missy. I'll be along directly."

She didn't believe him but the need to get to Colton over road everything. She sprinted down the hard packed trail toward the Old Man River. *What the hell were they thinking, little bastards? They know better, all of them.* Anger lent strength to her legs. She caught up with her husband where the trail dipped down a steep incline to the flats by the river's edge. Bella sat on her butt and slid down the sandy slope, taking the quickest way to the bottom. Scrambling to her feet she joined D who was ankle deep in the water, hat pushed back on his head as he scanned the water downstream.

"Where are they? I can't see them." Her nails bit into her palms. She pushed out further into the river, the current pulling at her knees.

"Ari, be careful!" D'Arcy caught her arm when she stumbled on the rocky bottom.

"I'm fine. Let me be. I can't see him," panic clogged her throat strangling the words.

He unceremoniously hauled her out of the river. "C'mon." He started following the river downstream, breaking a path through the bushes crowding the banks. Bella followed on his heels, eyes searching for any sign of the boys and their raft. *Where are they? They have to be there somewhere. When I get my hands on that boy I'm gonna kill him.* She stifled a sob and moved faster.

"Can you see them anywhere," Red huffed as he caught up to them.

She shook her head, not wasting breath on an answer. She rammed into D'Arcy when he halted abruptly.

"What did they use for a raft? Any chance it's actually still afloat?" The buttons on his shirt heaved as his chest rose and fell with his effort to catch his breath. "Answer me, damn it!"

"They was out on the river afore I seen them. Looked like inner tubes and a chunk of plywood. Damn, D. I can't say I'm sorry often enough."

"Plywood and inner tubes, the stupid little bastards. I told them to stay off the river…" D'Arcy ground his teeth, a muscle jumping in his jaw.

Bella pushed past the men and kept moving down stream, refusing to even think about the possibility there was nothing to find. A flash of yellow on the sand spit in the centre of the river caught her attention. She stopped and wiped a hand over her eyes, holding the hair back out of her face. Squinting against the glare of the late afternoon sun bouncing off the moving water she made out the group of boys huddled together. She wavered on her feet with the strength of the tide relief rushing through her.

"D! Red! I found them," Bella yelled never taking her eyes off the boys. "Stay there," she called over the rush of the river.

One of the boys noticed her and they all started waving their arms wildly. *Stay put, stay put.* What was left of the makeshift raft lay tangled in the roots of a large cottonwood snag embedded in the channel. If there hadn't been the sand spit…Bella snapped off the train of thought. *There is a sand spit and they're safe. So far, anyway.*

"Oh for the love of God!" D'Arcy arrived at her side, panting and disheveled. He eyed the churning water between the bank and the boys in disgust.

"Where are the little spalpeens?" Red caught up with them. When the old cowboy got excited or faced with a crisis he reverted back to the Irish idioms of his childhood.

"They're safe, for now at least." Bella found her husband's hand and gripped it hard. She looked to him for guidance. Colton was the only child they were likely to have and she had no intention of losing him to the Old Man River. "How're we gonna get them back?"

"I'm thinkin', Ari." Worry etched new lines in his face.

"The river ain't that deep right there, by the downstream end of the bar." Red pointed to a spot past where the boys were gathered at the edge of the water.

"The current's too strong for them to swim," Bella objected, fear squeezing her heart.

"But the channel is narrower there too. A rope might reach across." D measured the distance through squinted eyes. "If I can throw the loop that far they can tie it off to the cottonwood snag and we can anchor it on this end it'll keep the river from taking us downstream."

"Might just work, ya know." Red nodded. "Or we could go get Em and Hank, them big half-breed Clydes can swim and so long as the water ain't too deep and they had ta swim too far they're strong enough to fight the current."

"Well go get them, and some rope." Bella stamped her foot. "We gotta get them over before we lose the light." She glanced at the orange ball sliding down the sky.

D'Arcy glanced at Red, pale beneath his tan. He looked like he was ready to sit down at any second. "You stay here with Ari, I'll go get the horses and gear. Don't let those young idiots do anything stupid." He crashed off through the brush.

Bella felt suddenly bereft and empty without his reassuring bulk beside her. Red's labouring breathing eased a bit, she glanced at the wiry cowboy glad to see the heat of exertion leaving his face. She loved the old Irishman with all her heart and constantly worried he was overdoing things. Not that he'd listen to anything she said about that. Stubborn old coot.

"I shoulda told D to bring blankets, them boys'll be half-froze." He glanced up stream where D'Arcy had disappeared.

Bella bit her lip. He was right, even though the sun was hot, the river's source was in the mountains and the water stayed cold all year except in the shallows at the very edge. Time to worry about that once they got the kids back on safe ground.

"I'm gonna go fetch some wool blankets, you stay here so they don't think we've deserted them." Red shoved through the break in the bushes without waiting for an answer.

She wrapped her arms around her waist. What was taking so long? Colton's dark head was in the middle of the group of boys. He looked one of his friends and pushed back the hank of hair that always fell over his forehead. Bella's heart skipped a beat. *Oh my stars, it could be Vear standing there.* She pressed a hand to her heart. It didn't mean anything, of course he'd inherited some of his father's mannerisms as well as physical characteristics. *Good thing D is dark and tall, no one thinks twice about who Colt's da is.* Crackling brush and the crunch of hooves announced D's return. She whirled around and hurried to take the reins of the big bay mare he led. He swung down from the matching gelding's back and gave her a swift hug.

"Everything still the same?" His gaze was on the sand spit.

"Yup. Red went to get some blankets. Did you see him on your way?" Bella looked over his shoulder.

"He's back at the house. Told him to make some hot chocolate and fill a few of those big flasks. He'll bring them along with the blankets. Give the old fool a chance to catch a breath, too."

"Good, I'm worried about him, D'Arcy. He isn't getting any younger." She bit her lip. "Do we need to wait for him or can we get on with it?"

"Ma!" Colt's voice carried across the river. "Jake's right freezing. When are you coming?"

"Just hang on," D'Arcy cupped his hands around his mouth and answered his son. He glanced over his shoulder and then down at Bella.

"I'll go first, if we make it you come with the mare. If we can bring two at a time, it'll save time. Wait until I make a trip before you come across." D'Arcy urged the Clydesdale cross into the river.

"What about the rope?" Bella called.

"If we can do it with the horses we don't need to bother." He didn't pause while the water swirled up to his ankles.

Gathering up the reins, Bella hiked her foot into the stirrup and swung up on the bay mare. The horse was taller than the one she usually rode, but she settled in the saddle and accommodated herself to the much wider back of the draft horse. D'Arcy must have had to lengthen the latigos to get the cinch to fit. D'Arcy was half way across the channel now, the river only coming to the big horse's shoulders. She crossed her fingers. If their luck held the bottom wouldn't drop away at some point. Breath hissed between her teeth when the level suddenly rose to the man's thighs and the gelding raised his nose higher. Seconds later, Hank emerged on the sand spit water sluicing off him in ribbons.

D'Arcy turned and waved to her. She moved her horse to the water's edge and waited. He put one boy up behind the saddle and threw another of the smaller boys into the saddle. *What the bloody hell is he doing?* She bit her lip as he knotted the reins and put them over the gelding's neck. Holding onto the breast collar on the upstream side, he led the horse back into the current. The animal moved steadily toward the shore, her husband was lost from her sight on the other side of the horse. If he lost his footing certainly she'd see him being carried away, wouldn't she? Bella stood in the stirrups and strained her neck to look further down the waterway.

"What's happening?" Red staggered to a halt under a load of blankets and heavy flasks. "Boys okay?"

"He's almost across with the first ones. Get those blankets ready." Bella urged Em forward as D'Arcy stumbled out of the river hanging off the horse's side.

"Don't try that, Ari," he gasped for breath. "Current's too fast, almost took me a couple of time. You stay on the horse. Here, Red. Take this one." He hauled the shaking boy out of the saddle.

Jake slid down himself and wrapped himself in the blanket waiting for him. Red bundled the other boy up and plunked him down beside Jake. He gathered some dry brush and started a small fire in a hollow in the sand. Unscrewing the lid of the flask, he gave both boys a tin cup of cocoa. Bella waited to be sure D'Arcy was recovering before heading out into the river.

"Angle into the current," he called after her.

She didn't respond, too afraid to take her attention off the rolling water. The frigid temperature took her breath away as the river climbed up over her knees. It seemed to take forever to reach the sand bar and she heaved a sigh of relief as the water receded just before Em climbed up on the bit of beach. Throwing herself off the mare she hugged Colton hard and then set him back to glare at him.

"What sort of harebrained stunt was that?" She stuck her chin out toward the wrecked raft.

"I'm sorry, Ma. But I saved us—" He shut his mouth with a snap when he saw her expression.

"Get up on Em, now," she ordered him.

Colt backed away from her. "No, Ma. Take these guys first. The raft was my idea, so I'll wait til the last. Only fair."

From the stubborn set of his chin, so much like D'Arcy's when he had his mind set on something, Bella decided to let him salve his conscience. "Fine, but you wait for your Pa or me, you hear. No heroics."

He nodded. Bella turned to the other four boys huddled together in a shivering bunch. "Who's in the worst shape?"

"Sam, you better go," Colt said. "He's got a buggered wing," he addressed his mother.

"Colton, language! What happened to his arm? Is it broken?" She knelt beside the blond boy. "Show me where it hurts," she said gently.

Sam removed the hand clutching his opposite forearm. "It hurts like the blazes, Mrs. Rowan." He gritted his teeth and tried to be brave, but tears cut tracks in the dirty face.

Bella put her hands on the injured area, not sharp bones poked at her searching fingers.

289

There was a knot of swelling and she thought the alignment was misplaced. "Hang on a second, Sam. We'll get you out of here in no time flat." She stripped off the large bandana from around her neck and bound the arm across his middle. "Okay, let's see if you can get up, son." He took her hand and she pulled him upright. "Good job, Sam. Now, up you go." Bella grunted as she hefted him up into the saddle.

She scrambled up behind him, squeezing into the seat. Kicking her left foot free of the stirrup, she looked down at the other boys. "Who else is coming this time?"

Colt pushed Jared forward. "Go on, go with your brother."

He climbed up on a sandstone boulder and got his foot in the stirrup, Bella grasped his arm and helped him scramble up behind her. "Hold tight, boys. No matter what, hang onto the horse. You hear?"

"Yes, ma'am," they chorused.

"Mr. Rowan is coming now, Joey and Chance you go with him. Colton, I'll be back for you."

D'Arcy and Hank splashed out of the water just as she entered it. He gave her a brilliant smile and she realized he was enjoying the challenge presented by the river. Bella shook her head, what was it about men that made them love to walk that thin edge of danger? "Be careful," she called over the rush of the water.

"Always," he answered.

Em snorted and plunged into the current. It seemed stronger, but Bella figured she was just anxious because now it was more than her neck on the line. She wrapped an arm around Sam and was reassured by Jared's death grip on her waist. Using the small fire on the bank as a guide she turned the mare's nose into the current. There was a bit of a drift but they should make the shore close to where she was headed. Sam bit back a whimper when the huge shoulders bunched and got them clear of the river. Red was waiting to lift Sam down, careful of the bandaged arm. Jared slithered down on his own, following his brother over to the fire. She waited to be sure Red had things in hand before swinging the mare back toward the river.

"Wait, Ari. I'll go get Colt," D'Arcy was only a few feet from the bank with Joey and Chance clinging on Hank's broad rump. "You stay."

The mare was already in the river up to her knees. Bella laughed at him and sent her forward. "I'm not letting you have all the fun, cowboy," she called.

"Ari, wait!"

She lost whatever else he said in the roar of the water. Em surged forward, ridges of foam curling around her. The cold was getting to Bella, she could only imagine how the mare was feeling. Leaning down, she patted the neck. "This is the last one, old girl." It seemed to take longer than before to reach the sand bar. *It's just my imagination.* Her son waited at the water's edge, shivering with his arms wrapped around his thin body. *If I wasn't so glad he's okay, I'd kill the little bugger.* He managed a crooked smile when she halted beside him. "C'mon then, Colt. Let's get the hell out of here." He scrambled up on the same boulder Jared used and hauled himself up behind her.

"Let's go, Ma. It's colder'n a witches tit out here." His teeth chattered so he could hardly get the words out.

"Colton, where did you hear that?" Bella glared at him over her shoulder.

"Red," he muttered, burying his face against her back.

"We'll talk about this later, young man. For now let's get out here." Em snorted and danced at the edge, refusing for a moment to enter the river. "Get up, horse." Bella kicked the mare smartly in the ribs. "Hold on, Colt," she yelled as the mare bunched up under her and leaped into the current.

Water splashed everywhere, dousing Bella and obscuring her vision. One hand pinned Colt's arms to her middle, the other gripped the wet leather reins on top of the saddle horn. "Stupid bloody beast," she spluttered spitting sandy river water out of her mouth. "You okay, Colt?"

"Yeah, Ma."

She kept her gaze on the flickering flames on the bank. She allowed herself to relax a little as they crossed the halfway point. Em forged steadily ahead. They were a little further downstream than last time, Bella judged, but didn't see any reason they shouldn't come out near where she aimed.

D'Arcy stood up to his ankles in the water holding Hank beside him. "Ari!" His voice carried across the water.

"I'm fine, D. We're coming!" She lifted her rein hand to wave. The next thing she knew the mare disappeared from under her and the river closed over her head. The reins tore free of her grasping fingers. "Colt!" She swallowed a mouthful of river and no sound came out. *Where is he? God damn horse.* She floundered to the surface looking wildly for her son. The current shoved her along, fortunately close enough to the side to occasionally reach the bottom with her feet. A wet black head rose on a wave to her right, further out in the river. "Colt," she screamed and he turned his frightened face toward her. "I'm coming!" Bella flung herself toward him, pushing off from the sandy base underfoot.

She kicked off her boots, filling with water they were dragging her down. She caught sight of him, closer now and struck out with renewed effort. A swell lifted her up and then rolled her over under the brown waves. She rolled again and lost any sense of what was up or down. *Colton! God damn it, I'm not dying like this, and neither is he.* The river offered her a reprieve and she bobbed to the surface. Blinking the water out of her eyes, she swallowed another mouthful of muddy water.

Arrowing toward her against the current was a sleek black head cutting cleanly through the water. Floundering to stay afloat, she tried to shove the wet mop of hair out of her face. There were two ebony heads, not one, coming to her. The smaller one swimming at the larger one's shoulder. She went under again with not enough air in her lungs. The current tossed her about, she skidded against a submerged boulder but hardly registered the pain. She opened her eyes and watched fascinated as the bits of flotsam swirled around her. The sense of urgency disappeared and she gave herself up to the river's will.

Her head broke the surface and she gasped sharply. A huge body was bearing her back up river and toward the shore. At her shoulder, a small sable body sliced through the current like a hot knife through butter. *A seal? It can't be a seal. There aren't any hereabouts.* They reached an eddy and shallower water. The body beneath her shifted and strong arms held her safe, carrying her toward the bank. Through bleary eyes she peered at her rescuer. The hands holding her were human, but the narrow snout with bristling whiskers most definitely wasn't.

"Vear?" Her voice was husky and low.

"You're safe, Bella."

"Colton!" She struggled to get free. Colton was still out there somewhere, she had to get to him.

"Be still, Bella. Water will never hurt him."

A splashing at beside her caught her attention. A half-grown seal was working its way up the bank, flippers flapping clumsily. She lunged toward it and fell, collapsing half-submerged back into the river. On hands and knees she crawled up the shore. The seal turned around and looked at her.

"Ari!" Red and D'Arcy plunged into the water and hauled her out. She clung to her husband, never taking her eyes off the seal. "Where's Colt?" He looked over head scanning the river.

"D'Arcy, there." She pointed at the seal. "Look, oh my stars."

"Holy mother of God!" Red stepped back and crossed himself, making the ancient sign against evil with his fingers just to be sure.

The sleek ebony body rippled and shimmered. Bella caught her breath. She'd seen that before back in the cave in Cornwall. She sobbed in relief and struggled out of her husband's stunned grasp. Reaching his side just as the transformation was complete, she collapsed on her knees, gathering Colton in her arms.

"Oh, baby. I'm so sorry. Oh, baby."

"Ma, what happened? What happened to me?" His eyes were wide with panic, fingers digging into her arms. He looked down at his body. "What am I?" he whispered in disbelief.

"Colt, I can explain everything. We never wanted you to find out this way." She looked over his head at D'Arcy.

He got to his feet and sank down beside his son. "It's okay, Colt. There's nothing to be afraid of."

The boy burrowed into his father's arms. "I went under and then something weird happened and I could swim like a fish. But, I wasn't...I wasn't...me," he wailed. "What's wrong with me? Am I some kind of freak?" The boy sobbed hysterically.

Bella crawled over to him and put her arms around both of her men. Red was muttering decades of rosaries in the background. "Would you shut up?" she roared at him. "Go and get blankets. Where are the others?"

"Sorry, missy. I heered tales when I was a nipper, but heerin' it and seein' it is two different things. Them other boys are fine. I'll go fetch some blankets." He hurried off.

Colt bolted upright, looking about. "Where is he? Where is he?"

"Where is who?" D'Arcy frowned at his son and held him tighter.

"The other big thing, a big black otter, he looked like. Found me and turned me in the right direction." He stopped and stared at Bella. "It was carrying, Ma. Told me to wait and dove down real deep. Came up with Ma on his back and brought her to the shore. Who was that?"

D'Arcy caught her gaze over Colt and shook his head. Bella vaguely remembered someone grabbing her and bearing her to the surface. She jumped as the memory of Vear's whiskered face crossed her mind. "It couldn't be," she whispered. "I don't know, Colt. I think you're confused from falling in the river. Let's talk about it after we get you home."

D'Arcy got to his feet with Colt in his arms and Bella got up as well, shivering even in the warm air. The sun was almost gone from the sky and an evening breeze blew up the valley. Red arrived bearing supplies. She wrapped the wool blanket around her and followed the men along the bank back to the small fire.

"What happened to Em?" Bella stopped dead. Until that moment she'd forgotten about the mare.

"She's fine. Came out of the water a couple of hundred feet away from you and headed up the trail for home," Red told her.

"Thank God for that." Her teeth chattered.

The boys ran to meet them when they neared the fire. "Colt, is he…" Jared swallowed hard, his arm supporting his little brother.

Sam started to cry and the others looked ready to join him.

"He's okay. Just water logged. Now let's get you boys up to the house." Red herded the group up the steep incline. He put Sam up on Hank and led him behind the straggling line of subdued little boys.

D'Arcy and Bella brought up the rear. Colt stared at her over his dad's shoulder, a blank expression on his pale face. *Thank you, thank you whoever pulled us out of that fix. I don't understand how or why…but thanks.* How was she ever going to explain the child's ability to shape shift to him?

Chapter Sixteen

Bella cradled the mug of coffee in her hands, letting the warmth seep through her. The boys' parents were all aware of what happened, and all but Sam and Jared were asleep upstairs. Sam's dad called a few minutes ago to report the arm was broken but only a green fracture. Doc promised it should heal up well. *Thank heavens for small mercies.* She met her husband's gaze over the table.

"Well, I guess this answers our questions about what he did or didn't inherit." She let the words fall between them.

"I don't blame you, Ari. We knew from the start it was a possibility." He sounded wearier than she'd ever heard him.

"I thought I'd lost him," she choked on the words a sob forced its way up her throat.

"I thought I'd lost both of you...when the mare went down..." He scrubbed his hands over his face. "Lord God Almighty, don't ever scare me like that again, Arabella."

"Not like I planned it," she retorted.

"I know, I know. What happened out there?" He stared at her as if willing her to tell him they hadn't really seen what went down on the river.

"I don't know for sure. I thought I saw Colt and tried to get to him. The next thing I remember I was under the water scraping along the bottom. Something grabbed me and shoved me up. I saw…I saw…a little seal, I thought maybe it was an otter at first, swimming beside me. But something bigger was shoving me toward the bank against the current. I don't know what it was. I couldn't…I didn't get a good look at it," she lied. It was inconceivable that Vear could have saved her. It must have been her imagination. "But what Colt did on the sand, that was real, D'Arcy. I've seen his fa…I've seen Vear do it once or twice."

He shuddered. "Once is more than enough. Do you think he'll remember anything?"

She raised her shoulders helplessly. "I don't know. Maybe? I'll try and talk to him after his friends leave tomorrow."

"I just don't want the boy to scairt of himself. He might not be ready to understand."

"If he's mature enough to shift, he's old enough to know why, even if I don't know the how of it." She paused. "Where's Red?"

"I sent the old coot to bed. He was pale as a whore's ass and shaking. I made a big mug of the hot whiskey drink he likes so much. A hot'un he calls it. Just whiskey, sugar and hot water, but it's like mother's milk to an Irishman, I guess. I looked in on him when you were in the bath, he's sleeping like a baby, so it must have done the trick."

"I was worried about him out there. Thought he was going to have a heart attack." Bella reached across the table and wound her fingers around D'Arcy's.

"He's not getting any younger, that's for sure. When I tell him to cut back a bit he gets all ornery and reminds me I'm getting long in the tooth right along with him." He grinned at her.

"You're like fine wine, D. Or whiskey. The older you get the better you become." She smiled and was pleased to see the fire ignite in his eyes.

He released her hand and got to his feet. "I'm gonna go check the Clydes one more time." His stocking feet whispered on the floor boards as he carried their crockery to the sink. "I'll turn out the lights when I come in, you go on up to bed, Ari. I'll be up in a few." Warm lips closed over hers with a promise of better things to come.

"I'll look in on the boys before I turn in. Do you think we should check on Red?" She slid her arms around his waist and rested her head on his broad chest.

"The old man's fine. Take more than a little excitement to knock the stuffing out of that cowboy." He released her and disappeared into the night.

Bella paused in the door of the living room where the scattered lumps of boys wrapped in sleeping bags were still and peaceful. Faint light from the kitchen shone on Colt's ebony hair. Her heart twisted with love and fear. He was growing up. How was she supposed to protect him from what he was? *Worry about it tomorrow, Bella. Lord, I wish Sarie was here.*

She padded upstairs in her bare feet and stripped off her clothes before sliding into bed. The sheets were cool on her skin and she wished D would hurry. His huge body was like a monster furnace producing enough heat to warm her even when the blizzards were howling over the earth. The soft thump of his feet coming down the hall set her heart racing. A dim glow from the night light was the only illumination when he shut the door behind him. Dark eyes held her gaze while his clothes dropped to the floor. Bella drew the quilts back so her bare torso was exposed to his hungry scrutiny, the cool air pebbling her nipples. D stood by the bed looking down at her.

"God you're beautiful, Arabella." The words husky and catching in his throat. He bent to trace circles around the taut tip on one breast, his penis standing against his flat belly rising from the nest of hair at his groin.

"Come to bed, D'Arcy," she whispered, bringing his finger to her lips and sucking it into her mouth.

The mattress groaned and then his warm body was wrapped around her. Bella turned her fact up for his kiss.

* * *

Because of the excitement earlier, the evening BBQ was a no go. Bella decided a morning cook out would take the boys' minds off what could have happened on the river. In the kitchen, she stirred the batter for a big mess of Saskatoon berry griddle cakes. The small deep freeze D'Arcy brought home to surprise her earlier in the summer was a God send. At the time Bella thought he'd put out a horrendous amount of cash in exchange for the freezer. She soon came to appreciate being able to blanche and freeze fruit and vegetables without having to can everything.

Glancing out the window, she saw Red had the big old river stone BBQ ready and a fire shone in the fire pit as well. She grinned, he did love his coffee perked over an open fire rather than on the stove. D'Arcy appeared with an armload of wood which he dumped by the pit. When he placed the heavy iron griddle over the coals of the BBQ Bella picked up the pottery basin in her arms and lugged it out to join the men.

"I fried up a mess of bacon, missy." Red pointed to a deep tin plate set on the stone edge keeping warm. "All we need now is them cakes o' your'n."

"Where are the boys?" She glanced around the yard.

"I sent them to rub down Em and Hank and give them another mash. Least they can do, those animals saved their hides." D'Arcy took the heavy batter bowl from her and set it on the table.

"They did that. Those two have a home here 'til the day they die of old age," she vowed. "They never get shipped, you hear me?"

D'Arcy pulled her close, avoiding the batter spoon in her hand. "Yes, Mrs. Rowan. I hear you loud and clear." He kissed her cheek.

"See that you do." She waved the spoon at him dripping griddle cake on his boots. "Red, call the little heathens would you? These'll be ready in two shakes of a calf's tail."

He set off toward the corrals, a decided limp making itself known as he went.

"Man's got quite a hitch in his git along," she remarked. "Maybe you could persuade him to go see Doc?"

"Not much chance of that, Ari. But I'll try," he promised.

The arrival of five hungry boys distracted her from anything except trying to cook fast enough to keep up with their ravenous appetites.

It was amazing how quickly the youngsters recovered from trauma. Her gaze lingered on her dark haired son, while he was joining in the nonsense with his friends, there was an underlying stillness that worried her. "Here we go." She set another platter of fragrant griddle cakes on the rough picnic table. The hoard swooped on the stack leaving the plate bare in seconds. They settled back on the logs arranged around the fire pit, devouring their breakfast with the ferocity only teenage boys seemed to be capable of. Grinning, she turned back to the grill and spooned more batter onto the greased cast iron.

Deftly she flipped four cakes onto a plate and handed them to D'Arcy, before doing the same for Red. "Take these before the hollow legs over there descend on us again." Bella filled the griddle again. By the time the batter bowl was empty the boys were satisfied and prepared to disappear toward the corrals.

"Stay out of trouble," she called after them.

"Aw, Ma," Colton protested, turning to look back at her with an aggrieved expression on his face.

"Mind your mother," D rumbled, stifling any further comment.

"Is he okay, do you think?" Bella sat beside him on the log balancing a plate of hot cakes on her knee. "Want some, I saved a few for us." She offered him the plate.

Her husband rolled one of the cakes around a few strips of bacon and crunched it between square white teeth. "I reckon he's doing all right, Ari. You still planning on talking to him later?"

"Do you think I should let the hare lie?" She frowned up at him while picking at her breakfast.

He shook his head. "Don't rightly know what to say. Best if you just follow your heart." His hand closed over hers and squeezed.

"Red, leave those dishes. I'll get to them when I'm done here," Bella said.

He set down the stack of tin plates and glanced toward the corrals. "Reckon I'll go see what them scalawags is up to." The Irishman ambled around the side of the house.

Bella turned her face up to the sun and closed her eyes. The heat felt good on her face, she swore her bones were still cold from the dunking yesterday.

"Penny for your thoughts." D'Arcy kissed the end of her nose.

"I'm not sure how much to tell him. Or if I should say anything at all." She opened her eyes and stared at the blue-gold sky. "You're the only father he knows, how do I tell him you're not the one who sired him?" She turned to look him in the face and gripped his forearm. "You are his father, in every way that counts."

"I know that, Ari. I got over bein' jealous of some man I've never clapped eyes on a long time ago. Colton is my son and you're my wife. You tell him whatever your heart tells you to." He got up and his long legs carried him around the corner of the house and out of sight.

"My heart's all sixes and sevens," she muttered. "Get your arse in gear, woman. Time's a wasting." Bella got to her feet and gathered up the dirty plates, it took three trips to retrieve everything and a good hour for her to

306

set the kitchen to rights. There was laundry that needed doing and she immersed herself in the task to divert her thoughts from the discussion she knew she needed to have with her son.

Red had to make a trip into Pincher Creek in the afternoon so he volunteered to drive Colt's friends home, dropping them off in town or at their ranch gate on his way. The early evening sun slanted across the yard tinting everything with a pale orange glow. The sky overhead burned a deep brilliant blue. It seemed a strange way to describe it, but the colour was so intense and clear, filled with light, that Bella could never figure out any other way to try and capture the ethereal quality. "Alberta blue," she murmured tipping her head back to catch the golden dust hanging in the still air. It wouldn't be still for long, she'd learned that early on. Wind in southern Alberta was as sure as death and taxes.

Bella crossed the yard and leaned on the corral fence next to Colt. He was a hair taller than her already, her long legged son. Tall like D'Arcy, and like Vear Du. She swallowed.

"Hey, Ma." Colt hooked a booted foot over a low rail in the fence. His eyes never left the rangy black horse pacing in the enclosure.

"Hey, Colt. Chores done?" She scaled the rails and perched on the top one, boot heels hooked on a rail for security.

"Pa's just throwing some hay to the Clydes. Red said you ran away with that horse when you first came here. That true?" The brim of his hat hid the expression in his eyes.

"It was a stupid thing to do," she answered him indirectly.

"Why'd you do it?" He picked apart a scrap of baling twine caught in the wood rail.

"I was young and scared."

Colt swung up to join her on the top rail. "Scared of Pa?"

"A little, yes. Your Pa is a lot older than me, you know that. And everything here was so strange and I...I...panicked, is the best way to describe it, I guess. As I said, it was very stupid of me."

"What was so special about the horse? It's just a big ol' black horse." He tipped his head to look at her.

"He reminded me of my horse I had to leave behind. Raven was a handful and not many could ride her but me, and I loved that about her. I sure didn't agree with the way the men were handling the horse. I spoke to your Pa about it and he wasn't inclined to listen to me. So I decided to take matters into my own hands. I was pretty headstrong in those days." She laughed.

"Red says you were hotter'n a chili pepper." Her son's face coloured. "Not hot in that way, said you had a hair trigger temper and it wasn't good for a man's health to be in firing range," he qualified.

"I don't think I was quite that bad." She grinned at him.

308

Colt's amusement faded and his expression became serious. Ma, what happened in the river? I had this weird dream and I just can't make head nor tails of it. Do you remember what went on?"

Bella inhaled sharply through her nose. Tension gripped her belly and she had to remind herself to let the air out of her lungs. "What do you remember, Colt?"

"I don't rightly now, Ma."

"What do you think you remember, then?" She tried again.

"It's pretty clear up until you and me were comin' back on Em. Then, once we got dumped in the river, it gets all...all...muddled up." Colt shrugged and averted his gaze, staring off toward the cattle on the hills.

"How do you mean, muddled up? I lost sight of you when I went under the water and when I came up—"

"What was that thing what brung you up? When you went down I tried to get to you and grab your hand or something. But I couldn't get to you, the current kept taking me further away...and then...then...well, something happened I can't explain it...Ma, am I some kind of freak, or something?" His jaw was clenched tight, a vein jumping in his neck.

Bella put a hand on his arm. "Colt, why would you think that? Why are you worried you're a freak?"

"Because, something awful went wrong with my body, I...I...it changed..." his words were strangled. "Like I was me, but in some other body. Am I possessed by the devil like the preacher was goin' on about in church last Sunday?"

"Colton, honey. I can assure you that you're not possessed by the devil or anything else," Bella spoke softly.

"But then what do you reckon happened?"

"You know the stories Red tells sometimes? From the old country?"

He frowned, but nodded.

"Well, in all the old tales there's usually a grain of truth. In some cases more than a grain. Do you remember the one about the shape shifters, the selkies?"

Colt wriggled on the fence and turned to look straight at her. "That's the ones what can turn from a man into a seal?"

"That's correct. Selkies can be males or females, and they have been known to live as humans and marry mortals."

"What's that got to do with me?" Colt looked uneasy.

Bella took a deep breath. "It's possible you have inherited the ability to change shape. It appears when you were in the river and scared for your life instinct took over and you…shifted into seal form…"

"What?" Colt's eyes widened and his nostrils flared in disbelief and fear. "You're trying to say I'm one of them…them…shifter things? That ain't possible, Ma! I never did nothing wrong to cause that."

"Oh, Colton. Of course you haven't done anything wrong. If there's blame to be laid at anyone's door it's mine."

Her son edged away from her on the top rail. "Are you...one of them things?" he whispered.

"No, I'm as ordinary as dirt."

"Then how!" Colt jumped down and glared up at her. "If you ain't, and Pa ain't, then how...?"

Bella slid down to stand beside him. "Your Pa—"

"You're lying! Pa ain't one them things. Why are you lying to me?"

"Colt, listen to me. Calm down a minute and let me try and explain."

He crossed his arms over his chest stuck his chin out in belligerence. "I'm listening."

"I'd best start at the beginning. You know you're Pa is a lot older than me, and that I came over from the old country to marry him. Like a mail order bride, sort of."

"But you knew Pa before you came over, he met you in that England place and fell in love with you. Brought you home and you got hitched here on the ranch," Colt protested.

"That's what everyone thinks, yes."

"You're sayin' that's all a lie?" Colt looked outraged, his face white.

"I was young and foolish, I made mistakes, Colton. D'Arcy put that story around to spare me humiliation. I was pregnant with you when I arrived in Alberta—"

311

"But, that's okay, I guess. I mean, Pa married you and made you an honest woman."

"I was always an honest woman, Colt. Society says it's okay for a man to sow his wild oats but if a woman anticipates marriage they call her a whore. I don't agree with that at all."

"You ain't answered my question, Ma. Is Pa one of them things?"

"No, Colton. D'Arcy isn't a selkie. But your father—"

"Pa is my father! What are you trying to say?"

"I was in the family way when I married D'Arcy, but not with his child." She waited for the explosion.

"You're lying!"

"I'm not at all. Your natural father is a man named Vear Du. It's Cornish. I loved him very much, but it was impossible for us to be together. Your Pa, D'Arcy, wanted an heir, he agreed to marry me and claim you as his own. He loves you, Colton. He couldn't love you more if you were his flesh and blood. But, Vear Du, he's a selkie. It's kind of like magic. And it's from him you inherited the ability to shift your shape."

"Does Pa know? And Red?" Colt planted his feet squarely and glared at her.

"They do." She nodded.

"Why didn't anyone tell me?"

"I, we, were hoping there would be no need to ever tell you. But once we realized you inherited the ability, we agreed it was time to tell you."

"So, I'm a bastard? Like Nelly Strongarm?"

"No, you're not. I was legally wed to D'Arcy when you were born and nobody knows any different. Everyone but Red, D'Arcy, and I, believe D'Arcy is your father. I see no reason for them to know any different."

"Huh." He didn't sound convinced.

"Colton, I want you to think about something else. Is Nelly any better or worse a person just because she was born on the wrong side of the sheets? She's a sweet girl and goes out of her way to be nice to everyone. Does it really matter she doesn't know who her pa is?"

"She is right nice. I guess, it don't make no never mind about her pa. But them girls in town are some mean to her over it."

"We can't do anything about what others do or think, only how we behave."

"I reckon."

"Do you have any other questions for me, Colton? You can ask me whatever you want, no matter how embarrassing."

"I don't reckon I believe you, Ma. I don't know why you made up that cock and bull story about Pa not bein' my pa and some guy being a selkie thing really being my pa. I think I'm just gonna never go in the river again, or near any big things of water. I ain't no magic selkie thing. You're my ma and Pa is my pa. Ain't no such thing as magic anyway. I don't never want to hear about any of this crap again, you hear?"

313

Tears stung the back of Bella's eyes and she fought to control the quiver in her lower lip. "If that's what you want, Colt." She hesitated. "Are you angry with me?"

He regarded her for a long minute chewing on his bottom lip. The last light of the sun shone strong on his face when he pushed the hat back off his forehead. "I'm not mad, Ma. I don't rightly understand why you're saying all that weird stuff, but I'm not mad. I just don't want to talk about it ever again."

"Okay, right. You can talk to your pa, or Red, if you're curious about anything. They both know everything. I'm sorry what I did when I was young is hurting you now, Colt. I love you more than anything in the world." She hugged him and he returned the embrace.

"I'm gonna see if Pa and Red need help with night chores and then I'm gonna hit the hay. The branding is over at Murphy's tomorrow, gotta get up early. You're comin' tomorrow, right?" He stepped out of her arms.

"I am. I got a big pot of beans baking. You looking forward to seein' the Murphy girls again? Especially, the younger one, what's her name? Anna?"

Colt blushed in the faint evening light. "Um, yeah. Anna. She's in my class at school, that's all."

"She's a sweet little thing. Rides like she was born in the saddle. You still helping her with that barrel horse of hers?"

314

"Some. Mostly we just put some miles on the horses. I gotta go, Ma."

She caught his arm. "You sure you're okay, Colt? Really."

"Ma. I'm fine. Let's just forget we ever had this weird talk, okay? No crazy seal things, no magic, nothing changes."

"If that makes you happy, sweetheart. That's what we'll do. Tell your Pa and Red supper will be on the table in fifteen minutes."

Bella watched him stride toward the barns and swing up onto the high tractor seat. The machine roared into life and rumbled off toward the line of round bales. She bit her lip. Caution made her hesitate to insist he not deny what happened and shove the information she'd just provided into the back of his mind. *It's not healthy to ignore something like this. Maybe D will have better luck with him.*

* * *

"D?" Bella lay on her back and stared at the ceiling in the dark room.

"What?" Her husband huffed and rolled over throwing an arm over his head.

"I talked to Colt today. About the river...you know?"

"And?"

315

"He knows something strange happened, but he's determined to put it down to nearly drowning and being scared."

"Did you tell him the truth? About that selkie fella, and all?" He propped himself up on an elbow, his face hidden in shadow.

"I did. Everything, and he just doesn't want to hear it. Total denial. I don't know how to get through to him."

"Hhmmpf. Might be for the best if the boy just forgets about it." D'Arcy lay back down and rolled over.

"Can you try talking to him about it?" Bella snuggled up behind him.

"Do you think that's wise, Ari? Why don't we just let sleeping dogs lie?"

"I don't know, D. It doesn't seem healthy for him to just shove that kind of thing away."

"Probably what I'd do, iffen it was me."

"Really?" Bella sat up and stared down at him.

Her husband heaved himself upright with a groan and opened a bleary eye. "Yes, that's exactly what I'd do. But if it will make you happy I'll try to have a word with him in the next few days. Satisfied?"

She nodded and kissed his cheek. "Have you noticed the way that little Murphy girl has been following Colt around at the brandings? What do you think of her?"

D'Arcy flopped back on the bed and pulled the quilts over his shoulders. "Are you matchmaking already, Ari?"

"Maybe." She shrugged and lay down. "So, what do you think?"

"For the love of God," he muttered. "She's pretty little filly, all blue eyes and blonde hair. She ain't afraid of hard work, rides like she was born in the saddle…what's not to like?"

"Hmmmm. Do you think Colt's noticed her?" Bella poked him in the ribs. She squealed when D'Arcy rolled over and pinned her to the bed with his body, nuzzling at her collarbone, callused hands rubbing over her breasts. "What are you doing?"

"If you won't leave a man be and let him sleep, woman, you'd best be ready to keep him entertained." He nipped at the bud of her breast through the thin cotton while one hand slid up between her legs.

"D'Arcy, be serious." The words come out on a harsh breath when his fingers brushed the sensitive nub at the top of her thighs. "Has Colt said anything to you about Anna?"

"The boy has eyes in his head, Ari. Of course he's noticed her." He shimmied a little and the head of his penis replaced the searching fingers.

"But—" Bella started to pursue the conversation but lost track of the thought when he grasped her nightie and pulled, button shooting all over the bed as the material gave way and exposed her to his attentions.

"Ready to do your duty, wife?" He grinned and kissed the spot just below her ear that made her belly clench before licking his way down her body.

His mouth closed over a nipple and his large hands cupped her bottom, holding her steady while his penis slid into her. Her hands clenched on his forearms. He began to move inside her and Bella totally forgot about Colt and Anna.

D'Arcy was already gone when she woke up just before dawn. The smell of freshly brewed coffee wafted up the stair. Bella was dressed in short order and skipping down the stairs. She loved brandings, it was such fun to see the neighbors and once the hard work was done, eat and sit around the fire afterward with the stars burning in the wide dark sky overhead.

Red was still in the kitchen when she got there. The horses stood saddled in the yard. Murphy's was just the next spread over so the boys were just planning to ride over. Bella would need the car to bring the big pot of beans, pies and other things. He handed her a large mug and raised his in salute.

"To a good branding."

"To a safe day," she replied and raised her mug to clink against his.

The old cowhand set his mug down and stretched. "I swear, me old bones get creakier every day."

"Well, just take it easy today, old man." She grinned at him. "Thanks for the coffee."

"Gotta shake a leg, D and Colt are just about ready to head out. You comin' along soon?"

"Soon as I finish my coffee and lug all the food out to the car."

"You want some help with that, Ma?" Colt stood poised in the doorway. "I was just coming to see what was keeping Red."

"No, I'm fine, Colt. You run along with your pa and Red. Say hi to Anna," she called as he turned to leave.

"Okay." He half turned back to her, a perplexed expression creasing his young features.

Red grinned at Bella and gave the boy a gentle shove to get him moving again. "C'mon, son. Your pa's waiting."

Bella leaned a hip against the counter and savoured the last of her coffee. She made short work of the few dishes and put them away. Transferring the food from the kitchen to the car took significantly longer. She shook her head. *Those boys sure can pack it away.* By the time the men finished their noon meal the beans and sandwiches and whatever the other ladies brought would be devoured. Sally Murphy told her earlier in the week they were roasting a side of beef and a hog in the big BBQ pit for the evening meal. Bella's mouth watered at the thought. She made one last survey of her kitchen to make sure she hadn't forgotten anything and then headed to the car at the front of the house, pulling the kitchen door shut behind her.

Chapter Seventeen

A haze of dust hung over the corrals when Bella parked the big boat of a car alongside the various trucks and trailers. The bawling of cattle and the scent of burnt hair dominated the scene. She spotted the trestle tables set up by the fire pit and BBQ where the strong smell of cowboy coffee battled with the branding aromas for supremacy. She stepped out of the vehicle, jammed the battered straw hat over her unruly hair and lugged the heavy bean pot out of the back seat.

She neared the cooking area where Smoky was making use of an old chuck wagon to keep the sun off things. The lowered tailgate providing extra work space.

"Hey, Miz Rowan," he greeted her, removing his hat for a moment.

"Mornin' Smoky. Where do you want the beans?" She rested the pot on a bent thigh to ease the weight of it.

"Jes let me take that fer ye. It'll do right nicely snugged into the coals here to keep warm til the boys are ready." The large black man took the pot from her with a smile.

"Much obliged. I'll go fetch the rest of the grub." Bella headed back to the car.

"I'll help you, Mrs. Rowan," Anna Murphy offered as she matched steps with Bella.

"Morning, Anna. Looking forward to today?" She smiled down at the blonde haired thirteen year old.

"Branding's always a good day." The girl's long blue jean clad legs kept pace with the older woman.

"How's that barrel horse of yours coming along? I hear Colt's been helping you with him."

A pink glow blushed Anna's cheeks and Bella smiled inwardly.

"We're laying down some decent times. Colt's a big help."

Their arrival at the car cut short the thread of conversation. The two females loaded up the rest of the things Bella brought and carried them back to the chuck wagon where they gave them over to Smokey's care.

"Have you seen Colt this morning? Red and him and his pa rode over earlier." Bella glanced around. "I don't see them right now."

"Red's got the irons in the fire in the pen. I think Colt and Mr. Rowan went to bring down another lot of cow-calf pairs from the top field." Anna squinted into the glare of the morning sun. A small frown marred her pretty features and she turned to look up at Bella. "Is something eating at Colt lately? I mean, you can tell me to mind my own bees wax if it's none of my business, but I'm kinda worried about him." She scuffed the toe of her boot in the dust.

"What do you mean?" Bella held her breath and waited for the answer. Surely Colt hadn't said anything to the girl?

"Well, I don't rightly know how to say it...but he's been different, quieter since his birthday and the river and...He's okay, isn't he?"

Bella let the breath out. "Has he talked to you about what happened?"

Anna shook her head, braids bouncing on her shoulders. "Just that it was his fault and he feels responsible for Sam getting banged up and all. But, it's like there's something else, but he doesn't want to talk about it."

"I think it scared the heck out of all the boys. As far as I know, Colt's just fine. Give him a bit of time to get over it. That's the best advice I can give you."

"Anna! Where are you, girl? Get your butt in the saddle, I need you to haze some stock," Liam Murphy's voice bellowed over the ambient noise.

"Comin', Pa. Gotta go," she called over her shoulder to Bella. She ran lithely to her saddled horse and swung into the saddle with practiced grace. She wheeled the gelding and loped off toward the pens.

As if by magic, Colt materialized out of the thick dust and matched his horse's pace to hers. He turned his head toward the girl and the sunlight highlighted his face. Bella caught her breath, in another time and place she would have sworn it was Vear Du. Anna flashed him a brilliant smile and leaned over to answer whatever it was he's said to her.

"They make a nice couple, don't they?" Bridie Murphy's comment startled Bella.

"Hey, Bridie. A little young, don't you think. But yes, they do seem to make a good pair don't they?" Bella smiled at the little Scottish woman standing by her elbow.

"Boy's gonna need an understanding mate, what with his heritage and all." Shrewd blue eyes glimmered up at her.

"I'm sorry?" Bella stuttered.

Bridie laid a hand on her arm and drew her away from the fire pit to a bit of shade on the far side of the wagon. "He's got more than a touch of the fey about him, Arabella Rowan. No point in disagreeing with me. I've the Sight, you know. Passed down from me granny it was. Second Sight runs in our blood. Our Anna has it too, only she's pretty young yet."

"Dear God in heaven! What do you know?" Bella had the urge to sit down hard, but there was nothing nearby."

"I ken that tadpole isn't D'Arcy Rowan's get. He's all dark and sleekit, like a seal." She peered up at Bella daring her to deny it.

"How can you possible know that?" Spots danced in front of her vision.

"I tolt ye, girl. I've the Sight. Don't take on so, yer white as a sheet. I don't mean the boy any harm. Fact is, the boy's a God send. Our Anna is going to need a man what understands her magic and doesn't want to beat it out of her." Bridie shook her head. "Woe be to the man who ever tried that."

"Who else knows?" Bella looked over the woman's head, frantically searching for D'Arcy.

"Don't be carryin' on so. Just because I know something doesn't mean I go bletherin' about it. I know because I can see it, plain as the nose on your face. Anna senses something, but she's too young yet to understand what it is she sees. It's the magic that draws them together." Bridie patted her arm.

"He's almost a man. It scares the bejeesus out of me," Bella confessed, relieved to have the older woman to talk too. "Colt and your granddaughter have been close since they were running around in diapers."

"Like calls to like," Bridie said sagely. "Does your boy know who and what he is yet?"

"In a way, he does. But he's denying it with everything he has. Flat out told me when I tried to explain it to him that he wants no part of it. No such thing as magic, D is his father and he won't hear a word different."

"You can't force him, Bella. If he wants to deny his heritage, then he will. Maybe Anna will have some effect on him." She paused and looked straight through Bella. "They'll be jumping the broom in a few years, you mark my words." Bridie shook her head as if to clear it. "Those two young'uns will make a good match."

"Is that you or the Sight talking?"

"Both." Anna's granny grinned. "Knew a selkie once meself back in the old country. Handsome laddy he was too. You take care of that boy now, Arabella." Bridie left her standing open mouthed.

Bella turned back to the matters at hand and hurried to help the other women by the fires preparing the noon meal. She straightened from checking on the biscuits in the cat iron Dutch oven nestled in the coals and rubbed her back. Her gaze followed Colt and Anna working in perfect unison separating calves from their mommas in the pens. Bridie was right, they did make a good pair. She looked up to find D'Arcy at her side. She poured him a cup of coffee and handed him a sandwich. He leaned a hip against hers and smiled.

"Looks like the boy's latched onto his first sweetheart," he remarked looking toward the pens.

"So it seems. Bridie seems to think it's the real thing," she replied.

D glanced down at her. "Woman has the Sight, you know? The boy could do far worse than Anna Murphy. Girl comes from good stock and the land abuts ours, although the oldest boy will probably inherit."

"D'Arcy!" Bella slapped his arm gently. "The girl's not a brood mare you're matching blood lines with. The most important thing is if they love each other."

"Matches work out okay too, Ari. Look at us." He leaned down and kissed her soundly.

326

She smiled under his lips. Yes, matches did work out sometimes.

The End

If you enjoyed this book - please leave a review.
Authors need reviews. Please help readers find this author.

More Books by Nancy M Bell

Laurel's Quest The Cornwall Adventures
Book ~ 1
A Step Beyond The Cornwall Adventures
Book ~ 2
Go Gently The Cornwall Adventure Book
~ 3

Storm's Refuge A Longview Romance
Book ~ 1
Come Hell or High Water A Longview
Romance Book ~ 2
A Longview Wedding Longview Romance
Book ~ 3

With Pat Dale
The Last Cowboy
She's Driving Me Crazy
Henrietta's Heart
The Teddy Dialogues

Historical Horror
By N.M. Bell
No Absolution

Canadian Historical Brides Series
His Brother's Bride ~ Ontario

Nancy M Bell is a proud Albertan and Canadian. She lives near Balzac, Alberta with her husband and various critters. She works with and fosters rescue animals. Nancy is a member of The Writers Union of Canada and the Writers Guild of Alberta. Her work has been recognized and honoured with various awards. She has publishing credits in poetry, fiction, and non-fiction.

bookswelove.com